Odour Of Rectitude

Michael Eisele

Other books by Michael Eisele
Without Tears And Other Tales
Twelve O'Clock Sharp

Publisher: Michael Eisele

Printed in the United States of America

Contents

Page

Second Grace

The message arrived on a Tuesday afternoon.

"The interview can take place at four o'clock on Friday. Please arrive a little earlier and ask for me."

Rolf Keimer could hardly hide his satisfaction, for it was considered a triumph to be admitted to that place. For months he had striven to meet the widely known owner of the Karmak Company, of whom he had heard a lot. His wealth, along with a reclusive behaviour, formed the talk in the business circles, as much as in the media.

For years the enigmatic mogul had not shown his face in public; not even at trade shows, or at social gatherings. Many found such conduct peculiar, for after all he was considered to be a pillar, if not mainstay of the industry. A man in other words who was expected to serve as a label, advertising their guild.

Hair-raising stories circulated about him. Some insinuated that he was deformed, others imputed him with raving madness, due to continual drunken sprees. Suppositions whirred about like flies around a light. There were more than a few who maintained he was deaf and mute. Many accused him of this and that; in short of everything that scandalmongers were able to invent. One fact, however, they were agreed on: he was one of the richest men in the country.

By what means he had acquired that astounding wealth, opinions diverged. Rumours had it that as a young man he was plundering the diamond fields in Southwest Africa; others conjectured he might have been a ringleader of the underworld. The truth no one knew; except Franz Weil, friend and manager of the notorious Horst Kurin. The invitation bore Weil's name; in other words it was authentic.

At three-thirty Keimer announced his presence. Weil received him immediately. The two had known each other for years, not only commercially, but also socially.

"Ah, there you are," Weil greeted, extending a hand and sporting a smile.

Sincere joy lit up his face for an instant, before shadows of misgivings scurried across his brow.

"Finally it is going to happen, I can hardly wait to shake hands with our leader. I must say, Franz, it is high time. Where shall the meeting take place?"

"In his chambers. Don't worry, I shall accompany you," Weil assured his visitor.

In no time they were engaged in an animated conversation, for they had not seen each other for a while.

Weil glanced repeatedly at the clock on the wall, in a fashion as if trying to force the hands to stop moving.

"You are a bit jumpy today, I hope it has nothing to do with me," Keimer remarked a bit abashed.

Weil faced him squarely, evidently he was about to say something disconcerting to him. He creased his brow, stroked his chin, and puckered his lips several times, then remarked guardedly:

"You know of course, Rolf, that Mr Kurin has led a retired life for years."

"What are you referring to?" Keimer replied.

"He shuns people with a determination bordering on eccentricity. To be sure, reasons do exist for it," remarked Weil.

He glanced at him inquiringly, but he made no further comments, he just rested his eyes reflectively on him, sighing a few times, prior to saying:

"Before introducing you to Mr Kurin I would like to direct your attention to something."

"Alright, out with it," Keimer encouraged.

"Horst Kurin, my friend and chief of many years, suffers from convulsions."

Noticing Keimer's astonished, and somewhat amused stare, he added in a hushed voice:

"We are not talking about nervous twitches called tics, but of a constant paroxysmal contortion, which not only elicits surprise, but can be outright frightening. Therefore I entreat you earnestly to be composed before you cross the threshold to his rooms."

"Have no worry, I shall restrain myself," Keimer asserted, while turning his head towards the clock on the wall.

Another ten minutes the hands indicated.

Keimer chuckled self-consciously, then said smiling:

"I harbour no wish to appear obsessed, but I have put it in my head to shake the hand, be it only once, of this remarkable man. I'm in the dark what he looks like, faring no better than others in that respect. The name is known, but not the person. To my knowledge neither pictures nor drawings exist of him."

Weil nodded assent, thereby inducing Keimer to ask:

"What do you think governs this.... hm, should I say exaggerated inclination to live in seclusion?"

Instead of an answer Weil pointed to the clock.

"Time to be on our way," the gesture said.

Weil entered first, he bid Keimer to wait outside.

"It won't be long, meanwhile you may take a seat," he advised.

As Keimer sat there, ready to be called at any moment, his glance met an object in the corner where a miner's insignia stood on a shelf. He could not believe it; his eyes distended instinctively, a sort of paralysis almost overcame him. What he saw made him oblivious of anything else. He forgot where he was. Spellbound he stared at the mallet and tinner's hammer, crossed like St. Andrew's cross. What particularly fascinated him were two implements lying beside it. Whirling thoughts began rummaging inside him, they wandered way back into the past, to a faraway country, foreign and wild.

He literally shook in his skin. Why would a miner's insignia trigger such consternation in him? Memories of unforgettable days arose. No mistake about it, they warranted chuckles, the odd grin, and sigh, but robbing one's composure they should not. What adhered to these tools, which after all were used daily by countless miners?

Nothing remarkable, had it not been for the pickaxe and pointed hammer lying beside them. Those received his entire attention. The more he observed them, the more distinct unfolded a long forgotten incident before his eyes. No doubt about it, they had belonged to him once.

The realisation caused his head to spin; a regular dizziness seized him at the sight of these implements. He repeatedly rubbed his eyes with both hands, as if attempting to wipe away shadowy pictures, which refused to yield. No mistake, there on the shelf lay his property, he could clearly identify the characteristic helves made with his own hands, which bore the initials P.S.

But it could not be! for they were left behind, worlds away in a remote wild and lonely valley in British Columbia's Selkirk Mountains. Twenty years had passed since he and Peter Flander had pitched their tents at the banks of the impetuous Downie River. Not a soul except he and his missing friend had forced their way upriver in those days, to an exceptional rough and inaccessible region. Into the shadows, cast by towering ice fields, they had toted their gear. Stalked by grizzlies, and howled at by wolves, they searched for the mother lode. Yes, his one-time friend Peter Flander must have met his death somewhere in that vast inhospitable wilderness; where exactly, no one knew.

Just as he rose to take a closer look in order to convince himself whether he was dreaming or had become a victim of spectres of the past, Weil showed up.

"Alright, Rolf, Mr Kurin is ready to receive you," he advised not overly enthused.

Only with utmost efforts did Keimer succeed to turn his gaze from the shelf. Consoling himself with thoughts of a more thorough investigation later, he rose and followed Weil.

Then everything happened so fast, Weil reported, that even months later thinking about it, put his head in a whirl.

"You!" cried – no – roared Keimer aghast.

"You, you," croaked Kurin as if tortured.

In the next moment Keimer, uttering a feral shout of blind rage mixed with shrill joy, lunged at Kurin's throat with a panther-like leap. Weil stood frozen to the floor as if hit by a thunderbolt. Before he looked again, Kurin lay writhing and blue in the face at Keimer's feet, who still held his throat in a vice-like grip. Ever so slowly he squeezed the life out of Kurin's body.

All attempts by Weil to loosen the iron hold around his boss' and friend's throat, proved futile. Keimer's arms and hands seemed to be made of steel. He possessed the strength of a bear, and an avenger's determination. Finally he released his deadly grip on his own volition.

"There, that's done," he announced greatly relieved.

Weil stared at him struck dumb with horror, still unable to collect his wits. More bewildered than accusatory, he stammered:

"Rolf, do you know what you have done?"

"My name is not Rolf, nor is it Keimer," came a gruff rebuke.

"But – but, what is it then?"

"Philip Speer."

Kicking the distorted corpse on the floor, he added:

"This villain's name is Peter Flander."

In prison Speer had time to think. Not that it helped him much, for it was too late. One unfortunate moment was about to destroy his painstakingly structured life, which in many respects could have been termed successful. His tendency towards irascibility, for a long time an irritating thorn in his mind, he had learned to rein in. It was quite an effort, comparable to the knight's feat who bound Furor with a hundred ropes into a hundred knots.

Unfortunately the fetters got untied again in one unexpected jolt. But who would have been able to tame his emotions? Not Job, and certainly not he, in view of an encounter beyond belief. It brought occurrences to life, incredible perfidious, which leaped at him like a tidal wave. To be sure, some men would only have been stunned by surprise, but in him the sight of Kurin ignited the flames of hot fury.

The experience two decades ago came vividly back to him; it was painful enough even now to rob him of his composure. A deed, foul, unbelievable scurvy, which had been perpetrated against him arose life-like before his eyes at the unexpected sight of Peter Flander.

They were comrades once, close friends really, when this Ganelon ignominiously left him behind to die a slow torturous death. Well, it had not worked that way, he managed to dig himself out of a hoped for tomb, into which a whimsical destiny was about to hurl him again.

He was able to chuckle over that incident which happened twenty years ago, for after all it had not ended too badly; though finding a similar act of vileness would not prove easy. Yet he had learned to consider the whole affair with philosophical equanimity; at least so he thought, till Flander reappeared before his eyes.

In retrospect he regretted his rash act. At the same time, however, he blamed Flander for the unfortunate outcome. Why did the traitorous villain have to degenerate into a quaking weakling, who neither had the gumption to resist, nor possessed sufficient air in his windpipe to hold out a bit longer. Could he not have remained robust like himself, sturdy as before, and fearless as ever? He suffered from spasms Weil had revealed, no wonder in view of the bites of a guilty conscience, which must have gnawed the marrow from his bones.

But Flander always seemed to be tainted. He was a bleeding heart really, with plenty of heave on his lips, but little ho in his limbs. “May the devil and his dam fetch him,” he expelled between his teeth.

The remark made him snicker at the notion how Flander was being dragged already on both ears to that fiend’s den. That quailing milksop should have put up a struggle, seemly in a man, then things would have ended differently.

Concerning Weil he too had to shake his head, for there was something amiss in a man who watched idly, while his friend and patron perished writhing at his feet.

"There is another dodger," Speer snorted, "with a mimosa heart, which throws a shadow larger than the whole man."

He should have assisted his friend, not stand around rooted to the floor like Lot's wife. Entering the melee with flailing arms would have attained more than standing by with distended eyes. Of course he could hardly have divined the reason for Weil's enigmatic behaviour, nor why he came to his friend's aid only after he lay in his death throes. He learned all about it later, thus for now he still referred to him as a jack-a-dandy without get-up and spunk. Yet not for long; soon he was forced to change that opinion.

Speer drew a deep breath, images appeared before his eyes which could not be dispersed. "What a coincidence," he murmured repeatedly, to meet the man once so avidly sought, then completely forgotten in this faraway land. A lot of water must have rushed down from the great ice fields since those tumultuous days, when the Downie River had been his home. Even after two decades he could not forget the source of untold grief, mixed with memorable joy.

Closing his eyes, towering peaks crossed his vision, casting long shadows over that turbulent stream, which never came to rest on its journey from the Durand Glaciers to the legendary Columbia. While travelling eastward in search of his treacherous companion, he tried in vain, vicariously that is, to dump ugly memories and unworthy sentiments into the rushing water. Only time managed to heal the scars of wounded pride, it gradually effaced all traces of Peter Flander.

An encounter with him, once fervently desired, became increasingly unwelcome. True, at the beginning, after his miraculous escape, he left no stone unturned to find him. With a missionary's zeal he inquired here, investigated there, yet met nothing but negative gestures. No one knew Flander, neither by name nor description. Only in Revelstoke, the closest town to the spot of his incredible experience, did he stumble onto Flander's trail, but the man remained as elusive as ever.

That was hardly surprising in a town still graced with a lingering pioneer spirit. Inquiries made in a speculative manner were met by vacant stares and deprecating shrugs. These rugged men and courageous women had no stomach for telltales, and even less for betrayal; not yet, in any case.

Shooing away contradictory thoughts, Speer rose from his hard prison bunk. He forced himself to concentrate on his defence, for it alone deserved all his inner strength and undivided attention. Lawyer Kessler, scarcely a humbug as a man, and even less a slouch as an advocate, should arrive any time. A clear line of defence had to be arrived at, although he harboured few doubts which way it should go. First and foremost he would deny any imputations despite an eyewitness.

Speer belonged to a minority that never considered matters lost till he had foundered irresistibly. The manslaughter charge sounded more devastating than it actually was. Evidence may well be presented, but clever pleading, supported by astute cross-examination might bend, if not repudiate it. No amount of pessimism could label his situation as hopeless; certainly not if compared with that gruesome experience twenty years ago in the wild and forsaken Selkirks of Western Canada. There he was held in the jaws of death, closing slowly on him. But what a morsel he proved to be; a titbit that refused to be swallowed. In the face of certain doom, despite signs of hopelessness, he tenaciously clung onto life, desperately waiting for a miracle to tear him from the grip of fate.

The miracle did happen, or rather destiny rewarded his fortitude. She reached out a hand, as it were, which he grasped with a final surge of energy, and held on till he stood on firm ground again. True, that ground once more trembled in the balance. Detention afforded time to reflect. Evidence about his rash deed did exist, but whether it ultimately proved sufficient to convict him, remained to be seen.

The only hurdle in the path of a light sentence was Franz Weil, who would surely testify against him. But not all spelled gloom there either, considering the man's enigmatic behaviour. In any case Weil had to be tackled ruthlessly from every side, be it by fair, or shady methods.

Speer so far had neither made a statement to the police, nor gave anyone verbal or written information. Promises, cajoleries, or threats did not persuade him to do so. The lack of motive bothered many, most of all the police, who searched feverishly for a connection between him and Flander. They were fishing in troubled waters, unable to find a link, which only two men knew about. One was dead. Not a syllable of their fateful relationship had crossed his lips. True, his words uttered at the scene of the crime might have sounded incriminating, but oddly enough nothing to date indicated that Weil, the witness, heard, or understood them. Even his lawyer remained in the dark about their common past.

Speer chuckled. Their ignorance served him well. It must look weird to all concerned, why a staid businessman of mature years should lunge at the throat of a renowned magnate of the industry at their first encounter. It sounded absurd really, incredible in other words. The lack of logic must surely stick in the prosecutor's gullet like a fish bone.

Strange enough, not much was said about Weil, the only eyewitness. Seldom did his name come up; if so, it was mentioned with surprising nonchalance.

Sitting down again on his hard bedstead with his head against the wall, he mused about his predicament. No doubt, misery had found him again, despite his vow to leave its side forever. His luck once more was stretched beyond the limit. But what of it? It had happened before, and as then he refused to let resignation weaken his mettle. One more time he begged his guardian angel for a second grace, and then no more. It will be the last call, he promised, the last ever.

His unrestrained behaviour he rued profoundly; to undo it, however, lay not in his powers. But perhaps, just maybe the consequences could be mitigated. Fate had smiled at him before when all seemed lost, why not again?

For Flander he felt no sympathy. That treacherous scoundrel deserved what he got. Speer sighed deeply, thereby venting his discontent. He had forgotten that disturbing incident in his past, which now had come marching back into his life. Reminiscences about Canada, a land that left a mark on his soul, though wakened frequently, deliberately circumvented

Flander, his erstwhile companion. But there he was back again, setting his whole being on edge.

Shivering in the overheated cell at the thought of Flander's duplicity, he moaned repeatedly:

"How could anyone be so perfidious as Flander, moreover, so simple-minded like myself."

Not a vestige of suspicion had clouded their relationship. To the contrary; he had trusted Flander implicitly with life and limbs, body and soul. Five years they had wandered through that amazing country, tramping and riding from sea to sea, from the frozen tundra to the fruit belts at the American border. Through thick and thin they went together. At times battling for sheer life in tumbling rapids, other times enjoying days with hearts at ease, camping in a valley amid grazing wapitis. They had smelled the tang of Hecate Strait, and watched billows rolling in from far away Alaska. It pained Speer to think of the beauty of a land marked by dark memories. Yet more distressed he felt by the ignoble deed of his erstwhile friend.

Sadness, mixed with anger, gripped him, culminating in a desire to strangle Flander again and again. Looking back, he passed his hand across his brow, trying to recall the turning point of their relation. It had taken some time to sink in, yet despite telltale signs, betrayal refused to enter Speer's mind. Had someone hinted of his comrade's intention to hurl him into the fangs of doom, he would have laughed him straight across the prairie.

Speer started, he heard steps nearing his cell. Two guards appeared outside the barred gate, bidding him to come along to a room where his lawyer sat waiting. Greetings were short, Herbert Kessler lost no time.

"You are keeping something from me," he informed his client, who looked sheepishly aside.

"Oh, am I?" he muttered evasively.

The lawyer did not avert his eyes. Wrinkles creased his brow, the corners of his mouth dropped ever so lightly.

"You are concealing something from me which may be vital," he repeated with the mien of a man reprimanding an obdurate child.

He went on:

"Here is the situation in a nutshell: Two apparent total strangers, both of mature years, business men of high rank to boot, pounce at each other at their first meeting. One of them, meaning you, almost chokes the other to death. Ears, willing to listen to such hogwash, will be difficult to find. Surely not attached to heads of judges or juries."

After this introductory discourse, which evidently caused the matter-of-fact attorney some vexation, he started a regular devil's tattoo on the table.

Speer had pricked his ears at the word almost, which had set his mind awhirl.

"Did you say almost, or have I misunderstood you?"

Kessler stopped drumming. He opened his briefcase with characteristic deliberation, then took out some papers. He read through them painstakingly, concentrating on every word. He appeared to be oblivious to Speer's presence, thus signs of a curious agitation on his face remained unnoticed.

No doubt Speer was perplexed upon hearing the lawyer's arcane words.

"What do you mean almost?" he nearly blurted out. But he managed to bite his tongue. Sitting still, however, proved too strenuous. Thought after thought raced through his mind, one more stirring than the next. Staring at the lawyer calmly studying his papers, he felt like on pins and needles. He dared not interrupt for fear of the man's well-known punishing glances.

Finally the perusal ended, Kessler put the sheets back where they belonged. Visibly annoyed he asked:

"What was the question just now?"

"You said: Almost choked the other to death." Speer emphasised the word almost.

"I did," followed a gruff answer.

"But – but," Speer started haltingly when good sense overtook the impulse to tell a tale.

Reining in his tongue, he swallowed the rest. He wanted to say:

"But I have done it. Here, these two hands squeezed the air out of the rotter's lungs."

On Kessler's lips appeared an enigmatic smile, half scornful, half appreciative. He liked clients who knew how to button up, who did not blab, but kept their tongues in check. To be sure his client carried taciturnity a bit too far when dealing with him. Kessler advised:

"Here is the latest: In accordance with official findings, Kurin died of heart failure."

"Not of suffocation?" Speer burst out in surprise.

Once more the lawyer could not suppress a grin, when he noticed Speer's anxiety. Sparks of hope seemed to crackle across his face, which were doused instantly by clouds of disbelief.

"Not of suffocation," Kessler confirmed, then added: "Heart failure it was, and a creeping one to boot."

Bewildered Speer shook his head.

"I don't understand."

"Neither do I actually. Kurin's death, it appears, is not consistent with strangulation. It happened not instantly, but over a period of hours."

"Am I off the hook then?"

"Not likely. As you know the police are privy to certain facts. Your fingerprints as much as the welts around Kurin's neck are authentic enough. Concerning Weil, the only eyewitness, much confusion reigns. Your fortune will heave and fall with him. So far, however, I venture a guess that he might do more good than harm."

Seeing his client's bewilderment, Kessler continued:

"Surprised? I can imagine why. Let me say you are not the only one. Another thing. If Weil's testimony were not so contradictory, your goose would be cooked. The man has a hidden agenda, no ifs or buts about it."

"Isn't his testimony crushing?"

Shaking his head Kessler remarked:

"Not really. It could be, according to logic it should be, yet for inexplicable reasons it is not. Nevertheless, he is the prosecution's only path to conviction. Charges would have no legs to stand on without him. Were it not for the man's penchant to blow hot and cold in the same breath, you would be in for it."

Speer, by no accounts a tenderfoot, could see his ghost and hear him laugh. An odd sensation crept over his skin, as he recalled Weil standing there wrapped in cynical silence, expectant, waiting for something Speer dared not to name. Such indifference, unexpected of a friend in need, reeked of secret jubilation. Surely, I must have seen phantoms, Speer admitted, just as Kessler spoke again:

"The tender spot for the prosecution is the lack of motive."

Pausing, he directed his gaze squarely at Speer before he continued:

"Therefore you are well advised to keep mum about it."

When his client stirred as if to interrupt, he silenced him with a raised hand:

"Say nothing about it now, I will advise when the time is ripe. As I said, the authorities are in a haze about it – the reason for this murderous assault – they stumble from speculation to conjecture. Self-defence is one of their theories, albeit rendered criminal by the use of excessive force."

Jumping up, Speer cried:

"Self-defence?"

Kessler's withering look silenced his client. Frowning he spoke again:

"Please sit down. Let's sum up. Here are the facts: Kurin changed his name officially twenty years ago. Your legal name is Philip Speer, though you have called yourself Rolf Keimer for some time. You knew Kurin, Weil attests to it. According to him, mutual recognition took place instantly. He is positive about that. Both of you changed names many years ago for unknown reasons. One surely is entitled, upon due deliberation, to assume that a connection between you and Kurin existed."

Kessler again started his characteristic finger-drumming, indicating a measure of discomfort.

"Your defence is not a humdrum routine, we have some explaining to do."

Seeing his client's questioning glance, he explained:

"For an opener, why did you use a pseudonym all these years? Furthermore, why did Kurin aim a pistol at you on sight?"

Speer almost belted from his seat.

"He what?"

The lawyer's head came up in astonishment. Eyeing his client sideways, he remarked:

"That seems to surprise you."

It sure did, for he neither saw a pistol anywhere, much less was one aimed at him. But he was no fool, and quick-witted besides.

"In a way it does, because I did not believe that Weil would have noticed."

Grinning broadly, eyes half closed, Kessler nodded several times. He almost admired his client; he would do well in the witness chair should he decide to call him.

"I take it that you admit to have known Kurin," Kessler declared.

"Yes, but that was many years ago, it should have no bearing on the case."

"Let me be the judge of that," Kessler announced.

After arranging to return in one week, the lawyer took his leave. Not, however, before advising:

"When I come back, questions will be put to you, which must be answered."

Soon Speer sat alone in his cell. Despite strenuous efforts to put his mind at ease, he did not succeed. The wan figure of Flander, buried by now, obtruded itself again and again.

They met in Canada over two decades ago, at one of the mines under construction, five hundred kilometres north of Toronto. What a wild and woolly time that was, unforgettable even to the old-timers. There, above the wind-swept Georgian Bay, uranium had been discovered. Opportunities, hitherto unimaginable, literally popped out of the ground. The surrounding area from Thunder Bay to the Quebec border reverberated with promises and rumours. Men and women with empty pockets, and hope-filled hearts, thronged from all directions to the Eldorado of the fifties. Fortune hunters, their eyes distended by greed, rubbed shoulders with future captains of the industry. Manual workers hobnobbed with the higher echelons.

It was a motley bunch; boisterous, liquor-prone, and constantly at odds with themselves. The atmosphere in the hastily erected camps, as much as in the fast growing town, trembled downright in the glow of optimism.

The short summers in Elliot Lake, scorching hot, are followed by long cold winters. Brisk winds, gathering over Lake Huron, blow unhindered across the North Channel over the frozen land.

It was a wonderful time, in a country not yet in full bloom. A sense of freedom reigned that infected even the timid and stolid. The whole country was astir, rousing the young, and not so young, into action. Immigrants, arriving by land and sea, could not believe their luck. The ease of movement, making them leery at first, fearing a trap that might be sprung any time, soon deemed them a god given boon. They soon considered it their birthright.

It was a joy to be alive in those days. One could climb up a hill on a clear summer morning, look across the shimmering water, where far away a stretch of broken land rose invitingly, and say: “That’s where I will go next.” The world seemed young then, uncomplicated, beckoning one to dare.

Speer had met Flander in Elliot Lake in the middle of an unprecedented construction boom. They were still young. Both prided themselves to be of an intellectual bent. A friendship sprung up almost immediately between them, cemented most likely by a common language. Neither one felt enamoured by the rough-and-tumble life of the campsite. In fact, they referred to that diverse crowd as ‘hoipoloi’, with scarcely a grain of brains between them. In their minds they were nothing but a riotous, mindless band of people.

One morning in April they looked at each other, turned westwards, and nodded. In that direction lay the future, they felt it in their bones. Without much ado they started packing. After fleeting farewells they were on the road. Westwards they pushed, past Lake Superior, cold as ever, and storm lashed as usual. On they went, crossing the vast prairie, the piercing sun above their heads, the parched earth at their feet. A relentless wind, seemingly blowing to destroy, blinded their eyes with dust. Layers of soil appeared to be in the air, raised by the snarling wind. Then they reached the grassland of Alberta, the province with a reputation of either 'do or die'.

"This is the place to be," they said after a week's stay.

They liked the people, besides, business and employment opportunities abounded. A few days later they announced:

"We are Calgarians for life."

A month passed. The second one had just begun, when Speer noticed Flander gazing westwards. Not just once, but again and again.

"What are you looking at?" he asked one day.

Flander started as if caught in a compromising act.

"Nothing in particular," he replied sheepishly.

The second month had barely ended, when they were on the road again. Within days they had crossed the Great Divide, where they stood and gazed awe-struck at sights beyond belief. Downhill it went to Revelstoke, at the banks of the historic Columbia River. There something occurred which changed their lives. Incredible it may sound, yet it irrevocably shaped their future. At first they treated the whole incident with a measure of levity, and a dash of scorn. They joked about it, had a few chuckles and tried to forget it.

"What a weird tale," Speer announced more often than once.

"Told by an even more weird man," Flander concurred.

Yet without realising it they were in the hands of destiny.

It happened like this: Speer, the possessor of a throat in need of frequent oiling, passed saloons reluctantly. It is uncivil, he maintained, to turn one's back on a sign outside of an alehouse. He usually detected them from afar, like the one reading: 'Welcome to the Hotel Ephram'. Before Flander had espied the building, his friend read the inscription of the swaying shingle. The moment Speer said, "aha, aha," Flander knew the sequel. Sure enough, his companion made already a beeline for the entrance.

The room was packed from wall to wall. Calls to touch glasses resounded in several languages. In no time did Speer wade through the restless crowd. Holding in one hand a half-empty glass, the other extended in salutation, he walked ahead of Flander. Then he stopped abruptly and stared. Something had roused his interest which he should have ignored, but did not. It proved to be a fateful moment when he approached the object of his curiosity.

What followed was one of those epoch-making events many hear about, but few experience. In a remote corner sat a man who gave the impression of being steeped in misery. His stooped shoulders and Hippocratic face would have done honour to the famous picture of discontent. Sorrow seemed to ooze out of every pore, bitter disappointment enveloped the whole man.

"There sits distress," Speer murmured, as he approached the piteous figure somewhat amused, but also repelled.

"How goes it comrade?" he asked.

Instead of an answer the epitome of glumness just raised his eyes, which he fixed first on Speer, then on Flander. Afterwards he moaned as if he were in the last of Mathew. Flander could not explain it, yet the man, still relatively young, deemed him a messenger of doom. Something eerie surrounded that fellow, whom the other tipplers appeared to avoid. More than a few, however, cast admonishing glances towards them. He wanted to nudge his friend, to make him aware of these leery peers, but Speer had unlimbered his well-known social graces.

Despite the downhearted grouch's attitude, he began to overwhelm him with questions, which chiefly remained unanswered. His name was Jens Melrud, that much they learned; also that for years misfortune followed him like his shadow. Stumbling from fields of thistles to patches of thorns, he averred, without a single fault of his own.

Flander felt repelled by this odd fellow; he made signs to his friend to leave the misery soaked chap to himself. Then Melrud started to cast furtive glances all around. What now, they thought, when Melrud displayed a piece of paper with a mysterious air. Flander turned to Speer, who was unable to suppress an amused twinkle.

Melrud held the paper in both hands with a solicitude befitting a page out of Ptah-Hotep, the oldest book in memory. Warily his eyes shifted from one to the other, suspiciously he observed the tipplers nearby. Taking on a mysterious air, he acted like someone about to make an epochal disclosure.

"Boys, what do you know about tungsten?" he inquired while fanning the paper in front of their eyes.

The friends looked nonplussed at each other, neither one found a ready reply.

"Not much," they finally admitted.

Melrud nodded repeatedly, never averting his appraising gaze.

"Tungsten is a rare metal which makes gold look like rusty iron."

He then commenced an eulogy peppered with technical expressions, which conveyed them from astonishment to amazement. With glittering eyes and reddening brow he explained its chemical compositions to the last dot. Speer fell into a feverish restlessness during this discourse, which he found difficult to fathom. Were they listening to a charlatan, a confidence man on the prowl for victims? Or was the man sitting across the table a product of this wondrous country, where an impecunious man with pluck and an idea in his head, can turn overnight into a Croesus?

"Why are you telling us this?" Flander wanted to know.

That fellow was simply incapable to give a straight answer. He cleared his throat a few times, then hemmed under his hand, creased his brow till it almost disappeared, and finally raised his eyebrows as if aggrieved. After repeated sniffing and humming, he deigned to respond:

"Do you gents have money?"

There we go, they thought, the line is being cast. They could see the bait wriggle in front of their eyes.

"Not much," came a reluctant answer.

"Thousand dollars?"

He is aiming too high, they silently mused. A thousand dollars in those days was more than a mere song. More so in the fast moving west, where most lived from hand to mouth. Easy come, easy go, was the motto there. Putting money aside appealed to few, most never played with the idea of crossing a bank's threshold.

Both were still shaking their heads, when Melrud made an astounding announcement:

"I know where immense riches lie," he whispered behind a shielding hand.

"Where?" Flander burst out before his companion's censorious glance could prevent it.

"The money first," Melrud reminded.

When he noticed their disinclination, and even worse, a willingness to leave, he quickly added:

"Not far from here are treasures in the ground which eclipse any discoveries to date. I tell you it's a second Klondike, with the only difference that not gold but tungsten waits for the lucky ones. Believe me, little money can earn millions."

Interrupting Melrud's tirade would have proved difficult; the fellow lacked only a podium to break into a harangue. Attempts to object touched him not a bit, he continued unaffected in an insistent manner.

"I'm not talking through my hat, far from it. Comprehensive bore holes were sunk by myself, naturally under the seal of secrecy. Cores to be assayed were transported in a roundabout way to Calgary. Why in a roundabout way, you want to know? Be reasonable; far reaching discoveries like mine must be kept confidential by all means."

Here he directed his glance fully at Speer with whom, being the more robust of the two, he felt a closer kinship.

"You surely will understand why I acted with such circumspection. The ore body, being about fifty kilometres from here, can be reached in three days, despite a nearly impassable terrain, if approached in a direct line, that is. Yet it always takes me a week and a half to get there. Why? For what reason you want to know? Well now, think again. I walk the crooked path to throw any snoops off my scent. You appreciate such subterfuge, don't you?"

Melrud drifted from eagerness to fervency. Like a conspirator he leaned alternately towards one and then the other, talking in a hoarse voice, hoping to convince them. In his excitement he disregarded his paper, which lay unguarded on the table. It must be a plan, Speer presumed. Melrud got into the thick of things. He thumped the table, shifted his chair, and swung his arms to and fro. As a result the plan shifted away from him.

Then a sudden silence set in, as though every tippler had lost his tongue. Melrud noticed nothing at first, for he was busy to raise the intensity of his panegyric a notch or two. With lively expressions, and emphatic gesticulations, he attempted to weave a net of expectation around his listeners. Therefore he did not see the frightful figures standing in the doorway. How could he, since both his eyes were riveted at the two friends, and the left as the right ear were attuned to his soliloquy.

But finally he sensed the changed atmosphere. Following the glances of Speer and Flander, his eyes distended with terror. He did not tarry one second. Before the friends were able to acknowledge the astounding turn of events, Melrud streaked out the back door. The plan, which he left behind, Flander pushed quick-wittedly into his pocket.

Circumstances were soon aired. As the two unsavory fellows gave chase, explanations followed. Scorn marked the informants' voices, for they assumed that Speer and Flander had been swindled by Melrud. They grinned and nodded knowingly, saying to each other:

"They took the bait the same as Roster and Clover."

Apparently they were inveigled to buy a claim from the impostor, somewhere up at Jordan River, which a cursory inspection showed as promising. Presence of gold dust seemed evident; a fact, which raised their expectations. Consequently they paid Melrud's asking price without haggling. Soon, however, they averred, their anticipation was doused with a sobering realisation. No gold nuggets could be found, only bits of colour they were able to pan from the rushing river. Thus they felt betrayed.

Speer and Flander took it all with a grain of salt. Melrud had impressed them as being honest; a bit odd perhaps, but nevertheless meriting respect. In addition, Melrud's pursuers looked shifty to them, if not villainous. Their assessment gained strength when the two returned unsuccessful in their hunt, spewing venom, and promising dire retribution.

"Something is amiss here," Speer informed his friend, who answered:

"Terribly so. Oho, be on guard! there they come."

"How goes it, strangers?" the one called Roster said.

"You were hobnobbing with that scoundrel Melrud, we noticed," the other one, Clover, added.

Questions were asked, sounding more like an interrogation than polite inquiries. The two friends responded evasively, because both felt an instinctive resentment towards these boastful churls.

In the following days the air was adrift with rumours about Melrud. Carried by clouds of blind belief, stoked by trends towards malignancy, incredible stories started to circulate. The dog was given a bad name, but he had absconded, thus could not be hanged.

However, not everybody partook in these character assassinations. Some refused to collect stones for the rabble to throw. After all this was Canada in the fifties, where particularly in the west traces of sincerity and stoutheartedness still lingered. Self-willed men, though becoming a rarity fast, were now as then stomping around the wild mountains of British Columbia.

Such a man was Thomas Shark, an eccentric of the West. He had remained impervious to the fickle mores of conventions, a fortress impregnable to this day. He was well known in mining circles as an oddball, but of sterling character. Ten years ago he prospected up and down the Goldstream River, where he discovered the mother lode. Resulting prestige and prosperity did not change him, he went his way as before, because he knew of no other, nor did he wish to find one.

Despite approaching age he had remained fiercely independent, he bore the indelible stamp of a spirit that not so long ago graced the wilds of British Columbia. This incorruptible trailblazer stood up for Melrud, whom he knew. Their path had crossed a few times, and without exception they met and parted on friendly terms. Once they even prospected together without a hitch.

Shark found out about Melrud's troubles. Saddling one horse, loading the other with gear and provisions, he went on the trail leading to town. Arriving there he read the local newspaper. The write-up about Melrud hit his eyes and raised his ire. It was grossly unfair, and mendacious besides. Giving it not a second thought he marched in a beeline to the local press. Tying both horses to a nearby tree, he entered the premises. He knew the editor with whom he had crossed swords more often than once. Stepping over the threshold he hollered:

"Come on out, Brent, I have something to say."

Brent Howard, the editor, had little use for this antediluvian, as he called him. That's why he hesitated to make a move. Shark was in no mood to shilly-shally; he thundered:

"Show yourself, my man, let me look in your false eyes, and show me the hand that writes such tripe."

The editor knew from experience that ignoring Shark was not an option. A row would ensue, upsetting everyone for the rest of the day.

"I wish the great Fiend would carry that fellow off," he expelled under his breath as Shark stepped into his office.

"What do you want?" he snapped.

"A retraction," Shark bellowed.

"Retraction of what?"

"That calumnious article about the Swede."

"Melrud?"

"Yes, him. I want you to repudiate it."

Howard made a wry face. Glancing at his typesetter, who was unable to suppress a smirk, he advised firmly:

"I will do no such thing."

Shark pulled out a sheet of paper from somewhere which bore his handwriting.

"Alright then, print this in the next issue, it's the truth. I want to see it on the first page," Shark commanded.

The editor creased his forehead visibly annoyed, yet he took the proffered sheet and read it.

"Hm, hm," he murmured, and read it again, hoping to find something objectionable.

He was no stranger to Shark's high-flown style of expression, which left no doubts about his intentions. Howard was a fair man, certainly not vindictive.

"I will print it," he acquiesced, "but not on the first page."

They haggled a while, and what a demonstration that was. Shark shook the tree of righteous wrath, which was a treat to see. He stomped back and forth, cutting the air with one or the other hand, while berating the editor, who pretended to hear and see none of it. But if the truth had been known, he felt relieved, for it eased his conscience. Condemning Melrud to satisfy a perceived loathing by the public, had made him feel guilty. A rebuttal should balance the scale. They agreed to have the article, a letter really, to appear on the second page.

Flander simply was unable to turn away from the sketch before him. Despite Speer's rebuking glances, he kept poring over it.

"Peter, you are working yourself into a dither over nothing. Staring at that worthless piece of paper gets you nowhere," Speer chided.

Flander came close to admitting, tacitly that is, the truth of his friend's observations. He felt stumped, no two ways about it. Clues on the map were scarce. Beyond reference points, obviously meant as hints for someone in the know, neither names of rivers nor mountain peaks were given. No doubt the originator of the drawing intended to keep the location hidden from anyone but himself.

A visit to the mining office shed no light on the mystery. Apart from an acknowledgement by the gold commissioner, that the sketch certainly depicted a properly staked mining claim, they learned very little.

"Sorry, fellows, I am unable to help you, unless more details are provided. I could be toting ledger upon ledger for weeks in vain."

Looking at them quizzically, he inquired:

"Where did you get the sketch?"

Flander, endowed with a keener perception than his companion, answered quickly:

"We bought it from a stranger on our way from Calgary."

Did the commissioner believe it? Who knows. His demeanour afforded no clue. Smiling wryly he remarked:

"You have been gypped, no doubt, it happens all the time. Not a week passes without someone walking through that door, waving a presumed price catch under our eyes, which invariably turns out to be a fraud."

They thanked him and turned towards the exit. Before they disappeared the commissioner called out:

"You might try old man Shark. If anybody can pinpoint that spot, it would be him. He knows every square inch of terrain between here and Mica."

Flander stepped back inside.

"Where can we find him?" he asked.

"Up at La Forme in the old mining town, he lives there all by himself. Shall I give you directions?"

"That would be appreciated," Flander replied undaunted by Speer's withering look.

"I will draw you a sketch," the commissioner promised.

That was yesterday. Not a further word was said about it till the next morning, when Speer made no bones about his intentions.

"Peter, we should push on," he remarked.

"Where to?"

"Back to Calgary. That entire region, as we have heard, is afloat in oil. Let's pull up stakes and be gone."

Flander realised it would be the most sensible move, yet he lacked the necessary resolve to carry it out. Not before a serious attempt had been made to search for the mysterious ore body, extolled by Melrud, and depicted on the esoteric sketch. He had become captive of an inexplicable excitement, stoked by a prophetic awareness of enormous proportions. His notion to be near the threshold of fabulous riches could not be dispelled. He wanted to sound conciliatory for more than one reason. First, he was loath to go it alone; second, his friend was in better pecuniary shape.

"You are right, Philip, we should head back to Calgary."

"Good, let's pack up today."

Getting no immediate response, he looked at his companion expectantly. Flander tried to smile, with little success, however.

"Now, Philip, don't fly in a passion again, I do have a small request."

The words made Speer start angrily. More resentment no voice could have mastered than his when he snarled:

"Not the old litany again."

"Call it what you want, the answer is yes. Laugh if you wish, scoff to your heart's content, but listen."

Since his friend neither cut him short, nor turned away, he felt encouraged to say the rest:

"I think we should make one more attempt to unearth the mystery of this mine."

"Mine?"

"Claim, if you prefer."

"What have you got in mind?" Speer asked irritably.

"A visit to Shark up at the ghost town."

"You expect me to come with you?"

The conciliatory tone, besides surprising Flander, no less encouraged him.

"Yes, I should not think of going alone," he declared.

His companion then said something that made his earlobes tingle. It were the words:

"Alright, when do you want to go?"

"How about tomorrow, first thing?"

They had trekked four mortal hours by now on a narrow path, leading nowhere it seemed. Eastwards, up the mountains it went, on a trail left by the passage of time, leading to a forgotten world. But they plodded on, driven by a burning expectation on the part of Flander, spurred on by a sense of gloating in Speer's case. Being the more robust, he walked ahead and set the pace.

Their march had started in good cheer, engendered by the sparkle of a bright morning, and sustained by the sight of shimmering ice fields. Flander walked briskly on. Heartened by the prospect of forthcoming information, he did not spare himself. But as the sun rose higher, his enthusiasm sunk. Falling behind, he remarked:

"I say, Philip, the old fellow surely likes solitude."

Speer said nothing, he just hastened his steps. After a while he became aware of an inexplicable sensation rising within him, a perception he was unable to define. Perplexing it was, but raising his hopes nevertheless that this wild-goose chase might soon end. The odd furtive glance over his shoulders made him aware of Flander's growing edginess. He appeared to be on the verge of giving up; but he erred. True, his friend became visible vexed and weary. His normally glib tongue seemed frozen in his mouth; the initial brisk strides had turned hesitant. Indeed, the whole man exuded dejection and consternation. The exertion amid a savage land, made worse by rising doubts, was written all over his face. Chuckling to himself, he accelerated his steps.

Speer lacked prudence. He would have been well advised to take a closer look at his friend. Wiping that smirk off his face, and paying heed to his companion's transformation, might have been beneficial to his health. But little did he understand, nor care what went on in Flander's mind. To be sure, he noticed the striking change, appalling really, which gave his friend a Mephistophelian aspect. Gone was the wonted smile; the sympathetic air had yielded to clouds of malevolence, gathering ominously on his brow.

The first harbinger of impending danger had arrived. Yes, Speer should have suppressed his chuckles, innocent enough, over his friend's lack of physical stamina and mental constancy. For Flander noticed his condescension, albeit expressed in silence, he felt and saw everything. What he beheld roused the demons of a weak nature and vainglorious disposition. Ridicule, even expressed through gestures only, and meant to be benign, he could not tolerate. Little did his companion realise that he was trotting a perilous path. He should have been wary from thereon, but the guileless son of a Dortmund merchant carried on as before.

When they reached the top of a steep rise, a broad valley unfolded before their eyes. Speer was unable to stifle an appreciative whistle. It was a sight for sore eyes. As the sun pushed over the snow covered peaks, the voices of the wilderness broke out in a veritable crescendo. A more rousing greeting no king could have expected. Below them the rushing La Forme Creek seemed to grow more impetuous, as if being spurred on by the glory of a spring day.

Near the end of the valley, almost in the shadows of the Durrand ice fields, stood an assemblage of tumble-down shacks, which had seen better times. A more dreary picture could not have been imagined. Coming closer they espied a square built man in front of a less dilapidated hut, whom they instantly recognised as Thomas Shark. How could they have erred, after the gold commissioner's description and closing remark:

"Have no worries, when it seems that you are facing a two legged grizzly, that is your man."

There he stood, like a grim keeper, flanked by two staring mules, intent to portray an air of hostility, meant to frighten off visitors. He would have succeeded, had not an innate heartiness, suffusing the whole man, given the show away. For despite a gruff demeanour, honed by a forbidding surrounding, he did not fool them. A glint of joy, though suppressed, shone all over his face. When Flander asked:

"Are you Thomas Shark?" he was almost drowned in laughter.

"Well now, son, who else did you expect?"

Shark possessed the disconcerting habit of examining people with a blunt stare. His penetrating gaze, so it seemed, scoured every nook of a person's character. He must have found nothing wanting in the two friends, judging by what followed. While saying a few words to his attentive mules, he plunged both hands in one saddlebag after the other. Crying out: "Aha, aha," he pulled out a bottle from one of them. Eyeing first his mules, then his visitors, he sat the bottle on a nearby stump. Murmuring: "Alright, alright," he entered one of the huts, from which he emerged again with three glasses.

"We are not that backward," he announced, as he poured freely.

"Down the hatch," he said.

Setting his glass on a nearby table, he asked:

"Now, boys, what brings you here?"

Visibly embarrassed, Flander fished through his pockets till he found Melrud's sketch, which he held self-consciously in his hands. His request, even this trip, suddenly took on a silly aspect, unworthy of grown men. Amid stately hemlock trees, surrounded by towering mountains, Flander felt intimidated. An overpowering urge nearly made him turn around, and flee head over heels downwards again.

"Well, young man, the cat got your tongue?" Shark grunted.

"It's a delicate affair," Flander stammered.

Shark silenced him with a peremptory wave of the hand. He had no use for doughy airs and graces borrowed from books. His type either spoke straight, or shut up. Ahems or la-di-das found no resonance in a man of his stamp. As Flander continued to stare nonplussed at the shaggy recluse, Speer spoke up:

"We are seeking information about this plan."

With these words he snatched the sketch from Flander's hands and handed it to Shark who, after giving it a cursory glance, looked at them quizzically. Perusing the sketch closer, he started to mumble, then directed his gaze northwards.

"You want to know how to get there?"

Flabbergasted they asked in union:

"You know where it is?"

"I should think so. It is one of my old stomping grounds. Twenty-five years ago Matt Krenz and I scoured that area with pick, shovel, and pan. Six months we prospected in that godforsaken place, finding nothing but misery."

Chortling several times, he poured himself a stiff one.

"What a terror Krenz was. Should I tell you about him? Better not, except that he was German, the same as you fellows appear to be. Itching for mischief that critter was, and ever quick at the trigger. His sense of humour, so rare for men of his background, could make a mortician break out in belly laughs."

Sizing them up in silence, in an unmistakable manner of a man who knew more than he was willing to admit, he asked:

"You are serious?"

Speer shrugged his shoulders without saying a word. Contrary to Flander who, nodding vigorously, wanted to know:

"Can you tell us how to find the place?"

"I can, but be aware it is not easy, besides being fraught with dangers. Trails beyond Pelly Creek do not exist. It's axes and machetes from thereon."

Taking closer measure of both, he asked:

"How is your sense of direction?"

"So-so," Speer answered.

"Well, never mind, once you reach the mouth of the Downie Creek, you are on your way."

Seeing Flander preparing to say something, he added:

"You can not miss the spot. Just follow the main road till you hear the sound of a waterfall. Proceed upriver till it widens to a lake. Now, however, the difficult part begins. I better make you a little drawing. Handing Speer the sketch, he remarked:

"Remember, boys, once in there you might never return."

Little did that shrewd, far-seeing sourdough realise how prophetic these words were, especially in the case of Speer. Facing him squarely, the old man muttered:

"Be careful, son."

Eyeing Flander, who studied the sketch, he said more:

"Just be on guard."

That was it. Shark made no bones about his desire to be rid of them. Not in words, mind you, but with unmistakable signals, which spoke loud and clear.

On the way back hardly a word was spoken; their minds were occupied with thoughts which neither one was willing to share. Speer mulled over Shark's parting words, alternately deemed facetious, or augural. Were they meant as earnest advice? It appeared to be exactly that. Then why only to him, and not openly to both? Finding no ready explanation, he put it out of his mind.

Flander could hardly contain a smirk while fingering the charts in his possession. He felt good. A voice within him promised bright days ahead, which only Melrud, the Swede, could darken. He conjectured much, yet said little. As they neared Revelstoke, Speer announced:

"First we should visit the gold commissioner again."

"What for?" Flander bridled.

"Simple, Peter, we know the approximate location now, therefore a search should be feasible."

Flander balked at it with all his strength, till his friend declared:

"You go alone then. I'm not setting out on a wild-goose chase, especially in a remote wilderness fraught with unknown dangers."

"I don't follow you."

"The whole area might be staked and recorded by someone already. What then, I ask you?"

After some pros and cons, Flander saw the wisdom of his friend's assertion.

Next morning bright and early they showed up at the mining office. An assistant listened to their request, which he might have found strange, yet gave no sign of it. He appeared to be an old hand in such matters, a man blessed with many years of experience. One glance at their proffered chart made him sing out:

"What do you know, the old Downie Creek."

Surprised, Speer asked:

"Do you know the area?"

Taking a closer look, the clerk replied:

"Not that particular spot, but I sure am acquainted with this turbulent stream. In our younger years my wife and I used to hike up to Walter's cabin, where we spent a night or two. Ah, memories, memories," he muttered as he walked towards a shelf.

With an alacrity belying his advanced years, he appeared with a heavy ledger under his arm.

"There it is," he announced within a few minutes.

Indeed, there it was. A cursory glance revealed the fact that Shark's sketch drawn from memory resembled what the ledger depicted. The official plan, however, showed far more than the woodsman's pencil drawing. After some further perusal, the assistant wanted to know:

"What are you chaps up to?"

Now, that was an innocent question, besides being necessary, but it rattled them. The official, noticing their discomfiture, tried to smoothen things over. Tapping the opened ledger, he continued:

"This claim, you might want to know, may soon be in abeyance."

Speer, more proficient in English than his friend, had an inkling what that implied.

"How soon?" he inquired.

"By the end of the month, unless of course certain conditions are met."

Flander, who had procured a copy of the Mineral Act and Regulations almost immediately after their encounter with Melrud, vaguely recalled what that entailed. He quickly stated:

"That means the claim might become available to someone else."

"Exactly, provided they are qualified."

Speer, thanking the official, made a move to leave. Not Flander, however; he was of a more persistent bent than his comrade. Acquiring a most inveigling manner, he asked:

"Could we find out who the present owner is?"

"Jens Melrud, a well-known prospector," followed a ready answer.

The obliging assistant said more:

"From what I understand he has absconded, so chances are this claim will soon be public property again. I shall make you a copy of it, just in case you are interested."

Looking at Speer triumphantly, Flander appeared to be saying: "See, that's how it's done."

Thanking the assistant profusely, they left in a state of agitation.

Back at the hotel, a heated discussion ensued. Flander, although still awed by their extraordinary luck, was in no mood to listen to his friend's objections.

"I see it, Philip, the Swede needed a thousand dollars to maintain his property. And I sense something else: Melrud is no harum-scarum. In other words there is gold, rather tungsten in these mountains. Gird your loins, we are going to get it."

"How can we, you know Melrud is still the owner," Speer remonstrated.

"Not for long, me son, not for long."

"What if he comes back?"

"Don't be such a pussyfoot. I realise that we can not claim the property, not yet anyway, but surely we are permitted to look at it," Flander pointed out.

"Peter, I have a premonition."

"Oh, be quiet, let's be on our way."

That's what they did. Obtaining free miner's certificates proved to be easy. Tags and other necessities were purchased, despite Speer's objections, at the mining office.

"Just in case," Flander reasoned, "and quit being so negative."

Procurement of transportation and equipment turned out to be a bit trickier. They were available alright; as a matter of fact three outlets in town boasted to carry the most and best, and not too silently either. But prudence had to be the guideline here, for whenever someone shopped for outfits, no matter what reasons were given, they became an object of interest. Rumours circulated with the speed of light in that tightly knit mining town.

"We must do it gradually," Speer suggested.

Flander listened but did not hear, because his thoughts were racing ahead of good sense. Not a word did he utter about them to his unsuspecting friend, not one syllable about his intentions was aired. They were not exactly noble, but meant to give fate a hand. Their tags, if need be only his, would grace those posts before the target date. No last moment panting and running, and the devil fetch the hindmost. Getting around his companion? Oh well, let's wait and see, he promised himself.

"I have a better idea. Let's dazzle them with speed. Mules and gear can be obtained from Albert's place across the street. I say we give them a list today towards closing time, with instructions that all must be ready at daybreak tomorrow."

"We might be followed," Speer remarked.

"No doubt, but leave that to me."

Next morning, when the sun's rays had not yet touched the earth, they walked the short distance to the yard where their mules, fully laden, stood waiting. The establishment's owner greeted them in a subdued voice:

"There you are, gentlemen, all is ready. Provisions are packed to last over two months, provided you shoot the odd game. Have a nice trip."

Relying on outfitters in those days went without saying. Service, no less than discretion, were trademarks jealously guarded by them. A slip of hand or tongue could have meant the beginning of their end. They felt bound by a time-honoured code of trust. Just the same, the two friends exercised circumspection by initially travelling on a slow circuitous path. Criss-crossing, doubling back, they finally stepped on the main trail. Before doing so, however, they waited fully two hours. After intensive scouting up and down the path, Speer announced:

"The coast is clear."

Then commenced a long and arduous trek, fraught with obstacles no guidebook dared mention. Prolonged rainstorms soaked their clothes despite protective gear. Hordes of insects nose-dived upon them in between, seeking a spot on their bare skins, where they dug in with wanton speed.

After a week on the trail, they started to look at each other deliberately, silently inviting each other to say: "Let's go back." But they persevered; Flander out of greed, Speer sustained by pride.

Three days ago they had arrived in the area depicted on the sketches, without finding a trace of the mine. Just now, worn to a frazzle, nerves and tempers on edge, they were trying to circumvent a particularly marshy tract. It was getting late, the sun had tipped behind the western peaks rendering the air nippy, and their souls even colder.

As luck might have it, they stumbled on to higher ground which, being dryer, made Speer suggest:

"Let's camp here for the night."

Flander needed no further prodding, he accepted his friend's recommendation eagerly. In any case, he lacked the strength to be contrary. After unloading the mules, they slumped down exhausted, too tired and listless to set up their tents immediately. Speer, however, struggled to his feet again, for he had to get away from his friend's constant lamentations about fate's injustice, and undeserved punishment.

Walking upriver, jaded more on account of vexation than physical weakness, he almost tripped over a post sticking out of the ground in the middle of nowhere. In the waning light of approaching evening, he soon realised that it was a corner post of Melrud's mine. Disbelieving his eyes at first, he bent down to have a closer look. No doubt, the Swede's coveted mine had been found.

Than a strange sensation surged through him, a perception of impending evil, somehow connected with this discovery. For a few seconds he felt tempted to say nothing about it, but his ingrained sense of fairness gained the upper hand. Turning around, he hollered at the top of his voice:

"Peter, Peter, I have found it."

Flander, starting in surprise, not fully understanding, called out:

"You have found what?"

"Melrud's mine, you donkey," came an answer loud enough to make the mountains reverberate in a tenfold echo.

Flander's weary bones and languorous spirit received an instantaneous jolt. He bolted upright and ran towards his friend with pounding feet and throbbing heart. Striking some matches, for daylight had almost vanished, Speer read off the particulars. Claim Name: Second Grace. Locator: Jens Melrud. When he came to the last line, reading number of claim units, Speer whistled through his teeth:

"This claim is huge," he announced.

So it was. By all appearances it consisted of twenty units measuring five hectares each. Their excitement knew no bounds, it made them restless during most of the night.

By dawn the flames of ecstasy were flickering all around them, which soon, however, were doused by a grim reality.

"What an awful place," Flander muttered.

"True enough. Not without good reason did the old sourdough call it the tail end of a forgotten world," agreed Speer.

Indeed, the view in every direction was daunting. The entire region conveyed an atmosphere of dread. Never in their lives had the two friends felt so forsaken, seldom were two men more thankful for the presence of mules.

Just the same, anticipation drove them on. In a flurry they prepared and ate breakfast, then went on foot to survey the staked property. It proved to be an arduous task.

"Stupid us, we should have brought a compass," Speer repeatedly said.

True enough, in their haste they had not thought of it. By midday barely half of the units had been accounted for. Luckily all claims appeared to be on the west side of the river, for crossing that turbulent stream would have been near impossible. At the approach of evening they had found, and recorded every post. All twenty units had been identified.

"Just in the nick of time," Flander commented.

Absorbed as they were, the distance travelled had received scant attention. Their camp, hidden from view behind a bend would soon be swallowed by the growing shadows of dusk.

"We must be some ways from our tents," remarked Flander.

"I suspect so, three to four kilometres anyway," agreed Speer. "Time to head back," he added.

A three to four kilometre walk is a modest task for young legs and stout hearts. Yet two tired, hungry men can well consider it a daunting stint, especially on well-nigh impassable ground.

"Let's take a short cut," Speer proposed.

Flander, although not enamoured with the idea, nevertheless acquiesced. Darkness was setting in fast, saving ten, fifteen minutes therefore meant a lot. To increase their plight a stiff wind arose which, drifting down from the icecapped peaks, made them shiver to their bones. Anticipating a blazing campfire and hearty supper, they hastened their steps.

Then it happened so suddenly, that not even a cry of surprise escaped them. They had just reached the top of a small hill, when both lost their footing. Stumbling, gesticulating wildly, they tumbled down into a pit. Luck was on their side; they sustained no serious injuries. Beyond some skin abrasions and mild contusions, not much else went wrong. At least so it appeared at first.

After uttering strings of imprecations at themselves, followed by curses about the lack of prudence, they started to see the comical side of their little trip.

"Well, so much for a short cut," Flander mocked.

"Don't fret, we will be out and on our way in a jiffy," Speer countered.

Daylight had vanished by now, dusk yielded to darkness at an alarming rate. Flander started to walk around the pit, probing with his hands, measuring with his feet.

"We are imprisoned," he announced.

"Not for long, Peter, not for long," the ever optimistic Speer consoled.

But this assurance sounded not convincing, a tremor in his voice betrayed his fear. Both now searched frantically for crevasses or projections on which to gain a hold.

"These walls are like glass," Flander commented in disgust.

Moving around, probing here, kicking there, they reached a conclusion which Speer expressed:

"We are here for the night."

Utterly dismayed, Flander started muttering about being selected for punishment by the Fates. Speer paid no heed to his friend's lamentations. Weightier matters occupied his mind. Although he realised that nothing can be done till dawn, he nevertheless kept active. Groping around he estimated the cave's size at approximately three metres wide, six metres long, and at least four metres high. Reaching the top will not be easy, he surmised, certainly not in the darkness.

"Try to get some rest, Peter, that's the most sensible thing to do."

But sleep was not easy to come by; not only anxiety prevented it, but also the braying of the mules.

"They must be hungry," Speer conjectured.

"And lonely," Flander added.

They settled down for the night. Both grew silent, each pursued his own thoughts. At first they sat side by side, but gradually, as if by accident they drifted apart. Finally, being unable to sidestep each other further, they slumped down in opposite corners. There they crouched most of the night, nourishing a simmering resentment for each other. Flander squarely blamed his companion for their predicament, who secretly cursed the other's timorousness. As the night progressed, Speer's resolve to part company with him gained momentum.

Flander too had notions of his own. Though cowed by fear, they nevertheless were scurrying around a sinuous path of infamy. Every time a mule brayed, he looked daggers in his friend's direction.

When later towards the first shimmer of dawn the air grew nippier, thereby making him more miserable, his thoughts plunged into a miasma of self-pity. Then a terrifying thought assailed him, which elicited a piteous groan form his breast.

"Quit moaning," Speer snapped, thoroughly annoyed at his friend's snivelling.

That was easier said than done, for Flander appeared to be in a regular dither.

"What is it?" Speer demanded to know.

"Something occurred to me, Philip. Just think if a grizzly were to tumble down, that surely would seal our fate."

Speer made no reply, but the mere notion rattled him to the bones.

Dawn approached rapidly. At the first glimmer they were on their feet. After taking stock, a plan of escape was voiced by Speer.

"Peter, get on my shoulders and stretch your limbs till you obtain a hold over the edge."

"It's a long way up," Flander remarked.

"Never mind, we will make it. In any case it's our only way to freedom. Step right on my head and start groping. Once you gain a firm grip I will give you the old heave ho, and up she goes."

They were at it for over an hour, trying, swearing, and bellowing at each other, but it did not help. Speer had a notion to let his friend fall and give him a sound thrashing for his ineptness and lack of gumption. But then he called out:

"I got a good grip, Philip, push with all your might."

Gathering the remnants of his strength, Speer shoved with an Herculean effort. Fuelled by desperation, spurred on by a rising wrath, he managed to heave his friend over the edge.

"I will be right back," Flander promised.

"Don't forget the rope and the donkeys," Speer called after him.

Three hours had passed, Speer guessed by the sun's position. Then four and five, he presumed, but there was no sign of Flander. The mules had turned quiet a long time ago, indicating that they were taken care of. Silence reigned, only the wind made a rustling sound in the tall fir trees. Trying to keep his emotions in check met with scant success. He felt like Bunyan's pilgrims locked in the castle of 'Giant Despair' with not a sign of the key 'Promise' to unlock the sturdy gates. Suffering from thirst and hunger was hardship in itself, added to it pangs of distrust, rendered his condition unbearable.

Wild images raced through his head. Had Flander met with an accident? Did he lose his way? Was he just plain dilatory, or – or, had he been betrayed? Would his friend, or any man for that matter, leave him in the fangs of a slow cruel death?

Morning passed, so did the afternoon, yet Flander could neither be seen nor heard. As the sun dipped behind the peaks, Speer reached a state of terror. An awful premonition leaped at him, a foreboding that squeezed the air out of his lungs. This pit, skilfully dug out for unknown reasons, could well become his tomb. Utterly discouraged he slumped down in a corner. Shark's words came to his mind. "Be on guard" the old sourdough had said. What did it mean? Be on guard from whom? Surely not from his trusted friend of many years. Peter Flander perfidious? Impossible! not in a hundred years! Fickle, weak perhaps, but treacherous? Never! Yet that grizzled woodsman had a discerning air about him, as if endowed with second sight. In any case, where was Peter Flander?

Sapped by doubts, weakened by privation, he wistfully gazed at the dipping sun, which seldom before had been so fervently beseeched to stay. In the dwindling light of day he lost the remnant of his fortitude. But not quite yet, for suddenly he rallied. As if seized by Phocensian despair, he lunged at the bare walls. Again and again he tried to shinny to the top. Driven by desperation, spurred on by wrath, he assaulted these walls till his fingers bled. Rushing and roaring like a fury-blind buffalo, hurling himself up with tigrish leaps, he was unable to reach the edge.

Totally worn out, he collapsed on the damp ground. Darkness was setting in fast. To the man at the bottom of the pit it seemed like a pall descending inexorably on him.

There he cowered all night between the millstones of fading hope, and increasing resignation. Nevertheless, there were lucid intervals when he valiantly evaded the encroaching tentacles of despondence.

"Patience, courage," he alternately whispered to the starry sky, then moaned pitifully:

"Peter, where are you?"

Morning came and passed. His friend, the sole hope to life, remained absent now as before. No doubt he had become the victim of a fatal accident, he told himself one moment, only to repudiate it the next.

"The mules are too quiet, Peter is with them," he said again and again.

Something else had bothered him on and off all day, occurrences which until now he subconsciously tried to ignore. All day, since the crack of dawn, someone appeared to be prowling around. At times, as at the present, hammering and pounding could be heard, as much as crunching sounds made by walking on loose gravel. Footsteps, some heavy, others lighter, surely crisscrossed over the ground above. Hearing these noises at first sent transports of joy through him. Peter must be on the way with the mules in tow; rescue is in the offing, he sang out.

But after a while as footsteps and other sounds grew louder, then died away, and not a soul came near him, all hope took flight. Especially when after frenzied calls, that weakened his lungs, and lamed his vocal cords, no one stirred a finger to lift him out of his grave.

"Pure fancy, images of an inflamed mind," he then murmured disappointed and angry.

Nevertheless, no amount of denial could make these noises disappear. Someone busied himself up there; with what, he could not even guess. As dusk approached the hammering and shuffling abated, it grew fainter, till finally nothing more could be heard.

Speer, the man in the pit, understood none of the goings on, till he recalled the gold commissioner's words.

"After midnight at the end of the month, the property, should Melrud fail to update it, can be claimed by any qualified miner."

That was it! someone was just doing that, ahead of time; in other words jumping the claim. Many questions raced through his mind, to which no answers were found. Will he, or they, be back in the morning, or had the work been completed? How could someone be so close, yet not hear his cries? Then what did it matter anyway? He decided, survival rested with him, and nobody else.

Taking measure again in the dwindling daylight, he nevertheless concluded that only a miracle could save him. Yet miracles never come to the idle man, he knew. This realisation brought him to his feet, determined to challenge fate once more. Two metres stood between life and death, a distance he must find a way to bridge.

As his eyes searched for routes to escape, he became riveted to something above. What they saw, however, his mind did not register, yet it put him on his mettle. A sudden surge of optimism stirred his spirit. Assuming a conqueror's voice, he announced to the world above:

"Should I have to fight every sneering fiend of the universe, I will walk away from here. Soon, tomorrow maybe, the mountains will re-echo with peals of my laughter. Just wait and see."

Heroic words these were, vainglorious assertions, nevertheless repeatedly uttered with firm conviction. What instilled this confidence he could not have said, even less why his eyes remained engrossed with a nondescript object above, which was nothing but a pile of stone and gravel. Shaking his head he forced himself to turn away. Then it hit him like a thunderbolt: The path to freedom lay before his eyes!

In the fading daylight he realised the reason for his subconscious fascination with the mound of fractured rock and stone above the edge. This pile of excavated material, most likely blasted and dug out to make this pit, bore the means of his escape. Setting it in motion, not an impossible task, should bring enough material down to backfill the far end of his prison, thereby raising the bottom sufficiently to climb over the edge. Two metres, no more was needed to escape the clutches of death.

Darkness slowly engulfed the surrounding mountains. As always at this time, an eerie silence set in. The wilderness seemed to pause for breath. As if awed by the mysterious change from day to night, its feral inhabitants fell silent. Not for long, however. Soon the wolves would start howling, filling the air with sounds, frightening, yet at the same time setting one's soul at ease.

The night, though short now, nonetheless appeared never ending to Speer. Hunted by doubts, whipped by anxieties he found no rest. Spurred by a need to remain in constant motion, he strode and stumbled from end to end of his prison. Some moments his spirit soared at the prospect of imminent deliverance, at others a crushing load of hopelessness descended on him.

Finally dawn arrived, allowing him to set his plan in motion. Driven by impatience, he collected some of the larger stones from the bottom of the pit, and hurled them indiscriminately at the pile above. He soon recognised the futility of such blind exertions, as much as the need to husband his ebbing strength more prudently. Taming his rampant eagerness, he found a better way. To begin with he had to wait for the sun to rise above the mountains, which surely would improve his aim.

Waiting, not a small feat for a desperate man, turned out to be beneficial. His throws, more selective now, gradually became effective. True, success, though improving, did not manifest itself till many hours later. It proved to be a slow, cumbersome process, which he interrupted occasionally to strain his ears for signs of human life above.

Nothing could be heard except the voices of the wilderness, almost drowned out by the rush of the river, and intermittent sough in the treetops.

Speer kept at it for hours, despite few encouraging signs of success. When the sun moved across the zenith, scarcely the bottom of the pit's corner was covered. Amid increasing frustration, reward for his tireless efforts came suddenly, entirely unexpected. A small rock, hurled in a fit of anger, unleashed a veritable landslide. So much so, that the man below feared to be buried under it.

His misgivings proved groundless. What happened, no architect could have planned better. Nature achieved with ease what human hands had most likely to grapple with. The miracle, called in question by Speer, unfolded before his amazed eyes. Where a moment ago a sheer wall daunted his spirit, an inviting ramp lay before him. Clambering up that godsend passageway required little effort. Accepting his marvelous escape, however, turned out to be more difficult. There he stood among the living again, dazzled by the brilliant sunshine, stunned by a reality beyond belief. Tears welled up in his eyes, released by a delirious heart, beating in a rhythm as seldom before. The world was never so beautiful, gratitude imparted the rough wilderness a bewitching charm.

Tearing himself out of this trance-like state, Speer set out towards the camp. Using the river below as a guidepost, he found it within the hour. Being confused, weak and hoarse, attempts to call out remained fruitless. When he arrived at the site, he found it almost in the state they had left it three days ago. Not quite, he discovered on closer inspection. Some gear, plus most of the provisions were missing, as much as Flander and the mules.

It was late afternoon by now, leaving sufficient time to search for his friend. To his delight some provisions had been left, a gift from the Magi to a ravenous man. Eating on the run, as it were, he scoured the entire property prior to dusk. Not a sign of his friend or the mules could be detected. Sure enough, there were foot and hoof marks all around, which gave evidence of the presence of human beings, for these tracks were quite fresh.

Upon returning, Speer cut firewood to last all night. Soon a blazing fire lit up the surrounding, which he intended to keep flaring all night. He hoped it would show his friend the way to safety. For he must be lost, Speer thought, wandering around somewhere in the dense forest.

The mind was willing, the flesh grew weak. In less than an hour the licking flames resembled Poe's dying embers. Speer had fallen almost headlong into a swoon-like sleep, from which a bright sun roused him. Stung by guilt, he quickly set out again.

"I must find my friend, I can almost hear him moan for help," he announced to himself and the river.

He scoured the entire area till nightfall. The following day he forged ahead to higher ground into dense forests proceeding northward to a tumultuous creek, which prevented further ingress.

He tramped up and down these mountains for five days, without encountering Flander, their mules, or another human being. Only his dwindling food supply persuaded him to give up. With a heavy heart and guilty mind he prepared for the return trip. It was a sad farewell. Plagued by self-deprecation over the failure to find his friend, he vowed to come back better equipped, and accompanied by experienced trackers.

After fording a shallow creek, he cast a last glance around. Clearly, and in range of vision, stood one of the claim's identification posts. Now, any miner worth his salt would have stepped closer to investigate. Be it only out of habit, curiosity, or an ingrained desire to stay informed.

Not so Speer, who to some extend possessed a quirky nature. Having crisscrossed the entire property several times, thereby passing posts variously labelled, and trees visibly blazed, he never thought of taking a closer look. Had he done so, much chagrin would have been spared him. But such was his make-up; inquisitiveness had never caused the merchant's son an uneasy moment. Besides, his mind was occupied with weightier matters. His friend's fate stood in the balance, he might be hovering between life and death.

Holding on to his meagre provision, he walked westward along the bank of the Downie. He felt an affinity with that unruly stream of many voices. At times thunderous, then coaxing, always peremptory, never timid, and constantly in a hurry. Like the heralds in former times being eager to announce the king's proclamations, the Downie brooked no resistance on its way to one of North America's historic rivers.

Speer's desire to reach Revelstoke unnoticed remained unfulfilled. An old trapper, known as 'The Oracle of the Selkirks', spotted him despite his endeavours to remain unseen.

"Greetings, friend," words of that nature reached his ears before he saw the man.

"How is life treating you?" followed in a voice bespeaking pleasure over their meeting, a pleasure which Speer did not feel. He wished the old man into the fangs of the devil.

Soon, however, that attitude changed when he learned the most astounding news, so incredulous that it took days, if not months to digest. Even after many years the thought of it made his flesh creep. After customary small talk, expected by woodsmen in these parts, Speer, just to say something, asked:

"You haven't perchance seen a stranger pass by lately?"

"You mean the German chap with two mules?"

A bolt of lightning at his feet could not have given him a greater jolt than these words, especially when the garrulous trapper continued:

"A queer fellow that was, I must confess. Forever on the jump, fidgety as if plagued by a tic. By all the saints, I never met a man so rattled."

"When did you see him?"

"Hm, hm, let's see now. Four, five, no, six days ago. If you want to join up with him, I tell you, stranger, you need wings. At the rate that chap was going, he must be past Toronto by now; and that's an understatement."

"Did he mention his name?"

"No, but I can describe him to the last freckle."

He did. It was Flander alright, no doubt about it.

"But it can not be," he almost shouted at his informant, who seemed intrigued by this stranger's behaviour.

Speer, being loath to compromise himself, checked himself in time.

The bitter truth hit home when he arrived in Revelstoke, where he met Thomas Shark, the old prospector, gifted with second sight.

For some reason the matter-of-fact woodsman ignored him at first, but then changed his mind. Crossing the street he greeted him somewhat reluctantly, as though considering the encounter unwelcome. Just the same the subject of Melrud, more so his claim, arose in no time. Shark could scarcely conceal his bewilderment at Speer's nonchalant attitude, which to the seasoned sourdough appeared to be deceptive, if not offensive. He felt hoodwinked, made sport of in a way.

"Where is your partner?" he inquired in a tone gruffer than intended.

Noting Speer's discomfort over such an innocent question, Shark considered him closer. What he read in the younger man's face puzzled him. He seemed to be torn between a desire to unbosom himself, and a fear by doing so to become vulnerable. Shark, not inclined to pry, merely remarked:

"I see Melrud's claim has changed hands."

"Oh, has it?" Speer replied disinterested.

Eyeing him with unconcealed annoyance, Shark went his way without a further word.

On the next day Speer visited the gold commissioner's office. Shark was right, the title of Melrud's property had been transferred three days ago. The new owner was Peter Flander. So that was it, his friend had left him behind to die. Out of greed he intended to condemn his loyal companion to an ignominious fate. Shark's ominous words came to his mind; the old woodsman evidently saw a consummate scoundrel underneath the veneer of probity.

Speer's action from thereon remained enigmatic even to himself; it could neither be called logical nor credible. It could only be ascribed to a quirk in his nature. For two mortal weeks he roamed around Revelstoke looking for Flander whom he intended to murder. With throbbing temples and boiling blood he went from hotel to hotel, checked in every bar, questioned all who listened, still he found not a trace of his destined victim.

Amazingly the notion to enlist the law never occurred to him. He neither contested Flander's spurious claim, nor did he lodge a complaint with the appropriate authorities. His unsophisticated personality only desired to strangle him.

After two weeks searching high and low, Speer gave up. Flander was obviously off and away. Maybe the Oracle of the Selkirks spoke the truth when he said that the nervous stranger he met seemed to travel at the speed of road runners.

Still on the lookout Speer travelled eastwards, never relaxing, constantly fanning the flames of retribution. His vigilance proved futile, besides, engendering undue vexation. Finally he forced himself to forget Flander and this ignoble episode.

Returning to the country of his birth, he started a new life. It turned out to be quite a chore. Materially he soon flourished, mentally he suffered. For the land of the midnight sun, traversed by grizzlies and howling wolves, had touched his heart. There were sounds, stirring chords in his being that refused to be silenced. The splendid loneliness of that untamed, yet soul-soothing wilderness, had left a mark on his character, which no amount of adulterated civilisation could expunge. The seat of his cradle, Germany, now deemed him terrible commonplace; it deemed him a country peopled by inhabitants trying hysterically to be accepted.

Today his lawyer was scheduled to pay a visit, the last one, should his demands not be met.

"You tell me all I want to know, or engage another lawyer," Mr Kessler had put it to him in his inimitable way.

Within the hour two prison guards fetched him. He was let to a private room where Kessler sat waiting. Poised with pen and paper, his mien set, he looked a symbol of competence. Without preamble, nor any attempt at niceties he came to the point:

"Now tell me everything," came a curt request.

Speer started talking. He related what happened twenty years ago in the wilds of British Columbia. Kessler listened attentively, made notes at times, plus asked the odd question. His face remained inscrutable, no conclusion could be drawn how Speer's narrative affected him. He just listened and wrote. Only towards the end when Speer described their unexpected meeting after all these years, did he come to life. Lifting his head, he glanced at him as though he had just been caught lying.

"You stepped in Flander's rooms behind Weil, you say."

"I did."

"Then what happened?"

"I saw that miserable scoundrel standing at a desk."

"You recognised him instantly?"

"Yes, though changed considerable. Yet deformed he deemed me, I knew it was him."

The lawyer then became uncharacteristically agitated. Considering Speer closer, as if undecided how to say what was on his mind, knitting his brow, he asked:

"Did anything particularly strike you about him?"

"Hm, he seemed to be in a state of advanced languor."

"Like someone drugged perhaps?"

"Exactly," Speer cried.

"He also recognised you, I take it?"

"Immediately."

"Was anything said?"

"Yes. He stuttered: 'You – you,' then croaked, 'God help me.' "

"And then?"

"I lunged forward and strangled him."

At this admission Kessler winced visibly. He expressed his displeasure by drumming the table with his fingers.

"Did Flander hold anything in his hands?" Kessler asked.

"What do you mean?"

"Well, did he aim a gun at you?"

"No."

This unexpected denial earned Speer a censorious glance.

"Did you feel threatened?"

"By that shrimp? Ha, ha, ha, do you hear me laugh?"

Kessler ignored his client's attempt at bravado, he appeared to be occupied with decisive matters. When Speer took up the thread of his narrative, the lawyer raised his hand to silence him. Clearing his throat a few times, he explained:

"Your defence must proceed as follows: Despite extraordinary provocation when you faced each other, you maintained an exemplary composure."

Dismissing Speer's intended protest, he continued:

"Past injuries were forgotten and forgiven by you. However, at the sight of Flander aiming a pistol at you, action was called for. You attempted to wrestle the gun out of his hands, as any man would. A scuffle ensued, which might have gotten out of hand. No matter what, it was self-defence; no more, no less. Incidentally, Weil, the only eye witness besides yourself, concurs with it."

Speer shook his head vigorously.

"That's not what happened."

Kessler, a pragmatic man with a finely honed jurist's mind, could scarcely refrain from boxing his client's ears. Suppressing his indignation over so much obtuseness, he advised curtly:

"It is the best, if not the only basis of defence with any prospect of success. By the way, I propose not to call you as a witness."

"Because I am too honest?"

Looking him squarely in the eyes, Kessler replied:

"No. Too foolish. Weil is our trump card, we must play it to the hilt."

Chuckling, Speer murmured:

"Have it your own way."

Raising his eyebrows he asked:

"Tell me, why would Weil lie?"

"That's not my concern, neither should it be yours," came a gruff rebuke.

Then he added:

"In any case a loaded pistol, bearing Flander's fingerprints, was found at the scene of the crime."

Speer, dumbfounded by this revelation just shook his head in disbelief.

Alone in his cell again, he tried to piece together the fragments of this conundrum. He could have sworn on his mother's grave that Flander's hands were empty when he stretched them out defensively. So how could anyone have felt threatened by that quailing heap of misery?

"By all the saints, a man of my built, spurred by red-hot fury, could handle such twerps with both hands tied behind my back," he announced to the blank walls.

Weil's behaviour baffled him to no end. His willingness to commit perjury, thereby helping him, perplexed and harassed his mind. Surely not out of friendship, which did not exist. Because of an ulterior motive? Perhaps. But he, Speer, could not think of a single one.

The trial ended in an acquittal. Speer took up the threads of his former life, or at least tried to. An annoying fact soon surfaced. His past in Canada, jealously guarded till now, had of course become public knowledge. Some people seemed to be miffed by the notion that their staid business acquaintance of many years was once stalked by grizzlies, and chased across the tundra by polar bears. Whether from envy, or perhaps they were not made privy to it, Speer could not determine. He did not care. Filling his urn of vexation above its brim, however, was the curious conduct of Franz Weil, who seemed to avoid him deliberately. Try as he may, he could never catch up with him to express his appreciation in the most delicate manner.

Three months had past since he had stepped out onto the sunlit street girding the prison. He still wanted to meet Weil, driven more by curiosity than a desire to convey his gratitude. However, he did not succeed to join up with his elusive benefactor. Weil's testimony, false to the core, therefore remained draped in layers of mystery. But soon the veils would drop, exposing singular hypotheses, and no less incredulous revelations.

The hour was approaching when he and Kessler would meet at the Mohringer Klub. What a surprise awaited him there. Kessler, surrounded by finely clothed and bright-faced men, appeared to be cracking jokes. That was difficult to believe. To perceive the standoffish jurist exchanging banter with club members, flirting with waitresses, and, yes, even humming a tune. Speer, at first a bit self-conscious, soon fell into the spirit of things. When they sat alone at a private table the conversation drifted in no time towards the trial and Franz Weil.

"Have you seen Weil since your release?" Kessler asked.

"To my regret, no."

"Well, cease regretting."

"What is that supposed to mean?"

"He disappeared."

While Speer still tried to digest that morsel of information, Kessler explained:

"The police are trying to locate him for the past three weeks."

"What for?"

"Murder."

"Poor chap, whom did he kill?"

"Peter Flander," Kessler said with a twinkle in his eyes.

"You are joking of course."

"Hardly. The authorities are convinced, as much as I, he killed his boss and benefactor."

Speer, waiving that notion aside, said laughingly:

"I realise you are in a festive mood, but fables are fables."

Stretching out his hands he repeated:

"These hands choked the miserable traitor to death."

Kessler raised his glass in a mocking gesture.

"But you didn't, my foolish client. True, you strangled him, but not to death; Weil took care of that. By the way, the police might want to question you. Mum is the word if I am not present."

"That's understood. Now let's hear about your theories."

"What I am going to tell you is strictly confidential, for the moment in any case. As you recall the trial, sensational by any comparison, had been largely forgotten by the public as much as by the police."

"Then why the turn of events?"

"The police commissioner died suddenly about a month ago. His replacement, Horst Tauber, for some reason reopened your case."

Seeing signs of dismay on Speer's countenance, Kessler assured him:

"Don't worry, nothing can happen to you. Double jeopardy does not exist in our country."

"You said, for some reason?"

"I can only guess, but here it is: Tauber, the new commissioner, knew Weil. At a chance meeting during the trial, in this very same club by the way, he confided in me: 'There is something slinky about that man, which no amount of feigned affability can hide.' "

"Oh, you know each other?"

"Not really. Till recently one could have called us nodding acquaintances, nothing more. But lately Tauber has taken an interest in me because of your trial. In short, it bothered him, the proceedings that is."

"Did he say why?"

"For one, the pistol affair."

"There was no pistol," Speer interrupted in a tone of finality.

Kessler's high spirits were not dampened by that reproving remark. He eyed his erstwhile client with a mixture of benign disgust and suppressed jubilation.

"You have never been so wrong. The police found the gun alright, but they neglected to draw the right conclusions. That was beyond their competence. Giving credence to Weil's explanations proved far easier. His perjury, a godsend to you, arose from sheer necessity."

"I don't understand."

"Well, as it turned out, telling the truth about the gun would have been synonymous with tying his own noose. Therefore, his initial statement to the police, false to be sure, had to be repeated in court."

"You mean that Flander aimed a pistol at me?"

"Exactly."

"It never happened."

"No doubt; but that lie saved your neck. No better defence, in my opinion, could have been found."

Speer made no reply, his whole being took on a wistful air. A curious smile, quite involuntarily, flitted across his face, as he looked at the sumptuous decor of the establishment. Seeing the escutcheons on the wall, the stained glass windows, he could not help comparing the gracious surrounding with that lonesome pit and the Selkirk Mountains; forbidding, yet of an unforgettable beauty. The experience there, he realised, had given his life a meaning which he could never share with his fellow men. Sighing deeply he asked:

"Where does it stand now? Weil, you say, has skipped."

"So it appears."

Kessler perked up. Something, rather someone, had caught his attention. A man, no longer young, quite distinguished looking, had entered the club.

"There is Horst Tauber. May I invite him to the table?"

"By all means," encouraged Speer.

As Kessler rose to approach the commissioner, Tauber waved him back. His keen eye had already detected them, he steered straight towards their table.

"I hoped to find you here," were his first words.

"Now that you did, please take a seat," Kessler invited.

They shook hands. When Kessler pointed at Speer, the commissioner announced:

"No need to introduce your client, I shall remember him, and his trial to the end of my days."

Shaking Speer's hand with surprising vigour, he declared:

"You can set your conscience at ease, sir, your innocence has been established. An assault you committed, but not murder. No, Weil took care of that in a most vile fashion."

"Have you found him yet?" Kessler inquired.

"No. We probably never will, but we found compelling clues of his misdeed."

Noticing their astonishment, Tauber explained:

"The smell gave him away."

"The smell?" parroted both.

As Tauber nodded, a broad grin creased his countenance.

"Yes. A fortuitous remark hurled me on a trail of no return. The chief of police came to see me one day. As he stepped into my office he stalled, sniffed left and right, than said more to himself than to me: 'Gee, it just smells like that Flander fellow who got killed not too long ago.' "

Resting his eyes first on Kessler, than shifting to Speer, Tauber said, emphasizing every word:

"That casual, innocent comment kicked me into action. You see, I have spent quite some time, on and off, in the island of Haiti and Dominica, the home of a singular tree called Cashimar Zombi. It exudes a smell, sweet and unique, incomparable to any other scent. On my return from Dominica, a few days prior to my chief's visit, I had smuggled in some of that tree's bark. Ground down, it gives off a fragrance only the dead are not affected by."

Pausing for a moment the commissioner chuckled:

"I can see that you are not impressed so far. 'What is significant about a scent?' you might say. Nothing much on the surface, till one digs a bit deeper. This odorous powder, mixed with other ingredients, produces a most infamous concoction. Depending on the dose, it induces permanent death, or suspended animation. Its distinction is the fact that it can not be traced easily, if at all."

"What is the inference?"Kessler asked.

"I will get to that in a moment. As you are aware, counsellor, I did not agree with the coroner's verdict."

"Natural death due to heart failure, was it not?"

"Yes. By and large a correct diagnosis, but lacking a vital complement."

"What would that be?" Speer queried.

"Heart failure, that was willfully produced by unknown substances."

"In other words Flander was poisoned, you say."

"Poisoned by Franz Weil in the bocor fashion of Haiti."

Neither Kessler nor Speer were acquainted with these sinister rites and villainous practices, risen from the damp soil of Africa, transported westwards in the holds of slave ships. Tauber, no stranger to voodoo and obeah, sensed a silent encouragement to say more. Drawing closer to his listeners, he said:

"Two more discoveries, one by chance, the other through research, supported my hypothesis."

"What were they?"

"Weil, I learned from Dr Bancour, an acquaintance from Haiti, had been wandering around the interior of Dominica.

That seemed unusual for a casual visitor, but his reported meetings with the notorious Alamanda were outright suspect."

"A loose woman, I take it?"commented Speer.

"Not in that context. Her unsavoury reputation rests on viler laurels. She is decried as a secouya, practicing bocor. In other words, she prepares what is known in esoteric circles the infamous 'Drops of Farewell'."

"The poison you referred to?"

Tauber nodded assent. Kessler then wanted to know:

"What was the other discovery?"

"Listen to this: Weil, by virtue of a codicil, testated some time prior to your client's long sought interview, was made a major beneficiary of Flander's estate."

Kessler, raising his eyebrows, looked squarely at Tauber.

"Are you implying he finagled it?"

"I am convinced he planned everything, quite cleverly too."

"But not the matter of the pistol obviously?" prompted Kessler.

"That turned out to be a major false step on Weil's part. I suspect he had temporarily forgotten about it. So after the pistol was discovered under Flander's corps, he must have found himself in a dither to explain it away. His statement that it was aimed at your client made no sense. Flander did not know his visitor's identity. Why then would he keep a loaded gun at his side, which in any case he lacked the time to grab and point?"

Tauber, noticing Speer's assenting nods, as much as the lawyer's reproving scowl, was unable to suppress a grin.

"What happened in Dominica?" Kessler asked quickly.

"The first two days we got nowhere, for Alamanda was on one of her rambles."

Observing their inquiring looks, Tauber expounded:

"She gets drunk once in as while, then wanders down to Roseau, where she rampages like a corn levelling tempest. We did link up with her on the third day. Negotiations proved ticklish, to say the least. Only Dr Bancour's endeavours achieved results. Lucky for us he happened to be on the island."

"She trusts him, in other words," remarked Speer.

"Implicitly. She confided that Weil had purchased a phial of her brew."

"I be darned," Speer blurted out.

"You will be darned some more once the rest is known. An autopsy was performed at which Dr Bancour assisted. Sure enough they detected traces of Cashimar and other complementary substances. All fell into place, Weil's culpability became evident. He was sort of grooming you to become his hatchet man. He was privy to your and his boss' true identities. Moreover, he learned about your past in Canada from a scared, contrite weakling. By revealing what should have remained unsaid, Flander sealed his fate."

Shifting uneasy, Speer could not refrain from exclaiming:

"Weil's surprise therefore upon learning our actual names from me, was nothing but a false show."

"I am certain it was. I am equally sure he must have suffered agonies, when after your departure Flander rose from the dead, as it were. What now? a voice rising from the bog of despair must have screamed. A full hour elapsed between the time you left, and Weil notifying the police. A curious omission no doubt, vindicated by Weil with his frantic attempts to resuscitate his dear friend and boss."

"That I don't find too far-fetched," Kessler reasoned.

"We do. Something far more tragic happened. A drama unfolded in that hour worthy of Aeschylus' best. When Flander staggered to his feet, glad to be still alive, he most likely wanted to forget the episode. Unlike Weil, whose sole desire was to see his boss dead."

Turning to Speer, Tauber said:

"That man must have cursed you by bell, book, and candle for not finishing a job you were selected for. Flustered, Weil prayed for an inspiration; it came. Alamanda's 'Drops of Farewell', he suddenly remembered, were close by. The concoction of a dark, earthy people would succeed where the pale hands of civilised man failed. Quick as a flash he fetched the little bottle. Persuading Flander to swallow the proffered fragrant medicine proved easy."

"Conjectures, my friend, nothing but imagery, lacking the tenets of evidence," cautioned the lawyer.

Tauber eyed Kessler contemplatively. His mien expressed irresolution, but also an urge to say more. Shifting his glance to Speer, he decided otherwise.

"Unfortunately I am not at liberty to divulge our proof, but it is sufficient to obtain an indictment. Hear the rest. There, in that posh surrounding started a tug of war between two men praying to different gods. Weil, waiting for the poison to take effect, no doubt, secretly railing at providence, while openly reassuring his boss with words of encouragement.

"Flander, in time, recognised an awful fact: The commended medicine was in reality deadly poison. He felt his end nearing, but he would not depart alone; the traitor standing there was going to accompany him. He managed somehow to divert Weil's attention. Perhaps by asking him to fetch a document filed in an adjoining room. What a surprise was in store for Weil. When he returned he almost thrust his nose into a gun squarely pointed at him. Eternal hell must appear like a tickle compared to his momentary anguish."

"Momentary?"Kessler asked.

"I say so advisedly. We have reasons to believe that, just as Flander was about to pull the trigger, probably uttering a triumphant whoop, he collapsed; the end had come."

Pretending to listen to the music, the three men fell silent. Kessler, lost in thought, started the devil's tattoo. Speer's countenance clouded over. His creased brow left no doubt that something disturbed him. Casting sidewise glances from Tauber to Kessler, he cleared his throat, then asked:

"This potion, commissioner, can induce death or suspended animation, I understand."

"Indeed, it does."

"Hm, could Flander have been buried alive?"

"The possibility exists," came a laconic reply.

Speer turned his head, he did not want the others to see his satisfied grin.

Star-Crossed

The moment he saw the figure at the bottom of the hill he knew it was Marvin Hirt. No other man moved like that. Not for nothing was he called Marvin the Duck, whose gait he appeared to be imitating. Dan Merton had many faults; temporising was not one of them. Acting in split seconds when cornered saved his neck more often than once in his long chequered career. Hirt, like himself no longer in the blush of youth, would need at least ten minutes to reach the cottage, a lonely abode surrounded by tracts of grazing land. That should afford sufficient time to make the final preparations. Harbouring no illusions about Hirt's tracking ability, he had taken precautions, which only needed to be implemented.

Granted, in a sense he was caught between wind and water by Hirt's sudden appearance, but not seriously. From day one he had decided that running was not an option, hiding even less. Hirt, the veritable embodiment of a sleuthhound would find him in ultima Thule, or beyond. Besides, living in constant anxiety did not sit well with him, for he knew it sapped one's strength, and gnawed away the roots of life.

"Myra, Marvin is on his way," he called out.

In an instant a woman appeared from the house, dismayed, incredulity written all over her unlined face. She was no longer young, but nevertheless endowed with a feline suppleness.

"That's impossible, Marvin is still in jail," she countered.

"Well, he is out, plus a long distance from it. Here, convince yourself."

With these words he handed her the binoculars. One glimpse and she exclaimed:

"By God, it's him!"

Turning towards Merton, she stuttered:

"What now, Dan?"

"Now we act, I am ready," he boasted, bending reality a bit.

For although a plan had been hatched long ago, its fulfilment required a crowning touch. Merton harboured no illusion about his fate should his scheme fail. Dealing fairly with his erstwhile pal would earn him no laurels, but rather a term in prison. Hirt's baseness, more so his avarice was boundless, he knew.

As so often luck was on his side again. A fluky impulse two days ago prodded him to complete Hirt's 'Welcome Chest' as he called it. It was a fine piece of engineering, worthy of a Guy Fawkes, in his opinion. For this sudden inspiration he could have smothered his guardian angel with kisses.

"Wait here, Myra, I will be right back," he said, then entered the cottage from which he emerged in less than a minute with a small steel chest under his arm.

"Listen carefully, Myra. Take this chest to the bank, remove the strongbox from our safety compartment and leave this one there instead. Do you understand?"

Averting her eyes from the approaching figure below, she answered mechanically:

"Of course I do. You want me to exchange the boxes. What happens to the one in there now?"

"You remove it."

"Yes, yes, what then?

Noticing her head wandering towards the road again, he chided:

"Pay attention, Myra."

"I hear every word you say."

"Deposit the removed chest over at the bus station in one of the lockers, then wait for me."

Myra, neither surprised nor reluctant to obey, made no further inquiries. She had gotten used to his abstruse ways. Besides, questioning them invariably unleashed a hail of imprecations on her greying head. She did however venture to ask:

"What about you, Dan?"

"Never mind, do as I tell you. Hurry up, Marvin is almost at the gate," he urged.

She needed no second bidding, for the man down below terrified her more than all the fiends of hell. It was her former husband whom she had divorced against his will soon after his imprisonment.

"He is going to harm us, I feel it, I know it," she lamented.

"Not till he gets his hands on the securities," Merton chuckled.

Myra Turcotte, as she called herself now, made haste to get away. Meeting her erstwhile spouse; just the thought of it accelerated her steps. Marvin must be in a vile mood, she reckoned, knowing very well his abhorrence for any form of physical activity. Why he walked at all she could not even divine, for the road, not an avenue by any stretch of the imagination, was passable with many kinds of vehicles.

Would Marvin claim her again? Most likely. Would she find the courage to refuse? The answer to that question she preferred to leave in abeyance, for she had learned to heed Solon's words of wisdom. 'Know thyself' the Athenian had urged, which she reluctantly tried to do. Indecision coupled with submissiveness were two of her most annoying weaknesses. No matter how firmly she resolved to have her own way, at the end she always bowed to someone else's will. I do it for the sake of harmony. Isn't it a small token in return for peace? she consoled herself. Strange to say, peace, so fervently sought, eluded her grasp like an afterimage, forever present, yet never palpable.

Fate was in the habit of venting her whims on Myra Turcotte. Promising her a bed of roses, but leading her onto fields of thorns and thistles. True, the union with Dan Merton, while not ideal, could be termed a blessing compared to the brutish relationship with Hirt. Repose, however, for whose sake she would have endured any hardship, seldom graced her days.

Instead of dignified calmness, aspired to with all her heart, gnawing doubts and rampant anxieties were her lot. Yet, her strength being patience and optimism, she bore that lot with fortitude. She recognised the cause of that crackling tension which pointed squarely at her former husband Marvin Hirt, who served a jail term for robbery. When she suggested to Merton why not move prior to his release, abroad perhaps, he rebuked her roundly, always ending by saying: “Moving once more? No, and no again. It would resolve nothing, for wherever we go, an inescapable menace will accompany us. Marvin must be dealt with, no ifs or buts.”

The wheels to do so were in motion, she realised; where exactly they led to she couldn’t rightly guess.

“It’s been a long time, Dan,” Hirt called out, as Merton approached the gate.

“So it has been.”

“I have found you,” Hirt said, trying to suppress a sardonic smile.

“So you have,” Merton admitted. “I didn’t expect you for another six months,” he added.

“What have you been doing in all those years?” Hirt inquired.

“Keeping a low profile mostly.”

“In other words, hiding,” suggested Hirt.

“More or less,” Merton replied laconically.

“From me?”

“From the authorities,” Merton replied.

Hirt surveyed his past chum with piercing glances, searching with one eye for signs of trickery, sending menacing signals with the other.

Merton was not an easy man to gauge, he realised, he possessed traits which never crossed his own threshold. Presence of mind was one, inscrutability the other. He managed to remain calm where someone like himself plunged in all directions. No wonder he, Merton, continued to be at large, while bracelets bit into his wrists before he got a grip on the bags filled with securities. How Merton contrived virtually under the eyes of the law to spirit them out, bordered on a miracle. It certainly raised his respect for the man opposite him. Bargaining with him required a good measure of prudence, he admitted.

Merton shuddered imperceptible under Hirt's speculative gazes, which he knew so well. They contained vestiges of a ruthless mind and treacherous soul. Confronted by the thought that soon he should be beyond the range of these menacing eyes, he opened the gate. On the way to the house Hirt remarked:

"You stole my wife."

"She came to me."

"Where is she now?"

"Gone out east, visiting her folks."

This lie elicited a grin from Hirt, lingering on his face till they entered the cottage.

"Let's get to business," Hirt demanded.

"Yes, let us," Merton agreed.

Hirt, fully alert, ready to pounce, remained standing. It was a tense situation for both, marred by distrust, tarnished by a fear to be outwitted. Merton entertained no illusions about Hirt's intent, which his whole countenance advertised, despite an effort to conceal it. That malicious sneer, etched deeper by years of imprisonment, spoke volumes. The stakes being high for either one, Merton had more to lose, namely, his freedom. But all should go well, he consoled himself. Myra, although not privy to the entire score, must divine her errand's importance.

"You realise I have not spilled the beans," Hirt announced.

"You couldn't afford to," Merton reminded.

Ruing these words instantly he hastened to add:

"Anyway, I had not expected it."

Pretending to be mollified, Hirt inquired:

"How much was the take?"

Anticipating an evasive answer, he declared:

"From what I heard it approached two million."

"You heard wrong. At today's value your share amounts to about six hundred thousand, denominated mostly in government bonds."

"In other words gilt-edged and untraceable."

"Plus readily transferable," Merton assented.

Pulling himself up, Hirt growled:

"Well, let's have them."

"Don't be silly, Marvin, they are not here," Merton expostulated.

How two eyes, pinched to a slit, were able to whip up such waves of suspicion, defied description.

Straightening up to his full height, which could hardly have been called awe inspiring, Hirt grumbled:

"Not here? Where are they?"

"In town, in one of the banks, safely tugged away in a vault, ready to be collected by you."

"You are coming with me?"

This sounded more like a command than a question.

"Not on your life. Being seen with you would hardly be advisable. Who knows, you might be shadowed by one of those pesky private detectives hoping to be led to the second man."

Directing another menacing glance at him, Hirt sneered:

"You are not double-crossing me?"

"Could I afford to?" Merton chuckled.

Of course not, both agreed silently; one word from Hirt would send him up the river for many years.

Merton realised that he faced the horns of dilemma, rendered more perilous by the fact that unexpected circumstances had forced him to improvise. Hirt's untimely appearance imposed undesirable conditions, namely, Myra's participation. He felt apprehensive about it in retrospect, for although he knew her as an honest, loyal woman, her fickleness was always a source of concern to him. Distracting and leading her required little effort; added the reality that she seemed to be pursued by a string of ill omens, who could blame him for being worried. "I was born under an unlucky star," she maintained stubbornly. Possibly so, Merton had to admit, after witnessing how she stumbled from one predicament to the next.

But what should go amiss with an errand a child could carry out? Just the same he failed to free himself of a nagging premonition not quite definable. In any case the dice were cast; the Rubicon had been crossed, he had to go on.

Hirt had approached one of the windows through which he quietly surveyed the area. Clucking approval, he said:

"Great hide-out, Dan, perfect for a man on the lam."

"I am neither hiding nor running," Merton snapped.

The outburst elicited a fixed look and a smirk from Hirt, who countered:

"Keep your shirt on, pal, I was only musing. Anyway, let's have the particulars."

Merton showed reluctance to comply, for he wanted to gain time, since Myra had a tendency to dawdle. Attempts to engage Hirt in conversation proved futile, he wanted to be on his way. Besides, it raised his ire and fanned a lingering suspicion. Yet his departure had to be delayed to accord Myra a good head start.

Looking straight at Hirt, Merton inquired:

"Tell me, Marvin, did you mention my name to anyone, perhaps to another inmate, Myra, or anybody at all?

"Do you think I'm daft? Killing the goose before it laid the golden eggs? Not this father's son."

Nodding his head knowingly at Hirt's tacit revelation, an admission really of nefarious intentions, Merton hunted for a piece of paper, pretending that he could find none. A ruse, necessary, he told himself, to prolong Hirt's presence here. Myra needed all the time possible to fulfil her task, otherwise they might be heading towards a catastrophe.

Hirt grew restive. His countenance turned into a mask of annoyance as he glowered at Merton.

"A piece of paper you want? Here, take this," he barked.

Merton accepted it reluctantly as he racked his brains for another excuse to stall him. He couldn't think of any, certainly not on the spur of the moment. But Marvin had to be delayed, at least for another half-hour. Then he suddenly realised that there was only one way.

"I changed my mind, Marvin."

"About what?"

"Letting you go alone."

"You are coming with me then?"

"Not exactly, but I shall hand the chest to you in your hotel."

"That's more like it," Hirt commented with a grin.

"Give me your room number."

"Two twelve, write it down. Cattlemen's Inn, room number two hundred and twelve."

"Under what name did you register?"

"Murry Snag."

"You go ahead, Marvin, I shall follow later."

"Still don't want to be seen with me?" Hirt mocked.

"No, it wouldn't be prudent," came a curt reply.

Merton felt a strange sensation creeping up his spine as he watched his partner in crime ambling down the steep hill. Marvin is right, he granted, the cottage could be called a hide-out. Sitting on a hilltop amid tall ponderosa pine trees, the house was completely hidden from view. Though worlds away from the bustle of civilisation, the property was not remote. The town, spread across a huge valley, could be reached quickly. How Hirt had found him in this secluded spot, oceans, and thousands of miles away, bordered on magic, especially since he kept an extremely low profile. Did Myra secretly stay in touch with him? Keep her erstwhile husband informed of their movements perhaps? A preposterous notion, he immediately conceded, not worth another thought.

Merton looked upward where three hawks circled high above under a cloudless sky. Their effortless flight, inimitable for eagles even, never failed to fascinate him. Not today, however, for his mind was elsewhere. Plagued by uncertainty, riven by remorse over the course his life had taken, he wished to have wings like these graceful birds to soar to Elysian fields, and never return to earth.

Dan Merton was no ordinary felon. True, he partook in a robbery, termed the heist of the century, but that was an aberration, totally against his nature. A chemical engineer by profession, he led an exemplary life till Hirt took him in tow. They encountered each other by a fluke, in Merton's view, at the Lord Nelson Hotel, which Merton frequented for a long time. Being an introvert by nature, he scarcely paid attention to his surrounding. Had he done so, Hirt's never failing presence since six to eight weeks might have caught his attention. It never did, till that fateful night when he took the proverbial false step, after the bartender announced:

"Last call, gentlemen."

Glancing anxiously from the clock on the wall to the lounge's entrance, he added shortly after:

"Closing time, it's eleven o'clock."

Having imbibed beyond a thirst, Merton took exception to that reminder; he demanded in a belligerent tone:

"Never mind that, bring me another drink, one for the road."

When the bartender firmly refused, Hirt, sitting three tables away, invited Merton to a private place serving alcohol all night.

The gears were set in motion; the spider spun his web with skill and determination. It proved not easy to inveigle the upright technologist onto the crooked path. Promises of riches beyond the dream of a king of Lydia left the chemist unaffected; seemingly, it must be added. For his initial resistance gradually abated as he listened to the tempting words uttered by a master of subliminal persuasion.

The notion to commit a felony for gain, abhorrent at first, soon took on a hue of logic, and ultimately seemed like a duty owed oneself.

Hirt, who knew about the frailty of men, detected Merton's Achilles heel in a twinkle. Self-pity was the albatross around his neck, dragging him through the gates of discontent. Disgruntled men, Hirt has learned a long time ago, are easily led on.

"There is a bank in downtown Halifax dealing in high grade securities waiting to be removed," Hirt declared one afternoon at their secret meeting place.

"That sounds risky," Merton objected.

"Hear me out before you judge. I have been casing that bank thoroughly; I might add for over six months. My conclusion? To rob it should be a walkover, provided we find a way to circumvent the security system, which is beyond my comprehension."

Eyeing his newly acquired acolyte almost reverentially, he added:

"That's were you come in."

"In what way?"

"Did you ever hear about something called actino or aktino?"

"Yes."

"What is it?"

"A process whereby light rays induce a chemical reaction. Why do you ask?"

"That actino, whatever it is, furnishes the basis of the alarm system, I am told. Can you understand that?"

Thinking for a few moments, Merton declared:

"Yes. The faintest beam of light could release forces which are capable of opening or closing circuits, thereby sounding an alarm."

Smacking his lips, Hirt remarked:

"That means we must work in complete darkness, an impossible feat, if you ask me."

"Not necessarily, by all means, not necessarily," Merton consoled with an enigmatic smile.

The robbery took place two months later. Hirt got caught; Merton escaped with a sizeable booty. He slipped through the tightest dragnet ever woven around Halifax and beyond. Would Hirt divulge his identity? Were the authorities on his heels? He did not tarry to find out. Driven by a desire to put a great distance between himself and Halifax, he followed the setting sun till he reached Vancouver, where he laid low, till he discovered Stanley Park. He should have resisted the lure of that remarkable tract of land bordering on downtown Vancouver. But who with a heart in his breast, eyes to see, and ears to hear, could have withstood the temptation to stroll through that garden of Alcinous.

There he met Myra Turcotte, a stranger at the time. They instantly liked each other; both looked forward to the promenades along the sea wall. Their relationship flourished; they became intimate. Merton's joy knew no bounds; he felt like being wrapped in a web of delight. Youth, bid farewell long ago, reared its laughing head again. He was in seventh heaven from which he suddenly dropped with a thud.

One evening, mellowed by food and wine, Myra told him more than he wanted to know. Had lightning struck him it would have been less devastating than her revelations. Listening spellbound, undecided whether to bold or stay, he heard words which his mind refused to acknowledge. Unable to contain a rising consternation, he blurted out:

"Do I understand that you are Marvin Hirt's wife?"

Adding substance to his slip he remarked:

"Marvin Hirt, the bank robber."

"Was, Dan, was. I divorced him."

Myra, who could hardly be called quick on the uptake, raised her eyes and pricked her ears.

"Do you know Marvin?" she asked.

There seemed to be no alternative to admitting it.

"Yes, we had some business dealings in the past."

Showing no further interest, she just chuckled:

"What a coincidence."

"Indeed, it is," he commented, referring however to their own encounter.

That momentous conversation took place two years ago. Although its significance diminished, it never fell into oblivion for Merton. Two questions burdened his mind: Were they colluding with each other? Did Myra know about his complicity in the robbery? Granted, though she never indicated as much, she must surely divine it, he believed. He therefore observed her with eyes sharpened by suspicion, and ears rendered acute by doubt. Probing inquiries made now and then, produced not an iota of information; he detected no trace of duplicity or dissimulation. For a woman wearing her heart on her sleeve, possessing a tongue quicker than thought, concealing inner feelings would have been a Herculean task. In addition, considering her loathing for Hirt, not to mention fear, conspiring with him seemed unlikely.

With those reassuring thoughts Merton's distrust waned by degrees. Then again, having been taken unawares by Hirt's untimely appearance, left him no choice but to place trust in Myra. Her assistance became essential, regardless of her intentions. All should go well, he comforted himself on the way to town. Hirt would soon be found dead as a doornail, suffocated by a gas ten times more lethal than phosgene.

"A quarter breath kills instantly," his professor always said. Marvin would never know what assailed him, Merton gleefully envisioned. He could see him, bursting with impatience, greedily tearing at the lid of the chest, thereby releasing the deadly gas from a contraption rigged with inimitable ingenuity.

A quarter breath kills. It would forever seal the lips of the only eyewitness of his crime. A new life beckoned; soon the money he stole could be spend freely, without fear of detection.

To call Merton nervous when he entered the bank would have been an understatement. As he approached the vault, he felt exceedingly queasy, so much so that he entered the wrong code twice to gain entrance. Realising that a third abortive attempt would alert the bank's security personnel, he took a deep breath prior to trying again.

With his heart in his mouth and trembling hands, he reached for the chest in the private compartment. In his excitement he paid no attention to the wrap which was absent when he handed it to Myra. He practically fled from the bank and ran towards the hotel.

His knock at the door of Hirt's room received an immediate response.

"Come in, come in," Marvin hollered.

"All went well?" he inquired.

Considering Merton closer with gloating written across his face, Hirt mocked:

"Have you seen a ghost?"

"Why do you ask?"

"You look paler than a corpse, and shake worse than a man with palsy."

"There is your chest and here is the key. I must run. See you at the cottage tomorrow. The lid usually jams a bit, so give it a good yank."

Hesitating for a moment, Merton requested:

"See if the coast is clear. Since I might be followed I better take the back stairs."

It was a feint conceived on the spur of the moment which proved not worth a tinker's curse.

"Easy does it, pal, let's open the box and take a peek," Hirt suggested.

"Do it after I am gone, see you tomorrow."

With these words Merton strode towards the door. Quick as a flash Hirt beat him to it. With one movement he turned the key in the lock and slipped it in his pocket.

"You are not leaving till you open that box and help me tallying the contents."

"Marvin, I am certain of being followed. Let me out before it is too late," he pleaded.

"Hang it, man, I will open it then."

Saying so Hirt seized the key and inserted it in the lock. Merton, panicking, shook the door handle with all his might. With terror-stricken eyes he cried:

"Don't, Marvin, don't."

Hirt, paying no attention to his pal's weird behaviour, proceeded to lift the chest's cover. Merton, on the verge of a fainting fit, heard strange utterances.

"Ah, ya beauties, a sight for sore eyes ye are. Lovely, lovely, you warm the cockles of me heart."

Turning around, his eyes bulged and his mouth fell open when he saw Hirt rummaging with both hands through the box.

A terrible realisation hit him: Myra had dawdled again.

Steamboat Rapids

Julius Kerner and Lester Stewart were the most unlikely men one would have expected to become pugnacious; yet they did. Circumstances, so trivial to be laughable, gradually stoked their resentment for each other, which literally pushed them over the cliffs into the torrential water of the Columbia River. Fighting for dear life, which they could but lose, they continued to revile each other.

It happened prior to the inundation of a vast area in British Columbia. The historic river, originating in the flats of the Kootenay Range, still coursed untamed through narrows, gulches, past shores where not a single dwelling stood for hundreds of miles. Like on that ninety-mile stretch from Mica to Revelstoke. What a stupendous wilderness that was, still is, despite the flooding. It contained some of the wildest passages, inviting rafters from all over the globe.

Somewhat below the Silver Tip Falls the two acknowledged scholars got into a scuffle which made them oblivious to the steep embankment and the river below. While attempting to get their hands on each other's throat, they tumbled into the foaming stream surging southward, towards the Steamboat Rapids. Traversing that Charybdis unscathed, not a foregone conclusion for the best rafters, still meant facing the treacherous Big Eddy beyond. The chances of survival for two sedentary, elderly scientists, were pretty slim.

How two dignified men, learned to the fingertips, of mature years, ended up in such a predicament sounds unbelievable. Julius Kerner, a German Canadian, held the chair of mathematics at the University of Calgary. Lester Stewart, a native of Brighton, England, was the head of physics at the same institution. They knew each other for more than a decade; not intimately, given Professor Stewart's inclination to reticence, yet time did melt these layers of reserve. Over the years they gravitated towards each other to the delight of their wives. Dr Stewart seldom shared his emotions with anyone, in contrast to Dr Kerner, who could have been called an extrovert.

Though Gudrun Kerner and Arlene Stewart addressed each other by their first names, their husbands remained more formal. Professor, Mister, Doctor, were titles conferred on each other. To tell the truth, Arlene Stewart felt oppressed by all that erudition surrounding her. Her husband's standoffish personality, draped with veils of dignity, at times made her feel uncomfortable. That is why she sought the company of the Kerners.

Professor Kerner, in his early sixties, deemed her a burst of fresh air. That man loved to spin a yarn. His roguishness, unseemly for a man of learning, captivated and jarred her simultaneously. She sometimes felt tempted to partake in the merriment his waggishness produced, but fearing her husband's rebuke refrained from it. She knew that he would rather be swallowed by the earth than be caught laughing aloud.

Just the same, she found the company of Professor Kerner, dubbed Democritus, the laughing philosopher, rather refreshing. She was the first to broach a sensitive subject.

"Gudrun, remember you were telling me about a vacation you took some years ago?"

"Hm, let's see. Oh yes, you mean out west in Little Dallas Canyon?"

"As I recall that is the name."

"What about it?" Gudrun wanted to know.

"Is it still for rent?"

"We didn't rent, actually, some acquaintance made it available."

Looking at her friend with those blue, sparkling eyes, she chuckled:

"Are you looking for a place to spice up your marriage?"

Noticing her friend's pained expression, she quickly changed tunes.

"Forgive me, dear, I didn't mean to be tactless."

Nevertheless, Gudrun was unable to suppress a smile at the thought of that staid man turning into a gay Lothario under any circumstances.

After hemming several times, Arlene Stewart burst out:

"It's Lester."

"Oh, what's the matter with him?"

Haltingly her friend commented:

"I don't want to tittle-tattle, or burden you with my problems, but something is bothering me. Perhaps you can help."

"Well, tell me about it," her friend encouraged.

"You know Lester's preoccupation with achievements?"

"I do, there is nothing wrong with it."

"Perhaps so, but Lester is overdoing it lately, he is getting exacting beyond endurance."

"With his subordinates?"

"With me."

"Hm," Gudrun Kerner mused, anticipating her friend's familiar complaints, which however did not follow.

Something quite different occupied her mind. She quickly added:

"Let me explain, Gudrun."

"I am waiting."

"As you know, summer recess is approaching."

"Yes, yes," Gudrun prodded.

"Are you and Julius going anywhere?"

"We have no plans yet, why do you ask?"

"Well, to come back to my original question, it served a purpose."

"You mean about the cottage out west?"

Arlene Stewart nodded, then continued:

"As I said, Lester is going through hard times, he needs a rest. That latest experience with magnetic forces taxed his mental and physical strength as never before."

"I understand it hasn't been crowned by success."

Grimacing as if aggrieved, Arlene waved that aside.

"Be that as it may, he needs respite from his daily grind," she declared.

"In that remote cottage you mean?"

"Exactly."

"Do you want me to find out whether it is available?"

"I would be grateful."

Several days later Gudrun Kerner advised her friend that the little place stood empty.

"You and Lester can stay there as long as you wish," she remarked.

Well, it wasn't meant that way, Arlene Stewart let it be known.

"I am baffled," her friend admitted.

"Let me explain, Gudrun. The situation at home is a bit tense, a short separation would be good for both of us."

"So you want Lester to go there alone, I understand, but might it not be too lonesome for him there?"

"I realise it, but – but couldn't Julius go with him?"

A wry smile appeared on her friend's cherubic face. The notion of her husband, expansive, and inclined to levity, being alone with Lester Stewart whom he considered a pillar of graveness, made her wince. But being a good woman and loyal friend, she promised:

"I will manage my end, how about you?"

"I shall let you know."

It took some wangling to convince their men, but they ultimately succeeded. Lester Stewart balked at first; he found the suggestion preposterous. His wife, a woman of insight, sincerely worried about him, stuck to her guns. She expected opposition for reasons easily divined, but reluctantly cited. Her husband was loath to separate from the misery he abhorred. The path of many steps, although grinding him down, had become his reason for being. As mentioned, however, she prevailed.

The professors moved in on a sunny afternoon. Their hands were full with gear and provisions, their hearts were lightened by anticipation.

"A month of bliss, professor," Stewart announced.

"It will be that, plus more," Dr Kerner agreed.

Although these remarks were uttered with tongue in cheek, certainly by Professor Stewart, the prediction proved true.

It was a wonderful time to be there. The rainy period seemed to have ended; days were sunny and warm, and the nights delightful cool. Wildlife abounded all around; fish in the river could almost be caught with bare hands. True, the eerie silence, interrupted after darkness by the sounds of an untamed wilderness, intimidated them somewhat. But the novelty of a world contrasting sharply with their wonted environment, nevertheless enthralled them.

A week passed, a second one went by; their contentment increased from day to day. Fishing together and hiking brought them closer. Even Lester Stewart, ever distant, felt a growing comradeship for his vivacious colleague, so diverse from him. He visibly loosened up to an extent which dispelled professor Kerner's misgivings concerning that dreaded haughty reserve usually shown.

The third week arrived; on its heels followed heavy rain.

"That's a welcome change, my dear colleague," Dr Stewart observed.

"Indeed it is," agreed Dr Kerner.

Sitting on the covered porch, listening to the ceaseless patter on the roof, they felt at ease with the world.

"I hope it will last through the night," professor Kerner remarked, anticipating the rain's soporific effect.

It did, plus way beyond. A continuous, relentless downpour curtailed their movements; it kept them more or less imprisoned inside for the rest of their stay. The entire surrounding changed; an ubiquitous darkness prevailed inside as much as outdoors. Shifting clouds, descending ever lower, where now brushing the treetops.

"What a filthy weather," Dr Stewart complained.

"Ah, cheer up, Doctor, the sun will break through any moment," professor Kerner consoled, or in any case tried to.

Admittedly his exuberant spirit too had received a few nicks, yet he managed to put a brave face on a deteriorating situation. Not so his dour colleague, who started to grouse about everything.

"We should go back," he suggested.

"That is easier said than done, remember our arrangement."

"With the outfitter?"

"None other. They are slated to collect us at the end of the month," professor Kerner reminded.

"More than a week away," moaned Dr Stewart.

Things were going downhill from there on. Two days later professor Stewart ran from the cottage scolding like a fishwife.

"I can't stand it any more, God knows, I'm only human," he announced to the giant fir trees.

The imprecations were not hurled at the weather this time, but at something entirely different.

"That infernal noise will drive me over the brink," he informed the bursting clouds.

What made the sedate scholar act as if stung to the soul? It was this: Yesterday, while sitting in their usual places, muffled in silence, brooding about their loathsome situation, professor Kerner suddenly jumped up.

"I almost forgot," he declared to nobody in particular.

Hurrying to his sleeping quarters where he rummaged around muttering to himself, he cried out:

"There is the old gal."

Turning towards his colleague, he displayed an enormous mouth organ.

"Ha, Doctor, get out your dancing shoes, unlimber those castanets, we are going to have ourselves a party," he urged.

Then he played and played the entire day to professor Stewart's dismay, who felt like someone being slowly tortured to the marrow in his bones. But he was a courteous man, seldom prone to rudeness, unless overly importuned. He sat there quietly, trying to wrestle a smile from his lips, wishing to be somewhere else.

Professor Kerner, captivated by his performance, paid scant attention to his confrere's disposition, which in any case he deemed exalted on account of his merrymaking. But that was not the case. Professor Stewart exceedingly acquired the attributes of the proverbial sufferer Job. Misery was etched all over his stern face; wrinkles, not of joy, marred his brow. Being a decorous man however, he suppressed the urge to voice an objection, which in all likelihood would have averted a catastrophe.

Glancing towards his confrere to gauge his reaction, professor Kerner didn't like what he saw. Encouragement was in order. He called out:

"Now now, professor, lighten up, you look like a man chewing on the herba sacra. Here, this will cheer you up."

Saying so he struck up a lively mazurka. Professor Stewart, despite a rising resentment, repressed his nascent fury. Neither by gestures nor words did he manifest it. It seemed odd that someone bold and free in speech, not averse to reprimand or criticise, should not balk at this charivari, as he silently termed his colleague's performance; especially where no fear of abuse existed. For professor Kerner, despite his faults, was a gentleman and scholar of the first magnitude.

Did shyness prevent him to voice objections? No. Delicacy perhaps? Not in the least. The eminent physicist lacked not an iota of assertiveness. To the contrary; he had a penchant for imperiousness. The enigma's answer lay elsewhere.

Although incensed, bursting at the seams with wrath, he kept his temper in check. What force compelled him to suffer in silence? A simple gesture, accompanied by a few well-meaning words, playfully spoken perhaps, surely would have ended his agony. Yet he uttered not a syllable, he just sat there stoking the embers of hate. Not even when his zealous colleague, hoping to chase away the fog of dolour, stamped on the floor in the fashion of Polish folk dancers, did he protest. He just winced at every thud.

Again, why would a man, peremptory by nature, accustomed to call the tune, put up with something onerous that could be remedied so easily? It was an enigma which few would have been able to unravel.

His wife was one of them. Though unaware of the reason, she knew about this phenomenon. Her conventional husband, quick at repartee, suffered from a quirk bordering on absurdity. Being graced with a good measure of perception honed by dread, she discovered that her worldly-wise husband, resolute to a fault, showed a morbid reluctance to ask a favour.

It was a phobia really; silly, incomprehensible, yet true. Did fear of a rebuff count for it? Or a belief that it was beneath his dignity? She had thought about it frequently without reaching a conclusion. What of it? one might say, it's just a harmless caprice, so why fret?

However, Arlene Stewart was not in a position to revel in nonchalance. For her husband's affliction, mild, if not laughable, caused them both untold grief, which had left many scars on her psyche. His inability to make a humble request that needed to be made, rendered him ill-humoured and outright vengeful.

How she dreaded those dark moods, when the proverbial black dog's shadow appeared to be lying on his soul. He never talked during these doldrums, but his face spoke louder than words; it became a mask of seething hate.

Like at this very moment as he stood in the pouring rain, soaked to the skin, breathing revenge.

"I will learn that Knickerbockers, right now, and not a second later," he snorted.

Rushing inside, grunting like a wild boar ready to attack, he wrenched the harmonica from his colleague's mouth.

"What – what is this?" the startled player expelled.

"This is the end of my suffering," professor Stewart roared.

With a vehemence unexpected in a man of learning, he tried to break the offending instrument over his knee. Failing to do so, howling in pain, he plunged through the door. Hurling maledictions over his shoulders, he ran towards the river's bank.

"That blasted tin box is going for a swim," he hollered beside himself.

These were brave words uttered by a man no longer governed by reason. He didn't get far. Professor Kerner, bowled over momentarily, quickly recovered. He was a good-natured man, who normally would have treated his counterpart's tantrum as a lark; but not in this case, for the stakes for him were high.

The mouth organ, so rudely wrested from his hands, possessed an intrinsic value which no amount of money could replace. It was a heirloom inherited from his father, bequeathed by grandfather Kerner. When his confrere sort of manhandled the family treasure, professor Kerner, though annoyed, was not alarmed. But when he threatened to chuck it in the river, he acted with astounding alacrity.

Scarcely had professor Stewart raised an arm ready to hurl the harmonica over the bank, when he felt himself lifted into mid-air and thrown to the ground. That hurt his skimpily padded bones, but even more his heavily cushioned ego.

Jumping up with the agility of an athlete, he nevertheless raced towards the river. It proved to be a futile attempt, for professor Kerner, deeming his colleague quite mad, spurted after him. Fearing the loss of his treasure made him fleet-footed.

"Professor, no, give me back my property!" he thundered close to the other's heels.

"Fish it out from the bottom of the river," Stewart jeered.

He had shed every vestige of decorum. The next instant they were at each other again. Evenly matched, one agile and resilient, the other slow but powerful, they fought like cornered wolverines for the possession of the harmonica.

Both men had reached a state of desperation which rendered them oblivious to a significant reality: the proximity of the steep precipice above the coursing river.

The inevitable happened. They tumbled into the choppy water, and were swept towards the perilous Steamboat Rapids, which became their grave.

The Only Solution

These were heady days in Quebec, people's steps had a bounce not hitherto discernible. Smiles and laughter, never alien to the Québecoises, came easier now. Even inveterate grumblers, aged prematurely, were unable to hide their satisfaction. The young, and not so young faces, were suffused with a glow which inspired and irritated at the same time. The economy was in full swing, booming actually. That, however, bore not the reason for raised heads and shining eyes, which hope and self-respect induces. It was because the province, the French Canadian section anyway, lay in the grip of a movement called 'Quiet Revolution'.

Life in the province changed rapidly and drastically. The French Canadians, a vast majority, conceived as hewers of wood and drawers of water for hundreds of years, did something unthinkable: they started to cross the lines of exclusiveness drawn by English, and not so English Canadians.

The Leduceurs were some of those transgressors, who dared to enter the sphere of the self-appointed upper crust. Their construction company, Leduceur Cie, ventured into fields reserved for English Canadians and their fellow travellers. They took on larger industrial projects, avoided by their father, who some years ago transferred ownership to the sons. Gérard Leduceur knew his place. The company, started over forty years ago, built houses mainly, and sometimes undertook small service jobs. He, the father, conducted himself in a manner acceptable to 'Les Anglais'.

Not so the sons René and Gaston; they showed neither compliancy nor willingness to play second fiddle to anyone. They were into the 'Quiet Revolution' tooth and nail; not so quietly to boot. Tackling larger projects, increasingly of the industrial type, they hired only French speaking workers. Complaints were answered curtly:

"It's for safety reasons, besides, this is Quebec."

Snickering disdain by the elite was met with mockery and a tongue-lashing impossible to mete out in English. The father resented their maverick ways, the mother egged them on. They had bid, and been awarded a large subcontract at the Mirabel Airport. The main contractor, Baldwin Construction from Toronto, welcomed their interest for several reasons. First, their bid was low, too low perhaps; second, the owners were proficient in both official languages, a fact that alleviated some difficulties. For Baldwin's management, down to the junior engineers, were unable to utter ten French words; with one exception, however.

After three months at the site, Gaston, the younger one, came right out with it:

"René, we are in trouble."

"Maybe, maybe not," the older brother countered.

"Don't be such a goose, René, you and I know we are not going to make it."

Reflecting for a moment, René suggested:

"Let's not preach doom, but rather act."

"Tell me how."

"Cutting down the work force for instance."

"We are already behind schedule. Have you forgotten Baldwin's notices?"

René's sigh, resembling a moan, sufficiently answered the query.

"What about delaying payments to our suppliers?"

"Be reasonable, they are holding back deliveries as is. Come, think of something else."

"I will," René promised with little enthusiasm.

Being the older brother, plus managing director of the firm, he felt incumbent to find a solution. There were not many options, except that a bankruptcy was out of the question. First, it would break their parents' heart; second, the thought of friends and detractors pouncing on the whole family stirred his resentment.

"You see what happens when you try to soar with eagles yet have no wings," friends would whisper.

"Pshaw, what do you expect from froggies," detractors would croak.

No, it may not be. Their ageing parents, proud of the sons' seeming success, ought never be exposed to such ridicule and shame.

Pondering for days trying to find an answer, he nearly despaired over his inability to do so. They had entered a morass alright; even worse, they were knee-deep in it, he admitted. Continuing the project meant getting mired deeper by the day; quitting invited certain bankruptcy, plus eternal disgrace not only for the family, but French Canadians in general.

The Leduceurs' brash confidence, their boldness to stomp where others dared not tread, appalled many, and evoked envy in some of their kith and kin. They would surely rub their hands in glee should they stumble or fail.

"What a scrape we are in, and no doubt about it," he moaned. "The burden of atlantes must feel like a feather compared to ours," he conjectured.

The dejection lasted but an instant. Abruptly he straightened himself up. This was not the time to wallow in self-pity, he decided. Besides, the Leduceurs were not borne to suffer, he remembered.

"Thérèse, ask Mr Rivard to come to my office," he requested.

Lucien Rivard, the accountant, did not wait for a second bidding, he showed up momentarily.

"Tell me, Rivard, how do we stand, financially I mean?"

"Well, our accounts at both banks are overdrawn to the limits."

Cutting him short, Leduceur remarked:

"Never mind that, I want to know the status of the firm. A trial balance is needed, along with a realistic forecast, and don't forget the overbilling of the Mirabel project."

"How much should be allowed?"

Contemplating the accountant with raised eyebrows, Leduceur suggested:

"At least one hundred thousand dollars."

After sending Rivard on his way, Leduceur resumed his reflections. Momentous decisions must be made, affecting the very movement so vociferously advocated by themselves. They owed a duty to the 'Quiet Revolution' which under no circumstances ought to be compromised. How could they prevent the noose hovering over their heads from finding their necks? Indeed how? Racking his brains with might and main, he couldn't think of a single stratagem to elude disaster. Anger rose in him, it made him jump up and storm from his office, slamming the door almost off its hinges.

"Have you found a solution, René?" his brother asked.

"No," came a brusque reply.

"Are we making this week's payroll?"

"Barely."

The brothers had a long talk. Ideas were broached, repudiated, rehashed, and tackled from every angle; but no amount of juggling or self-deception could efface an unpleasant reality.

"Frankly, Gaston, there is only one glimmer of hope."

"What is it?"

"Having a candid talk with Paul Brodeur."

"You are too late."

Casting an inquiring gaze at his brother, he snapped:

"What are you talking about?"

"He is going back to Toronto. In fact, he is retiring at the end of the month. A letter is being sent by Baldwin's head office, confirming the fact."

Assailed by misgivings, apprehension darkening his face, René wanted to know:

"Who is replacing him?"

Reluctantly Gaston replied:

"James Pelter."

"Oh no," his brother burst out, justifiably so, considering the punishing enmity that existed between them.

James Pelter, the project engineer, seemingly now promoted to the highest site position, possessed a character best described in two words: swaggering chauvinist. A native of Ottawa, he prided himself to be the champion Francophobe. Anything deemed remotely French ran the risk of being drowned in bile and poison. He spoke not a word of French, a fact that filled him with pride, for he considered Canada's second official language mere gibberish, demeaning to a real Canadian.

"I would sooner shovel my own grave, than imitate that jargon," he loudly avowed.

Blinded by hate, spurred on by impelling forces, he intrigued against the Leduceurs from the beginning. Nothing loath he blackened their name and set obstacles in their path. Complaining to Brodeur, the chief, never ended. He took compromising pictures, recorded damnable incidents, all deemed detrimental to the Leduceurs, which he gleefully presented to Brodeur, who silently resented his engineer's machinations.

Brodeur, a Francophone from way back, still reasonable bilingual, felt sympathy for the Leduceurs. Besides, he knew Pelter's type well. Canada's bane, he called them, vainglorious rattlers of chains whose welts they bore themselves. Pelter, he realised, was riven by inferiority, which nothing but denigration of others could stitch. Just the same, he pretended to take note of his engineer's accusations, whereas in reality they went in and out of his ears.

"Now we are in a real pickle," René Leduceur sighed, as he walked away.

The letter arrived two days later, confirming Gaston's assertion. Come month's end, James Pelter, their nemesis and sworn detractor would be the project manager.

"Our goose is cooked," Gaston declared.

"I am not so sure," his brother remarked.

"What do you suggest?"

"Let me think."

Gaston, having heard similar announcements before, grinned sheepishly; inwardly, mind you, for he feared his older brother's, the chief of the firm, irascible temper.

Shortly after Pelter took the reins, the expected onslaught started with a vengeance. Instructions were given to Pelter's staff, intended to heap misery upon the Leduceurs. Somewhat couched, mind you, but leaving no doubt about their intent.

"Keep an eye on those Leduceurs, they are nothing but trouble," he cautioned the new project engineer.

The superintendent received strict orders:

"I want daily reports of their progress, plus a weekly schedule from them, approved by me, which must be assiduously adhered to."

Looking at his subordinates with eyes that meant business, he warned:

"Should they fall behind, be it only a day or two, I want to know about it."

Every morning at their regular site meeting Pelter asked his staff:

"Are the Leduceurs drinking?"

The standard reply by all: "I haven't noticed" visibly irked Pelter. His frown, directed at one after the other, implied gross dissatisfaction.

"I am sure they are, secretly, no doubt. Like all those Frenchmen they are hopeless sots, no mistake about it. Observe them closely, smell their breath, gauge their stride, and listen for slurred speech."

Unwittingly Pelter, bedevilled by animosity that needed constant nourishment, provided the Leduceurs, whom he wished to harm, the means to extricate themselves from the horns of a dilemma.

The superintendent took exception to Pelter's repressive attitude. Roman Hardy, born and raised in Montreal, had strait-laced parents who encased him in a corset weaved with the lisles of convention, and entwined with inherited prejudice that would sooner burst than stretch.

Associating with the Leduceurs felt like a breath of fresh air. Their unrestrained demeanour, so contrary to his, deemed him a salve that healed the cracks in his ego. He told Gaston about Pelter's intentions, who immediately informed his brother.

Expecting one of René's dreaded outbursts, he gazed in disbelief when quite the opposite happened. Instead of the anticipated scowl, accompanied by bloodcurdling imprecations, a smile brightened René's face. Instinctively bending forward to obtain a better look, he noticed a satisfied smirk settling on his brother's lips. Then a gleeful chuckle followed, as if joyful tidings had just been conveyed. When a peel of laughter rose from his throat, Gaston sighed in apprehension, thinking that stress had gotten to his brother.

"There, my boy, is the solution," René cried, rapping the table till the knuckles hurt.

"Don't you see it, Gaston?"

"See, what?"

"The key, slowpoke, the key that opens the door of opportunity."

Shaking his head, acquiring a compassionate air, Gaston repeated:

"René, I don't follow you. Key, door of opportunity, what do you mean?"

"I will explain it to you after work at the office."

As Gaston listened to his brother's notions, he grew more restive by the minute. To tell the truth he was genuinely worried; what René expounded sounded too weird to be taken serious.

"But – but," he stammered several times.

"No ifs or buts, I tell you, it's the only solution. Either that, or certain ruin."

Reflecting for a moment, Gaston granted:

"It sounds bizarre, but what have we got to lose?"

The Leduceurs proceeded with utmost prudence, saying neither a word to anyone, nor giving a clue about their intentions. Workers as much as supervisors were baffled as they became aware of a marked change at the site.

To begin with, René Leduceur, the firm's president and managing director, took a different approach. Till recently barely visible at the site, he now hardly missed an hour. More than that; he, along with his brother, took an active part in the work. They operated heavy equipment, issued orders to the men, and generally acted like sub foremen. They seemed bent on motivating the work force, plus assist in the advancement of the project.

René, prone to fly off the handle, behaved exemplary. He had sworn by all that is holy to keep his temper in check.

"No matter what, I shall grit my teeth, take a deep breath, count to ten, and 'yes' that blasted jingoist to death," he promised.

Indeed, he kept his word, telling himself over and over again: "The game is worth the candle."

Yet despite their Trojan effort the work fell behind. Baldwin's supervisors, enjoined to monitor their progress, at first concealed the slippage, hoping that the Leduceurs would recover lost ground.

It did not happen. The situation grew worse, compelling Baldwin's supervisors to update their reports. It looked grim for the Leduceurs, hopeless really, had the Fates not intervened.

As often happens they protect the foolhardy. Why? Because they are in love with them. The two mavericks, endowed with more courage than sense, tickled the fancy of the goddesses who control human destiny. As if by request, torrential rain fell for three days and nights, rendering the site into a mud field. All work ceased for a whole week. Pelter fumed, not on account of the delay, but because it took the Leduceurs off the hook. He was powerless to invoke the default clauses, since the delay could be attributed to force majeur, a power beyond anyone's control.

When the work resumed, strange occurrences were observed. At times the Leduceurs walked around as if on stilts. They cracked inane jokes, mumbled to themselves, and seemed to show an inclination for silly horseplay.

"They are drinking on the job," Pelter reported to his superiors in Toronto, who exhorted him to issue a stern warning to everybody involved. Pelter did more than that; he watched the Leduceurs Argus-eyed. The word soon got around:

"The boss is smirking, things must go well."

Indeed, they did; extraordinarily so. Pelter's mind did somersaults at the thought of impending success. These dumb Frenchmen played right into his hands; he couldn't believe what he saw, their carelessness had no equal. There they were, operating complex heavy machines which needed to be guided with absolute precision, taking swigs from nondescript bottles. The way it was done left no doubt about their contents. Casting furtive glances in every direction first, they quickly raised the bottle to their lips and took long greedy draughts. It had to be liquor which they poured down their throats, thereby contravening the tenets of the contract, plus of course the Workers' Compensation Act.

Pelter, feeling giddier by the day, took pictures on the sly, approached the Leduceurs in a conciliatory manner, plus grudgingly acknowledged their efforts. It was meant to reassure them of his good will, hoping they would be lulled into false security, thereby letting their guard down. Time was of the essence, for to his chagrin the work proceeded surprisingly well. Given the recent occurrence of force majeur, the project could not be considered in default. Pelter's aspirations, nourished with every fibre of his heart, ran the risk of becoming another spectre of the Brocken. Terminating Leduceur's contract looked increasingly dim in view of the favourable reports landing on his desk.

"They are close to schedule," the project engineer related.

"Workmanship too is improving," the superintendent affirmed.

Such statements affected Pelter like a man being hotfooted; it made him jump and cry out angrily:

"Performance is one thing, but what about safety? Their drinking on the job endangers the entire site, especially since for some strange reason they operate heavy equipment themselves."

"I will talk to them," the superintendent offered.

"You will do better than that," Pelter asserted.

Noticing Hardy's inquiring look, he expounded:

"Bring me a few of those bottles from which they are drinking."

Indignant, the superintendent shrunk back:

"I can't do that, besides, it's not my job," he protested.

"Yes, it is," Pelter snapped.

"It's theft, and I'm not going to do it."

Pelter, considering the superintendent closer, commented suggestively:

"You are chummy with the Leduceurs, aren't you?

Seeing craftiness written all over the new chief's face, Hardy hastened to declare:

"Not particularly, just fair and co-operative."

Grinning knowingly, pretending not to have heard, Pelter enunciated:

"Here is what you do: Remember we owe it to the company that pays and treats us well. Stick around the Leduceurs," your buddies he almost said, but he managed to check himself.

"When you see them taking sips from a bottle, step closer and ask them, innocent like, to pour out something for you into a vial, which you seal and bring to me."

"Wouldn't talking with them, no holds barred, be more affective?"

"I have tried that."

"And?"

"They laughed in my face. No, Roman, these – these, I won't say it, will bestow nothing but mischief on us, unless we take preventive action. Head office expects it. Sid Cowper, the president, will have our hide should anything untoward happen."

Hardy, though not cheering the assignment, grudgingly admitted it might be the only way to avert serious consequences. In other words, don't quibble, confront them with evidence, use a strong hand. Should what they are drinking prove innocuous, what of it? Their recent aberrant behaviour understandably compelled one to resort to drastic, albeit underhanded measures.

Thus mollifying his conscience, Hardy approached Gaston Leduceur. Did he see him? Not likely, judging by his actions. After looking on all sides, Gaston quickly produced a bottle from which he took several deep draughts. Smacking his lips, turning towards the superintendent, he said:

"Want some, Roman?"

Just as he was about to utter a sharp denial, he remembered Pelter's instructions.

"I wouldn't mind," he answered, not exactly eagerly.

Gaston stepped down from the machine. Handing Hardy the bottle, he remarked:

"René would like to talk to you when you have a minute."

"Any time."

"Let's go over there now," Gaston suggested.

"How goes the battle, Roman?" René asked with his customary exuberance.

"Not bad so far."

Looking at the superintendent as if taking measure of his mettle, René Leduceur spoke slowly:

"Roman, I take you for an honourable man, am I correct?"

"You are, why do you ask?"

"We need a favour."

"From me? Let's hear it."

"It might mean a heap of trouble for you."

Roman Hardy, brandisher of the Union Jack, believer in the white man's burden, meaning English of course, was no poltroon.

"What's the favour?"

"It's this."

After expounding the peculiar, yet innocuous request, René Leduceur added:

"One condition, you must keep mum about it."

Chuckling indulgently, as one does over a child's silly demands, the superintendent promised to remain close as a clam.

In the course of a week Hardy collected five bottles which, legally tested for ingredients, proved to contain thirty to thirty-five percent alcohol by volume. He never took a sip from a single one, he assured the project manager.

"I believe you," Pelter nodded.

The notice of contract termination followed on the heels of an odd accident. A truck driven by Pelter collided with a tractor on pads operated by René Leduceur, who, according to witnesses, had been carrying on erratically all morning.

Baldwin Construction, as empowered by the contract retained Leduceur's chattels. The word went around that the cheeky upstarts finally got their just deserts.

Three days later an action was registered in the Supreme Court of Quebec for breach of contract. This came as a surprise to many, since their misbehaviour, negligence, and security breaches were hawkers' news.

Pelter pooh-poohed the frivolous suit, as he called it.

"Just like stupid Frenchmen, throwing good money after bad," he snorted contemptuously.

Yet for some reasons he felt a bit queasy, especially after reading the statement of claim. When Sid Cowper, Baldwin's president, inquired what he thought of it, whether these demands possessed merit, Pelter almost heehawed his ears off. Cowper, no choir boy by any measures, who recently completed a stint in an Hamilton prison for price fixing, collusion, and perjury, sensed an undercurrent of bravado in his project manager's demonstrative demeanour. He didn't like it, but kept quiet.

The case came up before justice Lucien Archambault, a seasoned judge, who brooked no nonsense. Sid Cowper had decided to be present throughout the hearing. A disquieting realisation compelled him to do so. Pelter, he sensed, whose testimony was crucial to their defence, seemed to be guided by ulterior motives; he had an axe to grind.

Leduceur asked for general, special, and punitive damages, plus costs. They also wanted their chattels returned, or appropriate compensation. Pelter heehawed the demands; Cowper tried to snicker them out of existence, more so when he read their statement of claim, exceeding a million dollars. The lawyers just smiled condescendingly, and sanctimoniously wished them luck.

On the second day the guffaws turned to groans, snickers to coughs, smiles so cockily sported froze on the lawyers' lips. Something was amiss here. The sure-fire conduct of the plaintiff's lawyer as much as the Leduceurs' roguish demeanour, disturbed them. The presumed temerity of the complainants revealed itself as anything but an exercise in frivolity.

"They got something up their sleeves," Bruce Lamington, Baldwin's leading attorney announced.

Witnesses marched up to the stand, swearing to have seen the Leduceurs stagger, had heard their slurred speech, and noticed the repeated furtive drinking and suspicious behaviour. An impressive performance, well contrived, yet hardly possessing a puff of steam, the plaintiffs' miens expressed.

True enough, but heavier flak stood in the offing. A document issued by a certified laboratory was entered as an exhibit. It stated a simple fact: The contents of five bottles examined consisted, among other ingredients, of thirty to thirty-five percent alcohol by volume. A link of course needed to be established, connecting the laboratory's findings with the beverage consumed at the job site by the Leduceurs.

"Calling Roman Hardy to the stand," Baldwin's leading lawyer announced.

After the superintendent was sworn in, the attorney asked the customary questions, then shifted to the meat of the matter:

"Mr Hardy, over the course of a week you managed to wangle five bottles from René and Gaston Leduceur. Am I correct?"

"No."

That blunt response raised several eyebrows, even the judge's.

Taken aback, Mr Lamington rephrased his question:

"Didn't you hand five bottles containing various measures of a liquid to James Pelter, the project manager?"

"I did, but they were given to me, not wangled from them."

The assistant lawyer, maître Bromont, suddenly felt a cold draught crawling up his spine which bore an odour of calamity. He wished to stop the questioning, but plagued by uncertainty just raised his hand. A silent plea was sent to the bench, which justice Archambault noticed, but ignored deliberately. For he too saw clouds ready to burst with sensational tidings. A withering glance in the direction of maître Bromont kept the lawyer in his chair. Unaware of the frantic signs made behind him, Mr Lamington continued:

"So they were given to you voluntarily. What happened then?"

"I poured some of its contents, a small glass full perhaps, into a bottle which I sealed tightly."

Had a scorpion stung the attorney, his reaction would have been less violent than this revelation produced. He literally jerked upward. Turning first towards the bench, then casting beseeching glances in every direction, he visibly shrivelled before their eyes. But he couldn't leave well enough alone.

"So you ended up with two bottles. What happened to them?"

"One I gave to Mr Pelter."

As mentioned, Lamington could not leave well enough alone.

"The other, what did you do with the other?" he demanded to know in a tone that made his associate cringe.

"On the behest of René Leduceur I took them to a laboratory for testing."

Maître Bromont could no longer be held back, he bolted from his chair and approached the bench:

"Your honour, may I have a word with my colleague?"

Judge Archambeault, although tensely interested in the continuance of the questioning, nevertheless consented.

After a brief consultation Baldwin's lawyers requested a short recess.

"Thirty minutes," the judge granted.

As any lawyer worth his salt knows, the unexpected does you in. The witness, presumed to be amicable, proved anything but that. In other words he was about to tell the truth, the whole truth, and nothing but.

The defence lawyers acknowledged an awful truth: The Leduceurs had engineered a masterful plot, intended to save their skin, plus make them affluent for life.

"By golly, they have succeeded," the attorneys were forced to submit to Sid Cowper, who strenuously tried to repudiate such notions.

He tore into them:

"What a defeatist attitude, I won't have it. Our case is airtight. Didn't we submit evidence that they continually swigged almost raw liquor during working hours?"

Shaking his head, one of the attorneys advised:

"I bet that evidence is a fake."

Saying so he took a hard look at Pelter, who turned pale. Cowper bridled up:

"I don't follow you," he barked.

The lawyer sighed:

"You see, Mr Cowper, Hardy no doubt will testify that the laboratory reports, delivered to the Leduceurs directly, were based on the identical liquid which having gone through Baldwin's hands that showed alcohol contents of thirty to thirty-five percent by volume."

Shrugging his shoulders, knitting his brow, Cowper snapped:

"Are you implying that their samples show different results?"

"Drastically different. Talking to the plaintiff's attorney he advised that those samples, from the same beverage mind you, each and every one show zero percent alcohol, one hundred percent apple juice."

"We must settle out of court," Mr Lamington, the leading attorney announced.

Bristling with indignation, Cowper jumped up.

"Settle, accommodate these con artists? Not till hell freezes over," he stormed.

Looking daggers in every direction, he unleashed a hailstorm of invectives that never seemed to end. But they did abruptly when he turned to his project manager for support. As a matter of fact, he almost choked on his own words at the bewildering sight. The man looked like an apparition spit from hell; no other description could have done justice to the shape staring at Cowper.

Seeing Pelter's torpid condition, downcast eyes, and a face covered with layers of misery, an awful reality dawned on him. Stepping closer, stooping, jutting his head forward, he growled, emphasising every syllable:

"Did you spike those bottles?"

Mr Lamington, fearing an altercation, came to Pelter's rescue.

"We have no time for confrontations, the judge is waiting," he exhorted.

"Let him wait," Cowper retorted.

But on second thought he relented. Planting himself before the lawyers, he demanded to know:

"Do I smell trickery?"

"You might," acknowledged maître Bromont, not entirely certain what Cowper meant.

Lamington harboured no doubts about Cowper's exclamation; he hastened to explain:

"There are two issues here: Breach of contract, based on shaky, very shaky grounds, as we all know."

"That's one, what's the other?" Cowper growled, gazing at Pelter with eyes portending nothing agreeable.

"Criminal offences."

"Not by me."

"It hardly matters who committed them, Baldwin Construction breached the contract, and if found culpable must compensate Leduceur."

"The full amount?"

"Could well be, perhaps even more. It's entirely at the court's discretion."

"What do you suggest?" Cowper asked.

"Halting the case," Mr Lamington answered.

"An out of court arrangement, in other words."

"Exactly," fell in maître Bromont."

"Alright, let's try it," Cowper agreed.

The judge, being amenable, allotted time plus two private rooms for preliminary discussions. To Cowper's surprise the plaintiffs showed no inclination to co-operate; they appeared to be stuck with the notion of a court decision. Mind you, they said it not openly, but the obstinate refusal to lower their demands pointed towards it.

Baldwin's lawyers were equally amazed, initially that is. Although they privately agreed that a judgement in Leduceur's favour seemed to be foregone conclusion, amounts of an award are always unpredictable. Added to its aspect of appeals, plus sundry delaying tactics, which could defer payments for years, Leduceurs' obduracy made no sense.

Wanting a private discussion, Mr Lamington asked the plaintiffs to withdraw to an adjoining room.

"They are bluffing," Cowper announced.

"Perhaps not," countered maître Bromont.

"They must be daft then," Cowper mocked.

"It does sound odd, refusing a sure thing in favour of a pie in the sky," granted Mr Lamington.

"Not if you have a hidden agenda," maître Bromont proposed.

"What could that be?" queried Cowper.

The lawyers, who had more than an inkling of the Leduceurs' motive, looked at each other. Shall we tell him? their glances said.

"They are after someone's hide, Pelter's for instance."

"They can have him, warts and all. Matter of fact I will do the skinning," Cowper remarked, then added:

"But I'm still in the dark. Let's see now: Their claim surpasses one million dollars. We offer half, a magnanimous amount, if you ask me. Surprisingly they not only reject the offer but make no counter proposal. Why?"

"They want a judgement for two reason," he was told.

"Tell me."

"Obtaining an award by far exceeding our offer is one."

"The other?"

"Money is not the prime mover, but nailing Pelter to the cross is. For that, however, they need a trial transcript."

Sid Cowper, a rough-and-ready individual, led no charmed life. More than once he escaped disaster by the skin of his teeth. Educated in the school of hard knocks, he, like Meander of ancient times, was known to call a fig a fig and a spade a spade.

"Tell me if I am mistaken. Pelter is a stumbling block to a settlement which could save the company a lot of money, besides untold grief?"

Seeing both lawyers nodding, he turned towards Pelter.

"James, leave us, stay off the site till you hear from me," he ordered.

Cowper fell silent. As he glanced at the lawyers he repeatedly grunted: “Hm, hm.”

“What shall we tell the judge?” Mr Lamington prodded.

Cowper, with a sudden glint in both eyes announced:

“We shall settle out of court, ask for a week’s deferment.”

Justice Archambault consented in the teeth of the plaintiff’s objection. He chided them:

“Your attitude is unsupportable, a reasonable effort must be made to come to terms. I expect an answer Wednesday morning.”

Cowper took the bull by the horn. The following day, bright and early, he knocked at Leduceur’s door.

“Fellows, what’s your game?” he asked without a preamble.

Taken aback by his brusque approach, René Leduceur commented:

“Justice.”

“Good enough. I have tried to make amends by offering you instant cash, not a paltry sum either, yet you chuck it aside; what’s up?”

Receiving no immediate reply, he stated:

“You want to settle a score, is that it?”

“Mr Cowper, upon our lawyer’s counsel…”

“Fiddlesticks! You wouldn’t heed your mouthpiece’s advice if it were gold plated.”

Considering the brothers closer, Cowper came right out with it:

“You are after Pelter, plus me perhaps.”

“Not you,” Gaston averred before his brother could stop him.

“Well, Pelter did present us with a pretty kettle of fish. We acted solely upon advice for which you can not fault us. After all he has been a Trojan to the company for over fifteen years. To be honest, we heard some rumbling about his preoccupation with French Canada, but by golly, who would have thought that it is an aberration?”

Cowper harboured not the least desire to continue the trial. One never knows what can happen, he learned a few years ago, when he entered the Hamilton Courthouse sporting a smile, and left in handcuffs. No, he was not anxious to go back; neither did he see the necessity for it. The situation lay before him like an open book. Money was not the hurdle; contrary to Pelter, who might cost him an additional half million dollars, plus a lot of trouble. He knew of only one solution.

"The judge wants an answer Wednesday morning. We should make one more attempt to come to terms. Let's meet Tuesday noon at the Ritz Carlton for lunch, I am paying."

"That is mighty kind of you, we accept with pleasure. But be assured we shall not change our minds. Justice can only be obtained by a court decision," René Leduceur repeated.

"Quite so, quite so," Cowper assented.

Then, after casting significant glances at the brothers, he left.

On Sunday afternoon two strollers in the Gatineau Hills almost stumbled over a man lying face down, obviously quite dead. A pistol lay beside the prone figure, which gave rise to several conjectures.

"Don't touch anything, walk down and alert the police," the woman's companion advised.

James Pelter, just fired for cause, facing prosecution for fraud, evidence tampering, and perjury, had seemingly ended his life.

As arranged, they met for lunch. The subject of Pelter's demise, known to all, was intentionally avoided, as much as the court action. Good manners demanded it. Only after the meal, when brandy and coffee were served, drifted the conversation towards those topics.

"Poor chap," someone said.

"Miserable bigot," others remarked.

"Poor Sid," Cowper fell in.

The comment, appropriate enough, engendered a measure of merriment, it was conceived as a signal to commence negotiations which, with Pelter out of the way, should prove to be a mere formality.

It was not meant to be. The Leduceurs, René that is, insisted now as before on having the entire claim honoured. Maître Bromont, visibly perturbed, pointed out:

“But your direct losses, by your own admission, scarcely approach one third of your demands. Given the fact that you have been offered almost twice that amount, in all due respect, aren’t you unreasonable? Remember, it’s quick money.”

“Our claim will be paid in full,” René Leduceur maintained.

Cowper, losing his composure, bolted upright and barked:

“The devil it will.”

René, shrugging his shoulders, remarked:

“Let the judge decide.”

These words, uttered with infuriating nonchalance, stoked the flame of Cowper’s ire into a veritable conflagration. His face became a mask of suppressed rage. He started to hurl a string of imprecations at the Leduceurs and their attorney. Maître Bromont as much as Mr Lamington stared in disbelief at their client, wishing to be beyond earshot of his ravings.

The flurry of invectives came to a sudden end when the headwaiter, who obviously knew Cowper, stepped up to their table.

“Sir, there is a gentleman in the lobby with a message for you,” he announced.

Annoyed at the interruption, Cowper bellowed:

“Well, what is it?”

“It’s highly personal, he says, he can only deliver it to yourself.”

With raised eyebrows and a curse on his lips, Cowper rose. Within minutes he returned, or rather what was left of him. White as a shroud, with panic-stricken eyes, aged ten years, he staggered towards them. Everyone at the table stared aghast at the smitten figure. Was that the same man, robust a moment ago, who lit into the Leduceurs with the vigour of a charging bull? Sid Cowper, it seemed, had looked into the jaws of hell, which he tried to efface from his memory. Drained of all emotions except despair, looking dazed as if in doubt what to do or say, he collapsed on his chair. Complete silence reigned; not a word was spoken, all eyes rested on the prostrate shape.

Cowper, raising his head slowly, glanced in every direction, searching for signs that seemed not to be there.

Scrutinising every face suspiciously for a message that could not be found, till his questioning gaze fell on René Leduceur, who blinked first with one, then the other eye.

Cowper gasped, a shudder not unlike a convulsion, shook his heavy frame; he understood. Looking at his lawyers, he instructed:

"Draw up an agreement today."

"What are the terms?" Mr Lamington asked.

Turning towards René Leduceur, he said in a hoarse voice:

"Terms and conditions? Make it the original claim, payable upon court approval."

When they were alone, Gaston wondered aloud:

"What on earth happened?"

The brother, feigning ignorance, replied:

"Search me."

"Come, René, stop pretending. I'm neither blind nor obtuse. I watched you when Cowper returned, you know why?"

"No."

"Because when the headwaiter delivered his message you had a knowing smile on your face, so out with it."

"I see that you are observant after all."

"More than that, I have noticed your strange behaviour since the day Cowper visited us."

"So you have, so you have. I shall own up, but let me digress for a moment. Remember when I promised to find a solution to our financial predicament?"

"Well, you did."

"Thanks to a fluke."

"You never told me."

"I will now. After straining every brain cell in my head to find a way out of our fix, I got exactly nowhere. Then something remarkable happened. I suddenly felt an irresistible yen to see the Forum."

"The Forum? Didn't you tell me after the drubbing our team received from the Toronto Maple Leaves you will never go near that place again?"

"I sure did. But that morning some inexplicable force directed my steps. Before I knew it I stood at the gates of the

Forum gazing intently at a poster depicting Japanese jiujitsu fighters. It hit me like a flash. Wasn't that the sport where the weaker opponent can win the match by goading the stronger one to attack?"

"I don't see the connection."

"I did instantly. Pelter's seething francophobia needed to be nourished, thereby prodding him to act rashly."

"Aha, that's why you insisted that our men at the site speak French only."

"Yes. There wasn't much he could do about it, since our politicians in Quebec and Ottawa are brandishing the fleur-de-lis with brouhaha. But it certainly drove him over the brink."

"It sure did spur him on, all he needed was a pretext to expel us from the site," agreed Gaston.

"Well, we furnished one. It was a bait which he swallowed hook, line, and sinker."

"No doubt about it, but what about Sid Cowper, how did you manoeuvre him?"

Inclining his head in that inimitable way, he smirked from ear to ear.

"That proved not so cumbersome considering Cowper's proffered assistance when he visited us at the office."

"Oh, I was present, but saw or heard nothing of the sort," interjected Gaston.

"Let me ask you a question, Gaston."

"Go ahead."

"Do you know Cowper's moniker?"

"Never heard of it."

"Colonel Rough he is, and likes to be called. He is also known as Sid the Fixer, a title esteemed and promulgated by him. Understand, he took sole responsibility for that price fixing scheme in Hamilton, which earned him eighteen months behind bars. Why? To ingratiate himself with the heavyweights, but no less out of greed, for the big boys forked out with both hands."

"You did your homework, by the looks of it," Gaston praised, then added:

"But you have not answered my question yet."

"About Cowper?"

"Yes. What induced him to make that sudden about-face concerning our claim?"

"The pictures."

"Pictures? This is getting more mysterious by the minute."

"Let's leave it at that. What exactly happened will never be known anyway," René assured his brother, who couldn't suppress a broad grin.

"We could guess, René, couldn't we?" Gaston asked.

"I can try. Cowper's desire to continue the trial plummeted when Roman Hardy commenced his testimony. I saw the spectres of fear in his eyes as maître Bromont must have done, inducing him to interrupt the interrogation. You know the rest."

"The pictures, René, what about the pictures?"

"Oh, those?"

Saying that, René went to his private safe from which he removed a small envelope. Handing it to his brother, he said:

"Here, judge for yourself."

Wide-eyed, visibly stunned, he stared at the photographs.

"I will be..." he muttered repeatedly.

All three of them showed Sid Cowper bending over a collapsing figure, whom Gaston recognised as James Pelter. Amazed, still not comprehending, he noticed the gun in Pelter's hand, aimed squarely at his chest. The photographs exuded a stark realism. The pain distorted countenance of a dying man; the terror-stricken gaze of Cowper made Gaston gasp. Shaking his head, his face a question mark, he stammered:

"What does it mean?"

"That Cowper was present when Pelter died."

"You mean when he committed suicide?"

"Whatever," came a laconic reply.

Thoroughly confused, but no less awed, Gaston inquired:

"How did you get these pictures?"

"Someone gave them to me."

"Why didn't that someone go to the police?"

"He doesn't like the police. Besides, he took a sympathetic interest in our court case, therefore assuming these pictures would be valuable to us."

"They sure are," granted Gaston, then added:

"I take it that you and this – this benefactor staged that little drama at the Ritz Carlton."

Receiving no answer, Gaston said nothing further; he understood. His brother, ten years older, had come of age. The sentimental Québecois, wearing his heart on his sleeve, had ceased to exist; he had crossed the pale set over two hundred years ago by an implacable enemy, whose citadel he had entered.

As Gaston returned the envelope, he almost imperceptible inclined his head. It was the only tribute paid the older brother.

Odour Of Rectitude

Soon after Carlo Purento's arrival in the town of Marlin, the rumour mill started to turn. Ostensibly he came to assist his cousin Mario Pereira to set up a construction business. The reality, however, wore a different mantle: Purento had taken flight from his past. Two months ago, under cover of darkness, he left his native Kingston, intending never to return. Spurred on by his desire to lay the greatest distance between himself and his hometown, he headed west.

Progress, however, proved painfully slow, because of onerous burdens which held him back. What could they have been? Excessive baggage, lack of transportation, or inclement weather perhaps? None of it. The culprits were his travel companions: Hate, bitterness, and imagined wrongs. Hate wearied his limbs; bitterness sapped his resolve; and imagined wrongs choked his breath.

True, the injustice done him was grave, moreover, undeserved. Dark clouds, generated by unpleasant memories refused to lift, rendering a journey, which should have been enjoyable, highly miserable.

Purento, not a sophisticated man, in time figured out his dilemma. It proved not an easy feat, yet he managed to cast off one encumbrance after another. Thus the clouds started to lift from his mind, making him feel free and wholesome again.

Veils of discontent, which had obscured his vision, dropped by degrees, revealing the incomparable beauty of this wondrous land.

Carping voices rang less and less in his ears, thereby enabling him to hear the boisterous sounds of the wild, untamed world. At the sight of never-ending wheat fields swaying in the wind under a wide open prairie sky, smiles once more illuminated his face. By the time he had reached the Rockies he felt powerful hands tugging at his heartstrings. When he embraced his cousin out west, Purento was his old self again.

The cousins had not seen each other for ten years, so there was much to talk about. Being of a similar age, enjoying an almost identical background, words came easy.

"How long will you stay?" Pereira asked.

"Till I rest my feet and find my bearings. What do you think, are there any job or business opportunities here or nearby?"

"Actually yes, we find ourselves in the middle of a construction boom," Mario advised, "and watch out for the women though, they can be tricky."

"Pshaw, women, I have had enough of them," Purento snorted.

"For a while," Pereira chaffed, then added:

"I hear you got nicked."

"I sure did. Who told you?"

"Uncle Emilio. But you know him, quite often he makes more noise than sense. So tell me, what did happen?"

It was this: Purento loved grappa, but the ladies even more. He could not stay away from them. His delight in chatting them up, whether young, old, or in between, was only excelled by his joy to caress them with his eyes, and putting them in the mood with a lilting tongue. Few could resist his chivalrous attention; certainly not a female with blood in her veins and blush in her cheeks.

"Liking women led to my downfall," he complained.

"I hear you went to jail. Tell me, why?"

"Didn't uncle Emilio tell you?"

"Not exactly. You know him, he speaks in riddles at times, especially when talking Italian."

Carlo could not suppress a rippling laughter, for indeed their uncle was a queer fellow, whom they feared in childhood, but later liked and respected.

"What exactly did he say?"

"Something about getting ill returns for a favour done a lonely woman."

"Well, that is one way of putting it, but the judge as much as the jury were of contrary opinions. The service rendered, according to our uncle, earned me three months in jail."

"Was the girl under age?"

"Not at all, but my refusal to marry her seemed to unnerve the poor lass."

"Was she importunate?"

"Only after the local women's club took her in tow. I tell you, cousin, she learned fast. The kissing, cuddling nymph soon turned into a snarling vixen."

Pereira whistled softly.

"Aha, I sense the drift and smell the odour."

"More of a stench, I say, raised by crusading women, and fanned by men without an arrow in their quiver. Defiling the sanctity of the female, they called it, an offence unforgivable."

"What was the charge?"

"Carnal knowledge of a woman against her will."

"What does that mean?"

"Search me, but it must be a serious delict to lock me up for three months."

"They meant rape, of course," suggested Mario.

Purento snickered:

"Against her will, indeed. A lie concocted by a bunch of hissing snakes, and ultimately repeated by a confused and embittered girl. But that is all past now, I left the place for good."

Pereira glanced at his cousin for a moment, then directed his gaze down to the breaking waves of the Strait of Georgia. He was not exactly enamoured with Carlo's presence, for more than one reason. The town's people were of a peculiar stamp, who took pride in their Anglo-Saxon values, and did not readily cotton to strangers, especially if they looked and acted alien. More than a few had fled in disgust and anger from Quebec's 'Quiet Revolution'.

These expatriates, generally vociferous and influential, brought with them a mist of hate and discontent, which two decades exposure to the winds from across the strait were unable to dissipate. True, Carlo and Mario were born in this country, but their swarthy skins, topped by a shock of black untidy hair, made them suspect. Adding to it an irrepressible exuberance, plus the ability to speak a foreign language, Pereira's apprehension made sense.

Another reason why his cousin's appearance filled him with little enthusiasm could be termed incompatibility. Despite their common background they had grown apart, irreversible so. Carlo liked the country, but not its inhabitants, certainly not the Anglo-Saxon types. Mario, in contrast, felt an affinity for them, but showed no interest in the land. Many a squabble, followed by silent resentment, resulted from these divergent inclinations, which their parents had imbued them with.

Their families, both from the central Appeninos of Italy, were affected dissimilarly by the New World. From the day of their arrival the Pereiras eyes were directed towards work and business opportunities, and their ears stayed glued to the grapevine, strung along Bloor and Bathurst Streets, so as not to miss the faintest whisper about a break on the commercial horizon.

Not so the Purentos. From the moment they stepped off the gangway at the Toronto harbour, Enrico and Teresa Purento underwent a metamorphosis.

"Do you feel it, Enrico?" the wife asked.

"I do, I do," the husband replied.

"What can it be?"

Enrico Purento, Carlo's father, had no answer; not then, nor later, while walking through the streets of Toronto, feeling a stir under their feet and a fever in their hearts, that made them giddy.

"It must be the air," Teresa suggested.

"No, no, it is polluted," her husband countered.

"The people then," she conjectured.

"They are drab and listless," he replied.

"The city?"

"It's ugly," he cut her short.

Indeed, it was, compared to the quaint and ornate towns of the old country.

The Purentos developed a fierce love for the land which their children inherited. Even after more than four decades they sang of the country's remarkable days, when a joyous energy, hitherto unknown, almost swept them off their feet.

While Mario's uneasy gaze adhered to the pounding surf below, Carlo, not a stolid man, sensed his cousin's dilemma. A smile stretched his lips as his thoughts began to wander involuntarily. His father, gifted with a peasant's insight, and the tongue of a prophet, had a quaint way of expressing himself.

"I tell you, children, when we arrived there lay an excitement in the air that affected even the most phlegmatic. The streets of Toronto were aglow with promises," he narrated more often than once.

"And did we walk," his mother usually chimed in.

"We had to, burning feet or not. Some invisible power compelled one to go another kilometre, because surely, there stood the pot of gold. No one looked back in those days; there was no time nor an inclination for it. Because ahead lay untold treasures beckoning to be discovered."

His parents did not refer to material riches, but the wonders of the country not yet broken in. In his father's words a call seemed to reverberate from the green hills of Newfoundland to the wind-swept shores of the Queen Charlotte Islands. It sounded like an invitation to come and dare. He compared the country at that time to a mustang searching for riders. He said:

"It took us many years to figure out the lure of Canada; we finally did. It was the space to roam unhindered, but more so enough room, wherein an individual could think and act freely. And that has been the most precious gift handed us by this inimitable country."

His parents were dead now. Their end could well have been precipitated by his mishap. Their eyes, however, never failed to light up when they talked about Canada's past.

Meanwhile Mario had turned his attention back to Carlo.

"Does anyone know you are here?"

"Just you and I."

Mario nodded, signifying approval.

"It might as well stay that way, because, let me tell you, this town can turn vicious at the slightest whiff of – immorality," he remarked.

"I have done nothing immoral," Carlo protested.

"Quite so, but you don't know these church-going people. They bow their heads in contrition while kneeling at the pews, but once outside they sniff the air for the scent of a prey. If information were to leak out about your stint in jail, you might as well be gone; and don't forget to take me along."

Six months later Purento was hailed as a rising star in the business community. His construction company, started more as a diversion, flourished beyond expectations. His affable ways certainly helped, topped by solid trade skills, no wonder he soon became the talk of the town.

Within the year he was nominated president of the local Chamber of Commerce. The mayor, Ron Rowntree, took notice of him; he gave a gala dinner in his honour. It was a well-meant gesture, which unwittingly proved to be as treacherous as Uriah's letter. That event was the starting-signal of Purento's renewed grief.

It should be understood that Canada floundered in the throes of enormous changes. The west in particular lost its character quicker than could be digested. Not too long ago a pioneer spirit prevailed from the waving wheat fields of the prairie to the ice fields of British Columbia. That spirit now stood in the middle of a groaning death. A movement, aimless, leaderless, and nameless, scourged the country. Nameless? Not entirely; just shrouded beneath sobriquets like rectitude, morality, or a call to meet evil with courage.

Purento, although having smelled the odour raised by this movement, plus having felt its prickle, neither heeded nor understood the significance. Had he paid more attention, it might have spared him many wretched years. Indeed, there were forces at work which his ingenuous nature could neither fathom nor was able to regard with anything but nonchalance. Little did he realise that his beloved country, idolised by his parents, was being undermined by invisible tremors. Politicians danced to its vibrations; the media turned cartwheels in deference to them; and the police, despite their growing corpulence, made handsprings to show co-operation.

After an official reception a sumptuous dinner followed. Purento was cheered by many, and envied by a few, who looked the other way, except the man at the far end of the table. He never said a word, but stared at Purento with a constant smirk on his face. He is up to no good, it flashed through his mind several times.

After dessert and more toasts the assembly grew livelier. Carlo turned to Mario, sitting beside him:

"Who is that fellow at the end of the table?"

"The one that keeps looking our way?"

"Yes, he."

"Hm, I don't rightly know, he is a recent arrival, as far as I know. Why do you ask?"

"He looks familiar, somehow."

"Hm, could well be," Mario remarked in a disinterested tone.

"A bit offensive, I say, the way he stares at us."

"Oh well, he might be cross-eyed." Mario suggested.

Purento did not think so. Unwittingly his brow knitted into folds of annoyance, giving him a sombre expression quite alien to his nature. No doubt he had met that man before, out east perhaps, under circumstances, by the looks of it, which could hardly have been termed favourable. Yet he could not place him.

Racking his brains till it hurt, he was unable to ascertain where their path had crossed, or whether they had ever met at all. The mayor interrupted his musing:

"Ladies and gentlemen, I propose a final toast in honour of our man of the year. Rise and raise your glasses, and three cheers to Carlo Purento."

Everyone rose and drank to his health, except the man at the far end; he remained glued to his seat. Deliberately so, it appeared to Purento, moreover, in an ominous mood of defiance.

Observing him furtively from the corners of his eyes, he felt a faint shudder. The man resembled Fra Diavolo, whose miniature statue he remembered so well sitting on a shelf in his parental home. A grotesque, thoroughly ugly figure it was. A vivid reminder, his father often pointed out, of a person plagued by malignant thoughts. But this impression was only transitory, it lasted no more than a second or two. For the man was neither disfigured nor ugly, like that sorry looking carving. Quite the contrary; he had a smooth face, was well groomed, and he could actually be called handsome in accordance with prevailing standards. Yet a voice within Purento insisted: There sits Fra Diavolo, or one of his progenies.

Suddenly the man seemed to change before his eyes. His bland countenance took on a mask of mockery, a satyric expression that chilled Purento to the bones. Just as he decided to tear his eyes away from the chameleonic figure, the man rose and winked.

A few days later Carlo met Mario on the street. They were talking about inconsequential matters, when Pereira said:

"By the way, Carlo, do you remember that fellow who annoyed you the other night?"

"How could I forget him?"

Indeed, how could he. Fra Diavolo, the name stuck in his mind. The man even had appeared in his dreams, where he sat like a modern day Thersites at the foot-end of his bed, grimacing maliciously, and shaking a warning finger at him.

Mario announced:

"I found out who he is."

"Who?"

"Russ Baird, the new manager of the cement company."

"A newcomer, in other words."

Seeing Mario making signs of confirmation, he asked:

"Where is he from?"

Mario shifted uneasy from foot to foot. He turned towards some acquaintances passing at the other side, hoping they would cross the street and join them.

"Did you find out, Mario, where he is from?" Carlo insisted.

"Kingston," came a reluctant reply.

Purento was not overly surprised, he almost expected as much.

"That explains it," he murmured.

Both men fell silent. One like the other pretended to watch the foaming sea, and listen to the rustling in the trees. Pereira was reluctant to break the glum silence, not prior to arranging his thoughts, for he saw the handwriting on the wall. Not long ago a young man, quite a decent fellow really, was driven straight off the island, after his not so sterling past was revealed.

Mario decided to inform his cousin about it, just to keep him on the alert.

"You say this Baird fellow was leering at you?"

"He sure was."

"It could have been fortuitous," Mario suggested.

"Not on your life," Carlo shot back.

"Imaginary perhaps?"

Shaking his head Carlo replied:

"No, no, those gazes contained a message of evil delight.

Hesitating a moment, Mario remarked:

"Carlo, there is something you should know."

"Well, out with it."

"Not here, let's saunter over to Dollard's Place. Have you got half an hour or so?"

"Easily."

In the lounge they were greeted by Megan Haslit, the waitress on duty. Carlo knew of course about her and Mario, including their turbulent relationship. Not too long ago betrothal, followed by marriage, appeared to be a certainty. Then a baffling change occurred: Megan's ardour cooled. They drifted from disagreements to dissension; then, to Mario's chagrin, Megan grew indifferent. Yet according to his cousin they were back to billing and cooing again. One glance, however, convinced Carlo that Mario was gilding the pill, for Megan's demeanour, to him, expressed less affection for Mario, than an attitude implying he had been weighed in the balance, and found wanting.

Carlo waited patiently for Mario's comments, which were not so quick in coming. As they sat there absorbed in silence, Purento was vexed by a harrowing premonition with neither name nor shape. Yet his discomposure, as much as Mario's, was real enough. A peculiar uneasiness had seized his cousin, which he tried strenuously to disguise. Perhaps Megan's presence, with whom no doubt he stood in a state of flux, accounted for this demonstrable edginess. But Carlo felt subconsciously that was not the reason. No, Mario had made a discovery, startling and unsettling, which begged for disclosure. Smiling in anticipation he said:

"Well, Mario, what do you want to tell me?"

Hemming and hawing a few times, he finally gave himself a push and remarked:

"I say this with a measure of reluctance, Carlo, but your pleasant days in Marlin are numbered."

"Quit beating around the bush. If you know something, out with it."

"Alright. But first let me ask a question. Have you noticed a change in people's attitude towards you?"

"Not really. Besides, I would not give a hoot anyway. Mind you, now that you mentioned it, I do receive the odd sideways glances that could be termed intrusive."

Sighing deeply, Mario remarked cryptically:

"The vapour is rising."

"You are talking in riddles," Carlo objected.

"Your past has leaked out," Mario stated in a sepulchral voice, as if he were announcing the arrival of doomsday.

Carlo burst out laughing:

"Is that all? Pshaw, who cares? certainly not I," he snorted contemptuously.

Mario, taking on a prescient demeanour, observed:

"I used to share your views till I witnessed Tony Hicks' debacle."

Purento had no interest in Hicks' predicament, his mind was occupied with weightier matters. He tried to control a rising impatience, which had begun to acquire shades of annoyance. Crucify me if you must, he thought, but something is amiss here. Mario puzzled him, he behaved like a fish out of the water. His furtive glances mystified him the most; his eyes were forever on the move, wandering from Megan to him, and back again. There lay a scrutiny in those glimpses, at the same time embarrassing and disquieting. Try as he may, Carlo could not dispel the notion that Mario had steered him to this place for other reasons than implied. Almost unwillingly he asked:

"What happened to this Tony Hicks?"

Averting his eyes from Megan who blithely skipped from table to table, cheerful as always, Mario explained:

"He was a staunch fellow who arrived about a year before you. I got to know him quite well, it really hurt me to have seen him persecuted with such venom."

"By whom?" Carlo interjected with feigned interest.

"At first by the town's morality squad."

"Who are they?"

"Women past their prime, and men under their thumbs. I tell you, they are fierce."

"But no more teeth-baring than elsewhere in English-Canada. But tell me, how did it end?"

"He was forced to leave town."

It sounded familiar to him, but just the same he remarked:

"Forced?"

"Yes. You see, soon no one employed him anymore. The bank called his loan; merchants closed his accounts; and most townspeople shunned him openly."

Mario went on, but Carlo paid scant attention, for he was sidetracked by a creeping sensation. Before his inner eyes unfolded a chasm, where he stood on one side, and cousin Mario on the other. A realisation began to strike home, which he tried unsuccessfully to repudiate. Mario had a problem whose source he guessed in a flash. It was his association with Megan Haslit, the scintillating waitress, whose smile lit up the drab surrounding. But inexplicable this smile, a wreath of radiance, seemed to intentionally bypass her betrothed. Not all is well here, it shot through Carlo's mind.

As Mario talked more, Carlo listened less, for he was distracted by mysterious noises in his ears. Incomprehensible at first, they soon took on the form of voices, curiously subdued on the outset, then growing more insistent, till finally they hissed repeatedly: "Mario has a problem. Be on guard! Be on guard!"

Shaking off these confounding notions, he waited for an opportunity to interpose. When it came he remarked:

"Frankly, Mario, I care not a whit about this so-called vapour of malevolence. Unlike with Tony Hicks, poor chap, my life can not be fouled up again. I own a business in full gear, my income is derived from out of town work. I have neither a bank loan nor local accounts. So you see, these huddling brewers of discontent may poison the very atmosphere with the breath of the Philistine, for all I care. Let them create a Mohammedan hell where nothing grows for a hundred miles around, and you still won't see me shudder."

Pereira moved to say something, but he bit his tongue. However, he could not refrain from casting searching glances at his cousin, as if attempting to read his mind. Then his eyes strayed back to Megan, his bride to be.

"She is too friendly with men," he grumbled.

Carlo pretended not to have heard. He felt uneasy with Mario, who evidently vied for Megan's affection with spectres of his own creation. She was not a flirt in Carlo's eyes, just imbued with an animal spirit that no amount of reproach, hinted or expressed, could dampen. Her laughing mouth and flashing eyes, it deemed Carlo, were claimed by Mario as his sole possession. Out on the street, alone and baffled, he muttered:

"Mario has a problem."

Three weeks had passed since Pereira's prophecy, which remained unfulfilled. After a month Carlo twitted his cousin about it:

"There, old pessimist, nothing you predicted is happening, what a soothsayer you are."

Mario's immediate response was an enigmatic smile, accompanied by a sidewise look, which seemed to insinuate that despite the temporary calm something was brewing. It was too, albeit still backstage. The wings of Mario's feared rumour mill were in motion, turning the paddle wheel of malediction increasingly faster. Ingredients to be blended were not lacking.

Malice was supplied by the police, spite by the media, the 'Citizens who care' furnished the caldron to mix it in.

Not long after Purento's frivolous remarks, the news broke. The Marlin Weekender, one of two local papers, went into action first. Working closely with the police and women's groups, they performed the painful but necessary duty, according to the editor, to make the public aware of a disquieting situation.

The write-up, on the first page with Carlo Purento's picture, was a source of controversy that caused a belated publication. The problem? Purento's photographs. All of them exuded an aura not reconcilable with villainy. Of the many snapshots, some taken overtly, others covertly, not a single one served their purpose.

Finally, choosing the most averse, they angled it ingeniously, till it retained a measure of sinisterness. That proved to be no mean task. It required the expertise of technicians, artists, and psychologists; to little avail, however. As the chief typesetter remarked to his boss:

"I have turned this fellow's picture every which way, from tilting left to right to standing on end. But let me tell you, right into my face there always smiles a trustworthy man."

The editor, thoroughly vexed by now, ordered the artists to touch it up. He knew his readers well, certainly the most vociferous; namely, the 'Society of Christian Women' whose fire and brimstone services had more often than once been vented on him and his staff.

The leader of that group, Mrs Cartwheel, a mother of three, wan from virtue, and wrinkled from chastity, was imbued with St. Hilarion's gift to smell out evil. Once the scent of sin tickled her nostrils, she became unstoppable, like juggernauts of old. Should the offender be imputed with transgression against the sanctity of the female, her fury rose like a mass of burning vapour, which nothing but a promise of dire punishment could douse.

She was a conspicuous woman, surprisingly dolled up, as though expecting a feast, that she knew would never happen. She, as much as her helpers, never liked Purento. They called him a sneering devil behind his back, and a leering Lothario quite openly. They sibilated in many a maiden's ear to stay away from this Italian seducer, since he was false and amoral.

"Just wait, my dear, we will soon unmask him," they predicted.

Till recently, however, they were unaware of Purento's stained past, despite their relentless prying. Purento had covered his tracks with amazing success, not even a whiff of suspicion weighed on him. Till recently, that is.

As expected, Mrs Cartwheel, flanked by two female trusties who had not sinned in two decades, soon knocked at the editor's door. Despite a glow of satisfaction on their pinched faces, duly suppressed, the editor noticed streaks of annoyance marring their joy. He could well guess why. After a few words of praise, Mrs Cartwheel voiced their concern about the photograph:

"It gives a wrong impression," she suggested, while her companions nodded agreement.

"We have done the best we could under the circumstances," Mr Carter replied.

He immediately had guessed the reason for the women's raised eyebrows. More so because of his wife's reaction when she laid eyes on the photograph.

"What a handsome devil that one is," she cried out in honest admiration.

His daughter's remark didn't help matters.

"Hm, I could fall for him anytime," she admitted, sporting her most tempting smile.

The result of that meeting needed no oracle to predict. Mrs Cartwheel's piercing eyes narrowed as she advised:

"Mr Carter, the Society of Christian Women wants that photograph removed."

"It's too late."

"Hear me out, sir, we just received more disquieting information about this… this defiler in our midst, which warrants another report."

"Without the photograph," one of the other women hastened to add.

"And a bit more sting," her companion requested.

In the next issue of the Weekender appeared a regular broadside against Purento. It was necessary, the reporter wrote, the public needed to know. Especially our youth, he went on, deserved protection from someone infected by moral turpitude.

Purento paid little heed. The previous write-up amused more than it angered him. As he told his cousin, such exercises in malignancy left him untouched. He rather pitied these viragos, dried up prematurely in an emasculated world, but he nevertheless mocked them at every opportunity. For their spineless conniving men he was known to have a healthy dose of contempt. In any case, their dirty tricks could not harm him this time, he had rendered himself invulnerable.

So he thought, till a well-meaning acquaintance drew his attention to the latest exercise in yellow journalism, as he termed it.

"They have gone too far, Carlo, there may be grounds for a libel suit," he advised.

Purento, waiving this notion aside, replied:

"Let them, I have not even bothered to read it so far, and I don't think I will."

Yet his curiosity, once roused, left him no peace till he did read it; not once, but repeatedly. At first he dared not trust his eyes, then his senses, and finally his mind. Stunned, he stared at the caption, shaken to the core he scrutinised every word to the last syllable. Deeply hurt, humiliated and ashamed, he stammered: "How could they!"

Indeed, how could anyone stoop so low. Persecuting and denigrating him was all well and good, for in the eyes of society he had transgressed against one of its mores; that he knew and understood. But to drag his parents, god rest their souls, into it, went beyond the pale of his comprehension. To his unspeakable horror, the article cited incidents of their colourful lives, which no amount of grappa could have emboldened him to touch on. They were made to look like unworthy dabblers, courting mediocrity amid a sea of greatness.

He felt utterly debased; whoever intended to destroy him had succeeded. His adored mother and venerated father were portrayed with fiendish cunning, not exactly injuriously, but craftily enough to convey the notion that the son's criminal inclinations sprouted from seeds sown by the parents. Such insinuations were red-hot arrows piercing the centre of his heart. He instinctively knew that they could only come from the quiver of someone familiar with him and his ancestors. But who could that be?

For days he walked around in a daze, unable to concentrate, incapable to perform the least bit of work. He felt the slough of despond rising about him. Ever active, always energetic, he now hung lamely in the grip of inertia. Lifting a hand, be it only to greet an acquaintance, proved strenuous, besides conjuring up a cloud of evil jinn, deriding him without mercy.

An attempt to heap disgrace on the reporter and his informants, proved futile. Shame and guilt were his alone. A poisonous sting lay buried in his character, he believed, that caused so much vexation. Why could he not be like cousin Mario, compliant and conventional?

Mario! The name assailed him like a snarling tiger his prey. He was the traitor, for he of all people knew intimate details about his family, which were now broadcasted to the world. But then, looking at it closer, he repudiated such notions as aberrant, unworthy of a decent man. After all, Mario was family, an institution inviolable in the Italian tradition. He could not possibly commit the treachery that has no name in Italian life. Carlo oscillated for a while between inculpating his cousin mercilessly, and exonerating him contritely. Finally he decided that Mario would never sink so low. Never, never!

Early next morning Purento visited the cement company to make arrangements for his project in Port Hardy. Lafarge, the company, had a branch there. Russ Baird, the manager, judging by appearances, had to be the infamous telltale of his not so pure past. He wasn't going to confront him, not yet in any case, but taking his pulse, as it were, deemed him a good idea.

To his surprise Baird made a favourable impression. Not a trace of a sinister schemer adhered to his pleasant open face; not a hint of deviousness marred his friendly eyes. The whole man exuded sincerity and good will, so contrary to his original evaluation. Quite baffled, somewhat ruffled really, Purento listened to the manager's agreeable voice.

"We will set up the account today," he promised. Remembering Tony Hicks, Carlo asked:

"Will there be a problem?"

"None at all, you are one of the lowest risks in town, in my estimation."

Purento grew uncomfortable, he wished to be anywhere but there. Baird was either a consummate dissembler, or totally innocent. Only the recollection of the man's obnoxious behaviour that evening, precluded such an assumption. Having their business concluded, they shook hands. On his way out, Purento was called back:

"I hope you were not overly annoyed at my boorish conduct the other night," Baird remarked.

"I must say, I was," he admitted.

"Just forget it. I was drunk, blind to the world. Rising to my feet almost sent me sprawling across the floor," Baird said, chuckling at the thought of it.

Emboldened by this refreshing confession, Purento, turning fully around, commented with forced nonchalance:

"I understand we hail from the same town."

"Oh, where are you from?"

"Kingston, Ontario."

"Never been there in my life. I am a pure-bred Cape Bretoner. This is my first outing beyond the Strait of Canso."

Looking closer at his visitor, more amused than interested, he wanted to know:

"Whatever gave you the idea that Kingston is my hometown?"

"Pereira, my cousin," Purento almost blurted out, but he succeeded to hold his tongue.

Making further inquiries seemed pointless, certainly with Russ Baird. No amount of imagery could betray him as a telltale. His breezy manners, brusque but frank, made short shrift of such notions.

Out on the street Purento's equanimity dissipated at an alarming rate. What did it all mean? Had Mario simply repeated street gossip, or lay a more serious motive at the bottom of it? Hardly, he decided, so it is best to forget the entire affair. Let them talk, let them write, it would not handicap him. That was easier said than done. It resembled a reckoning without one's host, which in this case was a fiercely stubborn pride.

"Denounce me with every vituperative tongue in town; revile me with every pen dipped in vitriol; but my forebears, rest their bones, will not be maligned with impunity.

He decided to have a word with Mario, who might shed some light on this jumble. He also wished to apologise for his temporary lapse of trust and loyalty. Suspecting a close relative of vile designs against him, could hardly be called noble. It would also ease his conscience. Mario could not be found; it appeared that he had taken a trip to the mainland.

It was now late afternoon, time for a draught or two. The distraction might give him a rest from burdensome, never ending selfsame thoughts. Besides, a golden opportunity existed to take a closer look at Megan Haslit. He liked her. Hearing that sparkling wit, seeing those flashing eyes was worth a pilgrimage.

The waitress greeted him with evident joy, manifested by a startling exuberance. They knew each other, but not intimately. Being aware of Mario's green-eyed disposition, he trod carefully with her.

Just the same, seeing her skipping light-footed from table to table, exchanging banter with patrons, he couldn't help being enamoured of her. Alone her buoyant, graceful steps made him forget his troubles. For an instant he mused how wonderful she must be as friend and lover. In a twinkle, however, he repudiated such notions, for before his inner eye rose the picture of Roxana, the gal from Kingston, whom Megan resembled to an amazing degree.

Before he could place his order she talked to him. A change, surprising in its suddenness and intensity, took place. Her scintillating demeanour turned into a mask of ill humour.

"I'm sorry to see these scurrilous articles in the newspaper," were her first words.

Then drawing herself up with arms akimbo and sparks in her eyes, she expelled:

"In your place I would set a bomb under their noses, right this evening I would."

Taken aback by this passionate outburst, he was about to utter words of appeasement, when she bent forward and hissed:

"They did the same to Tony Hicks. A pleasant fellow that one was. Gallant to his fingertips, graced by manners that could set arthritic veins of a bedlam on fire. They are vipers, and the snake in the grass is no other than your cousin Mario."

"Megan!" Purento expostulated.

Waving his protest aside with one sweep of the hand, she said:

"Carlo, I must talk to you, but not here. My shift will end in an hour. Could we meet at Henry's Pub, right after?"

Carlo sat there on tenterhooks, both eyes riveted at the entrance. He neither knew what to make of Megan's display of anger, nor did he give credence to her wild accusations. No doubt, Mario had problems, difficulties ensnared in his nature, that could therefore not easily be overcome. He knew the sting, honed by traits imbedded in a foreign culture. Mario, of a vastly different background than Megan, stood not a chance on love's battlefield. Possessiveness pitched him headlong into the thorny hedge of Megan's rebellion, and jealousy made him vulnerable.

As Megan entered the pub, Carlo muttered instinctively:

"She is a second Roxana, a spooning purring tabby till opposed; then the velvet paws harden and out come the claws."

She wasn't quite so radiant now; in fact, a tinge of a scowl marred her comely face. She started talking before taking a seat.

"You seemed shocked when I told you about Mario."

"I can not believe it. We grew up together, not to mention our common background and kinship. Betraying one's family is unheard of in Italian life."

"Well, you hear it now."

"But why would he do such a thing?"

"I can think of two reasons."

"They are?" Carlo inquired with a measure of sarcasm that he didn't really feel.

"Jealousy is one," she replied.

"And the other?" he asked with tongue in cheek.

"Envy," she burst out somewhat vexed by his raillery.

Shaking his head, Carlo protested:

"I can not imagine cousin Mario being jealous of me, nor envious for that matter. I covet nothing that's not mine, and my possessions can be his for the asking."

Megan contemplated him closer, as if to say: "Is this man naive or just naturally dense?"

She asked:

"Did you ever hear what happened to Tony Hicks?"

"Yes, Mario told me about him, but I fail to see the connection."

Noticing her intention to interrupt, he signalled with his hand to let him continue.

"You see, Megan, I have nothing to fear. Contrary to this fellow Hicks, I do not depend on local business or employment, even less on credit. These machinations would not faze me where it not for the fact that my dead parents are being sullied."

"Oh, that? Pshaw, it's nothing but innuendoes. No reason to worry, in my opinion," she comforted.

Carlo made no immediate reply, but his mien said more than words; it bespoke inner turmoil. Something evidently bothered him. Scowls, alternating with forced smiles rendered his normally handsome countenance gloomy.

Eyeing him closer nearly made her gasp. The man across from her showed no resemblance with the ever friendly and relaxed Carlo. He looked much older, his face took on the grim aspect of an avenger of blood. The transformation gave her a jolt.

"You look upset, Carlo," she remarked.

Wincing, as if caught in a delicate act, he admitted:

"I am, Megan, I am."

Indeed, he was, for reasons she could never have guessed. He was burdened by a secret, which would accompany him to his grave. A secret known by few, betrayed by none; till now that is. Judging by the tenor of the recent newspaper write-up, it might soon be hawker's news. Megan interrupted his reveries:

"Do you care telling me about it?"

He harboured no such wish, but perceiving her sincere concern, he relented:

"I am plagued by a predicament," he said with a sigh.

"Not on account of that frivolous article, I hope?"

"Yes."

Stifling her intended protest by raising a hand, he added:

"Glossing over it as you suggest, is not my privilege."

Shaking her head reprovingly, Megan chided:

"Why bother? It's insignificant for someone financially and otherwise independent."

"True, but governed by ethics," he countered.

Taken aback she cast an inquiring glance at him.

"You heard about the laws of honour of course," Carlo asked.

"No, I have not. I didn't think such laws existed."

Carlo, with the mien of a suffering saint, explained indulgently:

"Not in the law books."

"Where then?"

"In the hearts of men."

"You are not talking about a vendetta?" she scoffed.

"It is in the Italian blood."

"Bosh! besides, you are not in Italy."

"True, but I am the son of Italians, inextricably tied to the code of the mountains."

Megan was about to snort derisively, but thought better of it. An inexplicable impulse, precursor of an idea, swept over her. The dancing imps of a moment ago left her eyes, which now expressed sombre contemplation.

"Carlo, do you know what really happened to Hicks?"

Out of humour because the question deflected from Mario's hinted perfidy, he replied testily:

"He disappeared without a trace, I understand."

"Without a trace, who told you that?" Megan queried with raised eyebrows.

"Mario did."

"Hm, he did?" she sniffed.

Bridling at her mocking tone, he remarked sharply:

"You sound incredulous."

Contemplating him with those eloquent eyes, shaking her head emphatically, she commented:

"Hicks was found dead not far from here at the bottom of a promontory."

"Hicks doesn't really interest me, Megan, I have weightier matters to consider."

"Perhaps not, once you hear the rest. There is a connection between your and Hicks' case."

"Well, go on then," he encouraged with scant conviction.

"Hicks was found with a broken skull one foggy morning by an early stroller. His picture was splashed over the front pages of every newspaper on the island."

"Are you insinuating something?" Carlo interrupted.

"Just that: Mario knows all about it, plus a lot more."

"Come to the point, Megan."

Leaning forward, lowering her voice to a near whisper, she observed:

"Carlo, there is something you should know."

"Tell me."

"The night before Hicks was found, he and Mario met."

"I don't see a significance there," Carlo pointed out.

"Their meeting took place on that bluff from which Hicks evidently fell," she emphasised.

"What are you trying to say?"

"Mario pushed Hicks over the edge."

Flinching as if struck a blow, Purento snapped:

"That's preposterous."

"May be so, but more than likely true. He either pushed Hicks off that rock, or he fell while engaged in a scuffle with Mario."

Purento narrowly suppressed a sharp rebuke that lay on his tongue. Casting aspersions at one's future husband could hardly be called seemly. But he desisted for no other reason perhaps than an ingrained tactfulness. It was just as well as it turned out.

Purento was aware of two facts: One, Megan could neither be called a scold nor a gossip; two, cousin Mario lay in the grip of that two-headed monster: jealousy, and possessiveness. But could that hissing fiend put him up to treachery, or violence even?

"You are suddenly quiet, Carlo. What are you thinking?"

"I am trying to digest what you are saying. Strange it is, very strange. It stretches one's credulity," he granted.

"Wait till you hear the rest," she declared, evidently happy to have a kindred spirit to whom she could unburden herself.

Purento interposed:

"First, Megan, what makes you believe that Mario had a hand in Hicks' death?"

"Two things: Hicks told me about their meeting, date, time and place. Apparently Mario intended to convey a message to him."

"At the spot where you say he was found?"

"Precisely. I know that bluff quite well," she confirmed.

Seeing Purento's raised eyebrows she hastened to add:

"I realise it's an odd place to transmit information."

"Late at night, according to you," Carlo stressed.

"That by itself made me bristle, but Hicks, having reached a state of despair, ignored my voiced misgivings, I can tell you."

"You mentioned two circumstances. What is the other one?"

Reaching into her purse, Megan produced a small object, which she laid on the table. Purento instinctively clasped a hand to his chest.

"Don't worry, yours is still there," Megan chuckled.

Flustered as if caught committing an indiscretion, he asked:

"What is it?"

Pushing the object, a small badge, under his eyes, she encouraged:

"You be the judge."

After shifting, turning and raising it towards the light, he declared:

"It's the insignia of L'Aquila, my parents' home town, worn by many, including Mario and myself."

"Mario wears it no longer," she averred. "It has been in my purse since the day after Mario and Hicks met."

"Did Mario give it to you?"

A sardonic smile appeared on her lips. In a voice dripping with sarcasm, she replied:

"Not exactly. I found it at the spot where Hicks plunged to his death."

Purento's discomfort grew by the minute. His mind evoked spectres, nameless and jeering that refused to go away. A wave of resentment rose within him, which he directed towards Megan, the messenger of evil tidings. How could a woman attribute such sinister deeds, falsely perhaps, to the man she is supposed to love?

Just as he was about to remonstrate with her, she leaned forward, then said in an undertone:

"Carlo, I can see that you are vexed, I don't blame you, for so am I. Before you find fault with me, listen to the rest."

"All right, go on."

"My head whirls, reason tells me one thing, instinct another. Mario came to see me right after the news broke of Hicks' death."

"Did he know about it?"

"Most certainly. The first thing he said was: 'Poor chap, he was such a nice fellow.' Then he added something significant."

Megan, shifting from side to side, paused. Then she commented haltingly:

"It was this: 'Why anyone would go to that Cormorant Bluff is a riddle to me.' "

"Sounds innocent enough," Carlo observed.

"Maybe so till you learn about a simple fact: The police did not disclose the location of Hicks' fatal fall until a week later. So how could Mario have known about it?"

"Did you point that out to him?"

Megan hesitated for an instant before she replied:

"Almost, until I noticed the missing insignia plus a rent on his jacket, where it used to be pinned."

At sea now, frowning openly, Purento inquired:

"Have you mentioned your discoveries to the authorities?"

"Of course not," came a brusque reply.

Purento, looking puzzled, shifting uneasily, remarked in a firm voice:

"Megan, I like to dot my i's and cross my t's. Why are you telling me this?"

Glancing at him as if uncertain what to say, she remarked:

"I feel compelled to confide in someone. To tell you the truth, I'm at the end of my wits, I hardly sleep at night, and my days are harrowing."

Startled, Purento looked up. Something is amiss here it shot through his head. Megan showed no traces of a harried woman. Quite the contrary; her chipper demeanour signified good health and an untroubled mind. Puzzled by this contrast he was about to make a comment, when Megan spoke again:

"To be frank, Mario is no longer himself, hasn't been since the arrival of Tony Hicks, whom he suspected to be my lover."

Seeing Purento's arched eyebrows, she chuckled:

"Nothing of the sort happened, we liked each other's company, that's were it ended."

Purento wanted to leave, he felt an overpowering wish, suddenly and unexpectantly rising within him, to depart abruptly. Something in Megan's demeanour perplexed and bothered him; she gradually changed before his eyes. The normally cherubic face took on a calculating, almost sneering aspect.

Dazzled by this seeming metamorphosis, he bent forward to obtain a closer look, then shrunk back in alarm. For an instant, an awful moment, he could have sworn it was Roxana glowering at him. It was the same unforgettable stare, seething with hate when he told her that matrimony was out of the question. But as he cast another glance the amiable face of Megan Haslit reappeared.

Suppressing a sigh of relief, he thanked the Lord that the apparition which gave him a jolt, was an evocation of frazzled nerves, nothing more.

Perturbed by the startling information, uncertain of her motives, knitting his brow, Purento declared:

"Let me reflect upon what you told me, then I shall talk to you again."

Why he offered these soothing words he hardly knew, for he still did not comprehend, nor could he concede the need for further deliberations.

That conversation took place a week ago. Purento's mind was in a jumble; he found no rest, especially after another scurrilous article appeared in the Marlin Weekender which minced no words. Under the pretext of performing a public duty, the reporter, a latter-day Thersites, squarely marked him with the brand of villainy. Reading again and again that exercise in scurrility, Purento reached the conclusion that someone intended to harm him, for reasons totally incomprehensible. Somebody familiar with his past, reaching beyond his own life to the Abruzzo Mountains, goaded the daughters of morality into action.

That by itself disturbed him not a whit. Neither the leers of withered termagants, nor the high-hatted smirks of their cowardly men, gave him a moment's uneasiness. Besmirching the memories of his deceased parents, however, was another matter.

Carlo Purento knew his obligations; he owed a debt which blood alone could redeem. Mario needed to be confronted, man to man, be it only to allay suspicion; that spewing, gnawing monster which shows no mercy.

But Mario was not to be found; he either evaded him, or had taken a long trip without informing anyone. He decided to bide his time while keeping eyes and ears open.

Then a bit of news came to his attention that shook him to the core. Megan Haslit and Mario Pereira announced their upcoming wedding. At first he refused to believe it, despite the nicely framed notice in the newspaper, which appeared in black and white, prominently placed. The wedding, the paper proclaimed, will take place at the fifteenth of the month, in other words, two weeks hence.

The news disturbed him mightily, understandably so. How a woman, hale in body and sound in mind, could marry a man she imputed with callousness, yes, even murder, was beyond his comprehension. Yet the fact could not be denied, since the marriage banns were also published in the church, where they intended to receive the benediction.

Purento shook off the temporary discomfort. Let the chips fall where they must, he told himself, there were more pressing things to worry about. Two weeks? Hm, not a bad time to steel one's resolve, and hone the stiletto just taken out of storage. Turning the dagger from side to side, raising it to the light, he wondered how often the glittering steel had found its mark. He remembered his father's words when he reached the age of majority:

"Carlo, you are twenty-one today, thus you must shoulder an ancient obligation."

Carlo knew only too well the sequel, but still pretended to be all ears.

"Yes, father," he said.

"Here, take the stiletto, it is a family heirloom since Olim's time, guard it well."

"Yes, father."

"Remember, use it when duty calls, otherwise leave it sheathed. Never raise it in jest or anger, neither to attack nor in defence."

How often had he heard this lover's litany, as he silently called it. He chuckled in retrospect at the thought of his father's contradictory nature. Frivolous in most ways, yet strangely solemn where the integrity of the family was concerned. For the hundredth time instruction were given:

"Don't forget! Parry with your left like so, and so. Thrust with your dagger hand like this, and that," his father advised as he lunged forward with lightning speed while making three or for jabs with the force of conviction.

Carlo recalled his father's face, tanned by the sun of the Abruzzo Mountains, darkened further by a sincere disposition. His countenance seemed to be always alive, a battlefield really, where the new and old fought over every pore, yet neither ever claimed victory.

Anger, fanned by doubts rose in him at the thought of being enjoined with an onerous obligation, dictated by traditions out of place in the New World. Why should archaic mores of distant lands be allowed to weave a collar around his neck that could prove fatal? But these were traitorous thoughts, quickly repudiated, till every drop of blood coursing through his veins demanded redress. Only a well-aimed stab through Mario's heart could restore his self-respect. Mario had to be confronted and dealt with in the fashion of their proud ancestors.

Turbulent days followed, where Purento faltered between compulsion and negation. Voices from the past cheered him on, murmurs of the present told him to desist. Mario's guilt, calmly weighed, could not be denied, for he alone far and wide knew about the family's skeleton in the closet. Why a full blood cousin should stoop so low eluded his comprehension. He finally decided, come what may, Mario must be challenged. This conclusion, however, turned out to be transitory.

Irresolution, that debilitating frame of mind, sapper of strength, and patron of irritation, kept him in a constant state of discomfort. Try as he may he could not, rather dared not, cross the Rubicon. Should he consult uncle Emilio? No, he quickly determined, for he knew the answer:

"You must do it, cousin or not, otherwise your father will find no peace in his grave!" he would surely be told.

Yes, uncle Emilio left no one guess where he stood. He regarded the New World with puckered brow, and biased eyes; a world he deemed inferior in any aspect except material things, a fact he granted with more than a grain of salt.

"I can see your father's ghost already, wandering to and fro, lamenting the day of his birth, hurling imprecations at the son who broke the chain which unites generations no matter where they sojourn. No, Carlo, it must be done!"

Talking to uncle Emilio would lead nowhere, the decision rested with him alone. But therein lay the rub; making up his mind that is.

Tantalised by conflicting emotions of duty and prudence, he walked around in a state of bewilderment. The unusual weather, generally equitable in the Strait of Georgia, heightened his discomfort. Seldom extreme, though wet at times, the climate had been erratic since his arrival. An exceptionally mild winter was succeeded by a hot and dry summer. People thanked the Lord for the steady breeze from the Pacific Ocean, finding its way through the Fuca de Juan Strait, that cooled their brows during the daytime, and made the nights bearable.

Purento received little comfort from the tempering wind that never ceased blowing. He wandered aimless through the day listening to whispers, telling him not to show the white feather. At night he tossed in his bed, racked by uncertainty, conscious-stricken one moment, snorting derisively the next. The devil fetch this notion of sullied honour! it has no standing in the land of the midnight sun. Was he not Canadian born? therefore owing no allegiance to any foreign country, or its outdated mores. Italy, whereon his shadow never fell, was worlds away. True, the bones of his ancestors rested in its ground, but to a son of the New World that meant little. Yet despite repeated attempts at vindication he could not muffle the voice that commanded: "Mario must be punished!"

Then a rumour reached his ears which changed everything. Megan Haslit, the grapevine said, harboured second thoughts about a wedding. Not only that. The whispering went she might even break the engagement. That was the nudge that pushed Purento off the fence, it gave him an idea. Chuckling to himself he murmured:

"That's the way out, the days of dither are over."

He suddenly knew how to disentangle himself from a vexing predicament, it sure was worth a try. Prancing around like Punchinello in his cups, trying to pierce each other with daggers? Not on your life! Such capers were beneath the dignity of a man possessing an abundance of grey matter. Work with what you have, he was taught since he could stand on two feet; and I will, he promised his mentors. I shall restore the family honour alright without employing the outlandish fashion of the Old World, which is dangerous if anything.

"Mario will be dealt a blow more devastating than a stab through his breast," he announced to the waves below.

"It's all so simple, it's all so simple," he muttered repeatedly as he threw himself on his bed, where for the first time in weeks he slept without interruption.

On the next morning before the air resounded with the piercing cries of seagulls, he jumped out of bed and started dressing. Gripped by a wild joy which he felt an urge to vent, he opened the window wider and let go with Verdi's 'Gloria all Egitto'. Let the neighbours cringe and curse, he repeated the finale several times. The sullen, fretful man of the past weeks had overnight been thrust aside by his usual exuberant self.

At lunch time he entered Dollard's Place with jaunty steps and a purposeful air. Sporting the well-known Purento smile, he greeted Megan with ingratiating words and admiring glances. Work with what you have, he was advised? By golly, he would! The notion to woo and seduce Megan received impetus when he noticed her eager countenance at the sight of him. Should he succeed, which not even Thomas Aquinas would doubt, what a bolt from the blue it will be for a man vain and possessive like cousin Mario.

Megan was unable to disguise the fact that she had something to tell him. Scarcely was he seated when she approached his table on skipping feet, with eyes twinkling from afar.

"Mario is still out east," she announced without preliminaries.

"When will he be back?"

"Middle of next week."

"In time for the wedding," he quipped.

Looking at him suggestively, turning her head cautiously left and right, she inquired:

"Carlo, can we meet again, tonight perhaps?"

Surprised at the husky tone, he responded:

"Of course, what time, where?"

"At Henry's Pub, say about eight o'clock."

"I will be waiting," he assured her with the mien of a paramour giddy with sweet hope.

They met as arranged. Megan, in contrast to her wonted upbeat demeanour, seemed strangely subdued; like a woman in distress, Carlo thought, or as uncle Emilio used to say: "Like someone on the Bridge of Sighs." She seemed undecided what to do or say. She hemmed and hawed, raised her head, drew herself up as if to make a comment, panted instead, while scanning Carlo's face. Interrupting her pantomime, Carlo asked:

"You wanted to tell me something?"

"I cancelled the engagement, the wedding is off," she burst out.

"What does Mario say?" Carlo, smiling broadly, inquired.

"He doesn't know it yet."

"That's just as well," Carlo almost blurted out, but checked his tongue, and asked probing questions instead:

"When will you tell him?"

"As soon as he returns."

"When will that be?"

"In about two weeks, as I just found out."

Good news, Carlo was tempted to utter, while chuckling on the quiet. That seemed sufficient time to effect his plan. True, rushing the matter would be imprudent, but dilly-dallying was unthinkable. The ball had to be taken before the bound; meaning the seduction must be in full flower prior the Mario's return. Best to start regaling Megan with that irresistible Italian charm instantly. But something in Megan's demeanour made him blink and take in his breath. Her comely face had acquired an expression that confounded and awed him. Guilt seemed to struggle with repressed longing. Her eyes, dim with restrained tears, had a haunted look. Carlo recognised the signs: Megan was a woman in love.

By the time Mario returned they had become ardent lovers, openly and unreservedly.

Carlo felt consumed with twofold joy engendered by love's delights and consummate gloating. Mario had been dealt a blow from which he could not possibly recover: His manliness withered right under the eyes of the whole town. What a disgrace to a proud and virile man that must be, to be thus dishonoured. Never again will he be able to lift his head, certainly not in this area.

But to Carlo's surprise he not only raised his head but held it high. Mario, fully expected to confront him, possibly fling down the gauntlet, did no such thing; in fact, the opposite happened. He became rather more companionable.

Upon his return he greeted Carlo effusively, invited him for dinner, and drank to his health. Not a word was uttered about the perfidy perpetrated, not even a syllable. Did Megan perchance neglect to own up? No, she didn't, he was assured. He is too stunned, decided Carlo.

"It hasn't sunk in yet," suggested Megan. "He thinks I'm coming back to him on all fours," she snickered.

All good and well, yet small consolation to a man plagued by a gnawing presentiment, Carlo concluded. Why was Mario so backslapping jovial with him? Why did he not take him to task?

Carlo, pensive at first, then annoyed, finally grew apprehensive. Was he being lulled into false security? Kept off guard, softened up for an intended crushing blow? Another disquieting state of affairs made Carlo's head spin: Megan thought of marriage. More insistently by the day, evidenced by silent entreaties that spoke louder than words. When she gazed at him with dolorous eyes, while sighing with quivering lips, Carlo pretended not to notice. Subtle allusions he evaded by claiming to be either on the run, or absorbed in the search of an important business solution.

So it went for a while. Importuned by Megan's no longer silent entreaties, confounded by Mario's sneering indifference, Carlo felt driven into a corner.

One morning Megan faced him squarely, her sober mien conveyed what the words expressed; further vexation for him.

"Carlo, when are we going to marry?"

This he sensed was less of a question than a demand. Bridling on account of her brusque manner and pushy tone, a sharp reprimand lay on his tongue. To be fair, marriage had been mentioned in passing at the beginning, but never seriously considered by him. The affair, though pleasing, served no greater purpose than getting back at Mario.

Checking his impulse to reply scathingly, he was about to cite reasons for a delay, when the shoe dropped.

"If you don't marry me promptly, I am going back to Mario."

The wedding took place on a beautiful autumn day.

Two weeks later surprising revelations manifested themselves. Like the veiled prophet of Khorassan, Megan had managed to conceal an ugly truth: Behind the facade of a Griselda lurked a Janus-faced vixen. To Carlo's horror she also displayed tendencies which would have made Messalina blush.

"What now?" he asked himself.

Feeling deceived, unable to stave off a nagging suspicion, he decided to have a word with his cousin. What he learned exceeded his wildest imagination. Megan did not jilt Mario, as she avowed, but was given the boot by him.

"I kicked her out of my life," Mario stated.

Although tempted to ask why, Carlo desisted, for he could conjecture the reason. His eyes narrowed, and signs of bewilderment flitted over his swarthy face. Bending forward, he remarked:

"Mario, for old-time sake, tell me straight. Did you sic the town's morality squad onto me?"

Totally at sea for an instant, Mario started to chuckle, then murmured:

"So, that's it?"

Instead of an answer, he posed a question:

"Did you know that Megan was born and raised in Kingston, Ontario?"

"No, but you haven't answered me."

"Did you also know that she and Roxana Turcotte are cousins?"

The rest was easy to figure out. Carlo moaned:

"The biter bit."

When Megan shed the last vestiges of respectability, by giving vent to her predilection for strong liquor, Carlo did not berate her; neither did he plunge deeper into the slough of vexation.

What happened? He decided to divorce Megan. Informing her about it elicited snickers and heehaws from his wife.

"Don't be a fool, check the law," she sneered.

Well, following that route seemed not advisable with an ill-meaning wife. True, Megan knew the law alright, but she couldn't divine the make-up of a scion of the Abruzzese.

Carlo's conduct changed miraculously. He no longer scowled at, or bemoaned his wife's behaviour. For some arcane reason he started to admire everything but her shadow about her; overtly that is. His covert actions took a different spin. While sporting a smile and caressing Megan with his eyes, he liquidated his possessions, and hers too in a way, and sent the proceeds to a bank account in L'Aquila. Taking on no further contracts, he fully concentrated on the project in Port Hardy.

A few days after the receipt of full payment, he disappeared. The hitherto harrowing question about cousin Mario's culpability bothered him not a whit anymore. His promise to give women a wide berth in the future, however, he considered etched in stone.

Laughing Eyes

Does a name influence one's future, or do individuals' characters give meaning to a name? Was Iona's sunny disposition a function of her moniker Laughing Eyes, or had she been named thus on account of her sparkling personality? She was a sight to behold; it made young men's hearts leap, and old men wish they were young again.

A Tlingit Indian, born near Teslin above the sixtieth parallel, she led an uneventful life, which changed drastically upon the arrival of Lars Elblang. He was on his way to someplace that he couldn't quite remember. All he knew, rather felt, was the never failing nip at his heels, urging to push on.

That urge, however, subsided when he glimpsed Laughing Eyes; he decided to stay awhile. Being young and vain he couldn't resist testing the waters.

Iona, reserved at first, soon sent out signals no man could misunderstand. By the time the wild laugh of the loon resounded across the lake, they had become lovers and steady companions. Iona was happy, her whole being radiated contentment. The northern sky, unsurpassed for seven months in a year, seemed even brighter in her presence.

They moved into a small house, a shack really, bordering on the lake. Marriage, though never discussed in depth, was understood to take place as soon as Lars had found his footing.

"I must establish myself first," he declared.

Of course that would not be easy in a small Indian village. Yet he, or rather they, went at it with the vigour of youth, carried on the wings of hope.

Iona, no stranger to work and hardship, toiled at his side. She never grumbled; quite the contrary. When afflicted by reverses her spirit rose, the serenity of a contented woman barely lost its sheen, not till the arrival of Lance Briggs. They knew each other, Elblang and Briggs, from a stint in Sudbury's nickel mines. After one glance at Briggs, Iona's features darkened; at the second, wrinkles marred her brow. She didn't like him; in fact, he made her feel uncomfortable. Why, was beyond her understanding; not that she wanted to examine the reason. Possessing neither sophistication nor psychological insight, she listened to her inner voice, triggered by an unswerving instinct. Briggs' presence spelled trouble, no two ways about it, she realised.

Her dislike turned to aversion when she noticed his efforts to drag Lars away from there; not that he stood much of a chance, in her estimation. Though he employed every ruse invented, she relied on Lars' innate distaste for wild goose chases, to resist his pal's spurious assertions. Briggs eulogized opportunities in places he never set foot in, or could find on a map most likely.

When she expressed misgivings about these assertions, plucked from the air, he chuckled :

"You know me sufficiently to realise that chasing a pie in the sky is not one of my faults."

Despite these comforting words she failed to be convinced; for good reasons, since they contradicted a dawning reality. First, her adored Lars grew more distant towards her; second, he sidled up to Briggs whose supposed prattle he found less and less distracting. In fact, he lent credence to his contention that fortunes were waiting on the plateau to be dug up, and crying for redemption at the bottom of creeks and rivers.

Her apprehensions were soon confirmed. One morning, when the sky resounded with the musical honking of Canada geese, Lars approached her:

"Iona, I am going up north," he declared in a voice meant to forestall opposition.

Having anticipated as much, besides, being demure by nature, she suppressed her disappointment and nodded.

"Can I come with you?" she asked.

"Not now," he answered curtly.

Seeing her saddened face, he added:

"I will send for you later."

She balked:

"Lars, I want to be with you."

"Not right away. After the groundwork for success is laid, we will be together again," he consoled.

Bothered by pangs of remorse, he promised:

"Then we will get married."

A doleful smile whisked across her stolid face, bearing witness of a woman's silent lament. She understood. Her devotion, though pleasing on the one hand, spun a cocoon from which he wanted to free himself for a spell.

They left early next morning. Did Briggs try to hide a smug grin? It hardly mattered, for her attention was directed at Lars, who appeared to be ill at ease. Contradictory emotions were reflected on his countenance consisting of joy, regret, and anger. With one shining eye, the other dimmed by inner conflict, he said:

"Goodbye, for now."

Iona, though saddened, felt strangely relieved. Life had taught her that once the inevitable unfolds, the dread is lost.

Spring had arrived, the vast wilderness stirred into life again; nature grew giddy under a rapidly climbing sun. A profusion of colours adorned waysides and meadows. The ice had receded, exposing the bluest water imaginable. A jubilation lay in the air that defied description. Wolves howled with renewed vigour, coyotes let go with abandoned joy.

Three months had past since her lover's departure, which deemed her an eternity. No messages were received, not a word had she heard about his whereabouts. July came and went, blue fireweeds, the Yukon's national flower, stood in full bloom. Iona had no eye for the splendour around her, nor did she lend an ear to the myriad sounds of the wilderness.

Since the snow had melted on the plateau, thereby rendering trails passable, people came and went. Iona stood on the wayside hailing men and women passing through.

"Have you seen Lars, a young Swede, blonde, with blue eyes?" she asked.

"No," some replied, while others shook their heads.

She grew anxious. Her laughing eyes took on a sombre aspect while casting uneasy glances towards the sun.

Summer drew to an end; the long shadows of autumn mirrored on the lake. Searching blindly for Lars in the wane of the good season seemed not prudent; spending the long winter without him deemed her unthinkable. Plagued by indecision, harrowed by fear of the unknown, she kept a constant vigil at the main road. Every traveller, man, or woman, was greeted with:

"Have you seen Lars, the Swede?"

On a late afternoon as the sun pushed over the Tagish Highlands, Lance Briggs appeared. They recognised each other instantly.

"Where is Lars?" Iona called out.

Briggs appeared to be at a loss for an answer, his sideways glances bode evil tidings.

"Where is Lars?" she repeated in a choked voice.

"Bad news, Iona," he finally muttered.

"Is he... is he hurt? Or...or..." she couldn't find it in her heart to utter the unthinkable.

"I'm afraid we lost him. In fact, he disappeared."

"When, where?" she gasped.

"A week ago. He plunged into a treacherous canyon near Carmacks, at the first bent of the Big Salmon River.

Iona, stunned to the marrow, still incredulous, trying desperately to stave off what may not be, made further inquiries.

"Has he been found?"

"Not yet," she was told.

Then Briggs made a remark whose significance eluded Iona momentarily. Inclining her head towards him, she exclaimed:

"What did you say?"

"Lars didn't fall, he was pushed," he repeated.

"Pushed! By whom?"

"By Les Hunt, his partner. By the way, Lars might never be found."

Noticing her inquiring stare, he explained:

"His fall triggered a landslide which probably entombed him till eternity."

Iona listened to every word uttered by Briggs. She learned about Lars' and Hunt's partnership in several claims upriver.

"The agreement, which I have seen, stipulates that upon the demise of one partner, his share falls wholly to the other," Briggs explained.

Iona saw the drift, more so when she learned about their rancorous relations, plus Hunt's threat to do his partner in.

"Besides, an old Indian witnessed everything," Briggs advised.

"Did he make a report?" she asked.

Observing her rebukingly as if to say, "stupid question, you know the way of Indians," he replied:

"No, and he never will. In any case he left the area."

Iona embarked on the first boat to Carmacks. She travelled light, for what needed to be done should not take long. Standing at the railing she periodically reached inside a bag to feel the cold steel of a dagger. It was a formidable weapon, made for its intended use.

On the following day she disembarked in Carmacks, a small village where miners and treasure seekers spend their free time. Though adversely affected by the raucous hubbub, Iona nevertheless found it opportune. After securing a room at the hotel she went for a walk. Leaving the dagger behind for later use, she decided to survey the lay of the land.

Finding Hunt proved easy. To her surprise he made an agreeable impression. Quite contrary to Briggs' description, he looked clean-cut and decidedly trustworthy. To her dismay he also seemed to be imbued with the strength of a bear, and no less his agility.

"I will never overpower him," she said to herself.

Iona kept her own counsel; she neither asked probing questions, nor gave revealing answers. Odd to say, Lars' name was nowhere mentioned. Her discrete inquiries about him were met with shrugs. This came as a surprise, yet not as much as the realisation of Hunt's indifference to her amorous advances. It seemed odd, considering that women were scarce for hundreds of miles around. In fact, men vastly outnumbered them, thus were apt to shower even an old hag with cooing attention.

Iona, a sight for sore eyes in the flower of youth, had made an instant stir among men. But not with Les Hunt. Though evidently pleased by her come-hither approach, he nevertheless shunned her silent invitation. She couldn't understand it. Not only did her womanly self-esteem founder, but also her plans to ensnare Hunt in a web of passion, ply him with liquor, then do the job at a propitious moment.

Distraught she walked around all day in a cloud of uncertainty. Gnawing doubts impeded her steps; growing anxiety dimmed the laughter in her eyes, which suddenly opened wide. 'Squaw Dance' a sign said, nailed up on the hotel wall. For no particular reason, perhaps to while away the time, she went inside. Pointing at one of the prominently displayed posters, she inquired:

"What does that mean?"

"Ladies choice," the publican boomed.

Seeing her puzzled look, he explained:

"It's a custom. Once a month the tables are turned, women invite men to dance."

"Is it held outside?" Iona asked.

"Weather permitting, yes."

Lingering for no apparent reason she turned her head in every direction. Though disinclined to partake in such shindies, as these events were called, she nevertheless showed a glimmer of interest. Why? Not even a mind-reader would have known, let alone an artless denizen of the great outdoors.

Casting furtive glances at the man behind the counter, she sidled towards the back door. Reluctantly, as if obeying an irresistible impulse, she stepped outside. The entire area, enclosed by a low stone wall, was covered with heavy planks. The location afforded a breathtaking view, unexcelled anywhere. Indeed, amid a region famous for its stunning landscapes, visited by people from every corner of the earth, it could justifiably be called nature's triumph.

Iona approached the bulwark built just high enough to prevent an accidental fall into a bottomless canyon. The dance floor, as it were, gaily festooned, unusually situated, cast a spell over her. Frightened, yet equally fascinated, she became unaccountable agitated. Persistent voices from somewhere belaboured her. One, pleading to hurry away; another one, equally insistent, urging to remain. Pausing to take a closer look, she instinctively recoiled when she bent over the parapet. The sight of the sheer drop beyond sent a shiver up her spine. Not for long, however, her wonted poise returned in a trice. A confidence, which she had not felt for weeks, made her cheeks glow. When she stepped outside, Laughing Eyes once again did justice to her moniker.

Today was Friday. Tomorrow at sundown eager men, scrubbed and spruced up, would anxiously wait to be chosen. It should be remembered that every woman could take her pick ten times over. Thus, men needed to look and act their best to be considered.

Iona, having decided to partake, discarded her European clothes for traditional Tlingit attire. Make-up she didn't need; nature had taken care of that while she lay in her mother's womb.

She arrived punctually, the show was about to begin. Her appearance caused a stir among the crowd. Men, from beardless youngsters to fully whiskered sourdoughs craned their necks. Women, some jealous, others struck with nostalgia, whispered to each other.

Then the music started, bringing women to their feet, and making men take positions. The rousing sound removed the last vestiges of restraint. Men whooped and hooted with abandon; the women had a field day. Not exactly bashful normally, the occasion served as a pretext to unleash their sensual proclivities. Rigged to the nines, fired up by liquor, their faces were suffused with a glow that permeated layers of rouge. They ogled their partners suggestively and tantalised them with silent promises. As the evening progressed, virtue, the fifth order of angels, took its leave.

Amid the increasing brouhaha, plus her own excitement, Iona paid no heed to the pricks of misgivings, which intermittently made themselves felt. Had she not been on pins and needles in anticipation of the fulfilment of her plans, she might have noticed a puzzling occurrence: The women seemed not enamoured with Les Hunt; in fact, they positively shunned him. Strange to say, but true, none except herself went near him, despite his pleasant aura enhanced by a manly virility. Another factor should have made her leery; he drank sparingly. While every other man had entered a state of wooziness, Hunt remained cold sober, thus jeopardising her scheme. That was not all.

Something more disquieting manifested itself: Hunt proved impervious to womanly allures. The man appeared to be a latter-day Joseph of Potiphar. When she snuggled up to him he bristled, her lover's hugs were not returned; quite the contrary, they made him shrink back. What an odd fish, she thought, but just the same kept up her endeavours. For tonight was crucial; her beloved Lars, entombed under tons of rubble would find no peace till his treacherous end had been requited. But how could it be done under these circumstances? Who in the world ever heard of a Northlander disdaining proffered love or available liquor?

Iona grew desperate, hope was about to leave her. All was arranged. After reaching a state of babbling intoxication, and being besotted by simmering passion, she intended to lead Hunt to a chosen trysting place. The spot, carefully selected, was situated above a steep narrow gorge wherein Hunt would find his grave. That was the plan which now trembled in the balance. The notion of stabbing had been discarded, it deemed her too messy, plus fraught with pitfalls and obvious danger to herself.

As midnight approached, thus signifying the party's end, Iona's despondency vanished suddenly. An inspiration struck her which lifted her spirit, yet also knitted her brow. She came to a decision that alternately made her sad and blissful. This was the only way out; it had to be done. Did she not make a pledge when they embraced for the last time? She remembered every word and gesture. When she beseeched her lover to be careful, he chuckled:

"Don't worry, nothing ever befalls a Swede."

Seeing her relieved smile, he added mischievously:

"Unless of course...."

"Unless what?" she burst out.

Taken aback he said the first thing that entered his mind:

"Someone harms him."

What happened next made him jump back. Quicker than lightning she whisked a dagger from the folds of her skirt. Making two, three split-second upward strokes, she exclaimed:

"Anybody harming you will be skewered like a pig."

Surprised, aghast really, Lars considered her closer. Her serene face, bespeaking a pleasant disposition, had acquired the cruel gaze of an avenger of blood. Emotions, which he never thought her capable of, frightening in their intensity, disfigured her features. In front of him stood a creature he had never met. As he turned and walked towards his waiting pal, Lars muttered:

"By golly, she means it."

"Last dance," a call came.

Iona knew what it would be; a hoedown polka, just right for her purpose. Uttering a fast and fervent prayer, silently that is, she rushed towards Hunt who met her halfway. He liked these lively steps far more than those cheek on cheek shuffles.

Hoedowns, never scorned by Northerners, are particularly welcome at closing time, like now for instance. The noise, increasingly becoming riotous, drowned out all other sounds till a sudden unearthly cry rent the air. Men from down under took it for the eerie cooee of an Australian aborigine. The music stopped, as did the dancing. Every head turned in the direction of the wail's supposed origin. One man, more alert than the others, ran to the edge of the parapet and looked down. Rubbing his eyes he moaned repeatedly:

"No, no, it can not be."

What he saw made him recoil. Turning towards the others he gasped:

"It's Les and the Indian maiden."

Almost everyone rushed to his side, aghast, but no less curious. In the starlit night, as the echo of the weird screams died away, they made out dark shapes tumbling downwards.

"What a terrible accident," the consensus was.

About a week later Lars Elblang entered his favoured saloon at the outskirts of Stewart Crossing. For a change he seemed to be in a jovial mood. The saloon keeper looked up, then cast sideways glances towards the patrons, as if to say: "Are my eyes deceiving me? Lars whistling again? Hm, he must have found the mother lode."

Nothing of the sort had happened; resoluteness alone revived Elblang's spirit. Gone was the knitted brow of recent weeks, signs of vexation caused by indecision had disappeared; in other words he had jumped off the fence. It occurred suddenly without warning. When he woke up this morning he did not linger in bed as usual in the past; to the contrary, he rose with a leap.

"Hang it, I will fetch Iona," he announced to the bare walls of his cabin.

Dressing in a jiffy, gathering a few things, he set out. First of course he decided to hoist a glass or two at Charly's Nugget.

It was now mid-September, a time of chilly nights and cool days. Snow started to accumulate at higher elevations, which inexorably pushed downwards. The landscape slowly acquired an aspect of fading beauty. Birds of passage, having flocked together for awhile, had either left or were in transit. Herds of porcupine caribou returned from their calving grounds on the Arctic coast, which was a sure sign of winter's approach, presaging unremitting cold, short days, and long nights.

Though out of the doldrums, Lars felt disinclined to chat. He just waved at everybody prior to sitting down at a table distant from the others. He wanted to be alone in order to deliberate. His mining property at Ethel Lake, while not exactly a windfall, nevertheless showed promise. He acquired it from Les Hunt in exchange for his share in the Salmon River claim held equally with Briggs.

Raising a hand to hide his chuckle, Elblang thought of an adage popular with sourdoughs: You never know a man till you empty a sack of flour together. How true, Lars granted, these old-timers sure knew a thing or two. In their case the sack stood more than half full in a corner, when Lars realised a simple fact: Remaining with Briggs another week would drive him into the arms of despair. They parted on terms neither amiable nor inimical; anyway, so it deemed Elblang. How his erstwhile partner felt he neither cared nor inquired about. Especially not at the present, for his thoughts were with Laughing Eyes.

He intended to travel by coach to Carmacks, then board the next barge plying upriver to Teslin. The street of Carmacks, as much as saloons and shops rebounded with narrations about a freak accident which had happened right here in this town. Lars paid scant attention, for in this part of the world, he knew, commonplace occurrences turn into flesh-creeping horror stories quite easily. He did however prick his ears for an instant when references were made to an Indian woman, but being surrounded by natives, ascribed little importance to it. Yet having Les Hunt's name mentioned, who apparently fell to his death, excited his interest. He decided to investigate.

Making a beeline for the hotel, Lars approached the barkeeper in a measured manner. Northerners generally dislike being rushed he realised, they feel discomfited by effusive behaviour. After dispensing with customary preliminaries, Lars remarked casually:

"It seems you had a bit of excitement lately."

"More than I appreciate," the barkeeper agreed.

"What exactly happened?"

Shaking his head in disgust he exclaimed:

"Something I still don't understand, it sure has all the trimmings of a scheme gone awry."

Seeing his listener's raised eyebrows, the bartender declared:

"I will expound on it later. Let me tell you first what happened. At the recent squaw dance held right here, out on the terrace, terror suddenly struck. At the final turn when dancers, as much as musicians, were in fine fettle, out of the blue the air was split by a bloodcurdling cry. At the same moment Les Hunt and the Indian girl disappeared in front of our eyes."

"Disappeared?" interrupted Elblang.

"There is no other word for it. One moment they were there, the next they had vanished. Without that ear-splitting scream, who knows whether their absence would have been noticed at all. When we heard Big Moe shouting: 'Les and the Indian went over the wall,' many rushed to the spot. Helping them was out of the question you will agree, after looking at that sheer drop. It's a one-way down to kingdom come."

"Too much of the good stuff, I reckon," Elblang suggested.

Eyeing his listener appraisingly, the bartender advised:

"Both were cold sober."

"Who was the woman?"

"A young Indian we hadn't seen before. She turned up one late afternoon, said little, plus kept to herself."

Elblang, now as before unsuspecting, nevertheless felt a tingling sensation within him that curiosity alone could not have evoked. The bartender, glad to have found a willing ear, acquired a conspiratorial air. Leaning forward he insinuated:

"That lass hadn't come for her health."

"What do you mean?" exclaimed Elblang.

"Make no mistake, her visit served a purpose, which soon became fiddler's news."

"What was it?"

"To nestle down with Les Hunt. She was sweet on him; if I am wrong, I'm a Dutchman."

Elblang, anxious to be on the wharf, yet also desirous to learn more, made an observation.

"A moment ago you mentioned something about a foiled plan."

"I did, but first let me explain. Les Hunt neither drank as befits a man, nor disported with women. Besides, he never worked."

"How did he make his living?"

"As a confidence man."

Noticing Elblang's astonished glance, the bartender asked:

"Did you know him perchance?"

Hesitating for an instant, Elblang replied:

"No."

Why he uttered a senseless lie, he would have been hard pressed to say. Especially in view of his recent honourable dealings with Hunt.

The bartender continued:

"Here is my theory: This Indian woman, pretty in a fashion, came looking for Hunt who showed signs of dismay because she found him. He visibly evaded her, but not so successfully. She might have been in the family way, for all we know, for which reason he intended to get rid of her. When the hotel announced an upcoming squaw dance, he heard opportunity knocking."

"I don't understand," interjected Lars.

"You will in a moment. The wall outside, a breastwork as can be seen, gave him an idea. Towards the end of the festivities with everybody's perception dimmed by an alcoholic haze, he intended to hurl his pesky appendage into the abyss of no return."

"But the biter was bit, I hear," suggested Elblang.

"And then some; she took him with her."

On the way to the wharf Lars was hailed:

"Swede," somebody shouted.

Turning towards the caller, Lars exclaimed:

"Skukum, what are you doing here?"

"Collecting Laughing Eyes' belongings."

"Laughing Eyes? Do you mean Iona?"

Sensing Lars bewilderment, the old man said:

"Haven't you heard?"

"Heard what?"

"About the accident," Skukum explained.

He was a Tlingit from Teslin, one of Iona's uncles actually. In a flash Lars realised an odd fact; he never once had inquired about the name of the unfortunate Indian woman. Horror-stricken he lowered his head. Could it be? No, no, impossible! Not the Laughing Eyes whom he was about to marry. Yet it proved true; his bride rested at the bottom of a canyon.

"I can't believe it, Skukum."

"Swede, it is so."

For an instant Lars felt tempted to apprise the old man of the bartender's incredulous narration, but decided against it.

Skukum's countenance displayed neither sorrow nor anger; the untimely end of his niece seemed not to concern him. Yet Lars knew better. Emotions, arising from a depth unknown in the New World, stirred in these prehistoric people's hearts. Despite Skukum's inscrutable face, Lars sensed his disquiet.

"What is it, Skukum?" he asked.

"Swede, something does not add up."

Before Lars managed to ask a question, the old man disappeared among a milling crowd. These words came to haunt him, he soon felt enjoined with a task which could not be avoided. While debating with himself whether to continue his journey or return to Ethel Lake, he arrived at the dock.

Still lost in thought, with half an eye he saw one of the river boats ready to steam upriver. Impelled by an inexplicable force, he jumped on board. Later he thanked his guardian angel for this decision, which turned out to be the first step leading to an amazing discovery.

In Teslin he learned about Briggs' visit, which in itself hardly ruffled his equanimity. Considering subsequent events however, it acquired a sinister meaning.

When Elblang stepped off the boat in Carmacks again, he was greeted by ear tingling news. Gold! men could be heard shouting to each other. The saloons were packed with people of different nationalities, speaking tongues unintelligible to others, with one exception: the words gold and mother lode. Liquor, never stagnant along the Yukon, flowed with added impetuosity. Voices, grown raucous by an untamed nature, loud enough to make the rafters quiver, shouted at each new arrival:

"Have you heard?"

"Yes, yes,"

Indeed, how could it have been otherwise, when the entire village appeared to be adrift in a sea of these tidings. Lars too felt a lick of excitement, although he took no particular notice, till someone mentioned the location of this putative discovery.

"It's near Frenchman Lake," a man known as Frenchie announced.

"Hold it, isn't that your old stamping ground?" a voice from somewhere whispered, then turned into a shout upon learning the mine owner's name.

Lance Briggs it was, his former pal and partner. The property? The very same he once shared with Briggs he found out. Despite the hubbub in the hotel, heads turned, brows drew into wrinkles, when they saw a man, chuckling under his hand, rushing towards the exit. It was Lars Elblang seemingly gripped by uncontrollable merriment.

It was getting late in the season. Anxious eyes scoured the northern sky for telltale signs of the first snowstorm. In these latitudes one can never foretell when it arrives; contrary to the certainty that arrive it will, with a vengeance to boot. Most years the snow remains on the ground at least seven months, kept there by bone-numbing cold temperatures. The frigid air, however, though blanching one's skin, is the lesser evil of a Yukon winter. The bane of existence in these months many consider to be the prolonged darkness. Lars neither paid heed to the approach of winter, nor tarried another moment. He had things to do.

As often happens when we try to solve a puzzle, every part must fit, plus be supportive of the next one. Logic alone without sequence can lead a master sleuth astray. Elblang, pricked by Skukum's musing, spurred by the knowledge of Briggs visit in Teslin, started to arrive at notions. First he considered the facts, which proved to be an easy feat. Iona danced with Hunt the better part of the evening. She must have done the choosing, since at squaw dances it is the women's province. Both dancers, Hunt and Iona, tumbled to their death unaccountably, as much as suddenly. The eerie cry meant little to Lars; he had heard it before, emanating from a Tlinglit's throat, expressing joy, surprise, or anguish. But in that unwonted surrounding, amid people from whom she usually fled, such utterances, as much as her presence, were totally out of place. Why did Iona give vent to a scream termed shrill and savage by some, and strangely jubilant by others?

Lars grew uneasier by the hour, for more than one reason. The bartender's narrative, most likely true, barring his conjectures, confounded him thoroughly. Her presence in Carmacks, albeit unexpected, could stand scrutiny, but not the rest. It's conceivable, Lars granted, that Briggs informed her of his whereabouts, thereby inducing her to come looking for him. But why she would, or could for that matter, behave totally out of character that evening, Lars was unable to fathom.

Some credence must be given to these accounts, he conceded, not everything was pulled out of thin air. She danced all evening with Hunt, a stranger whom she most likely had never met before. Why? What purpose did it serve, partaking with gusto in an event whose mere mention made her bristle with disgust? Yet dance she did; besides, showing overt affection for Les Hunt, so people maintained. Such alleged sentiments flew in the face of reality. Would a young woman, who repeatedly asserted that he, Lars, was her first and only love, throw herself at another man? Not only did she affirm her love in words, but showed it in deeds. Was she a wanton, pitted by perfidy beyond imagination? No! he almost shouted, aghast at such outrageous notions.

Then he recalled Skukum's words, which gradually acquired prophetic meanings. How did he say it? "Swede, something does not add up."

No, it didn't, Lars agreed as he reflected once more. The bartender's speculations deserved neither kick nor scoff, they were meant to entertain, no more, no less. Hurling Iona down a ravine in front of a hundred eyes? Not likely, Lars sneered. Manhandling a pack of Tasmanian devils would be less cumbersome than manoeuvring this sinewy wildcat to her death. Lars had witnessed more than once her amazing agility.

Like at the time when they said farewell in Teslin. What an exhibition of swiftness, strength, and resolve that was. He would never forget how in a single movement she produced that dagger, which she thrust out with lightning speed and force that propelled her forward. He remembered expelling a sigh of relief, and thanking his maker for not being the object of her wrath. Even in retrospect he winced at the recollection of her words: "Anybody harming you will be skewered like a pig."

Indeed, he flinched, as he did now, when a terrible realisation hit him. The fog started to lift, a mystery, thought insoluble, unfolded before his eyes. These remarks, inane to say the least, like Mother Carey's chickens, came home to roost. They triggered an avalanche which hurled Iona and Hunt to their death. Far-fetched it may sound, but it provided the vehicle used by Briggs to eliminate his partner with impunity.

Elblang sighed ruefully, then chortled and snorted in derision. Impunity? Maybe not entirely. Briggs scheme, doubtless deemed foolproof, had a major flaw, which soon would manifest itself. What a treat it would be to be present when Briggs found out.

As Elblang reminisced about that fateful day at the Wolverine Property, a desire to howl in despair arose in him. It started innocent enough. Having concluded an arrangement which concerned them both, Lars set out to inform Briggs what had occurred. But he never did, for reasons best described as bewildering. Upon arrival he encountered a cloud of malevolence, raised by Briggs demeanour, not unlike a grim keeper's whom no sop would pacify. He looked decidedly defensive, his inimical bearing was meant to drive off the bravest soul.

Lars, who had his ears near the ground, knew of course that something was brewing on the Wolverine Property. Strangers, according to the grapevine, were busy surveying, taking cores and making assays. Despite the wall of secrecy surrounding these activities, Elblang stumbled over some evidence, conclusive enough to rouse his interest. But he remained mum about it, not a syllable of his haphazard discovery was aired. Scowling, suspicion oozing from every pore of his face, Briggs inquired:

"What brings you here, Lars?"

Neither cherishing Briggs defensive attitude nor accusatory tone, Elblang decided to respond in kind. Not exactly knowing how, he muddled along, till ultimately he made the proverbial false step which cost Laughing Eyes' life.

Fishing a mickey of rye from his pockets, he offered it to Briggs with the words:

"Have a snort, Lance."

Reluctantly Briggs took a draught. As the bottle's contents receded, so did Elblang's customary reticence. What got into him he was unable to say in retrospect; but it happened, his tongue raced ahead of his wit.

"Lance, do you ever want to get rid of someone?" he asked out of the blue.

Taken aback, Briggs replied:

"Not I."

"Well, if you do, I know of an easy way."

Raising his eyebrows, screwing up his face, Briggs responded cautiously:

"Sounds like a lark, but go ahead, tell me."

"Just inform Iona that someone has, or intends to harm me."

"I don't understand."

Elblang smirked while relating Iona's grisly avowal.

"Good for a laugh, no more, no less," countered Briggs.

"You think so?"

"I do."

"Hm, did you not notice Iona's demonstration in Teslin?"

"No," Briggs lied.

Elblang, thoroughly annoyed, took his leave.

So, that was it, Elblang mused. After Briggs obtained the results of the assays, indicating a windfall, his thoughts no doubt were occupied with Les Hunt, the potential sharer in this newly found wealth. His riddance, no doubt, became more desirable by the hour; yet how to effect it took some pondering. Buying him out might be the answer, but that could be fraught with pitfalls, such as enormous costs, or roused suspicion. Then, so Elblang mused, Briggs must have remembered his imprudent prattle about Iona's emotional antics. He could almost see him slap his forehead, and hear his sigh of relief.

"There now, that's the solution," he likely called out.

The risk, practically nonexistent, by far outweighed inevitable gains. If the plan went awry, meaning Hunt remained unscathed, and his message proved to be ill-founded, what of it? Beyond accusations of rashness, negligence even, he could not be faulted. Ill intentions on his part, though divined in some quarters, were neither supportable nor indictable. He had done his duty as perceived, and the devil fetch the hindmost.

Clever thinking, Elblang granted, excellent planning, which was almost amply rewarded. Snorting derisively, he said aloud:

"You see, pal, there is a big fly in the ointment."

Indeed, there was, which fact Briggs was about to discover. He had kept a low profile for understandable reasons. Attracting attention seemed not advisable, for a while anyway, acting precipitately even less. Yet the records needed to be revised. Changes of ownership, although unassailable, nevertheless must be recorded at the title office. For until they appeared in black and white in the big book they were deemed to lack authenticity.

Briggs visited the gold commissioner's office in Dawson City on a Friday morning. Signs of approaching winter were everywhere. Ice started to form on the water of the Yukon; ominous clouds hovered over the Continental Divide presaging snow. Soon the valleys would be covered with snow for six to seven months. A chill lay in the air that made people scurry and puff. Columns of smoke rose from every chimney, followed at times by crackling sparks. Men were busy sealing chinks in walls, and boarding up openings. They exchanged banter, interrupted by the odd hoot when a hammer missed its intended mark. Craning their necks towards the snow-capped mountains, one or the other announced:

"Boys, she is coming down soon."

"Ah, not this year," someone quipped.

They were a breezy lot, not easily daunted, intoxicated by an odour of adventure that gave them no rest.

Equipped with Les Hunt's death certificate, Briggs entered the gold commissioner's office. He approached the counter in measured steps, trying neither to look officious nor overly eager. He had learned a thing or two in the north where people balked at the slightest hint of pushiness. Just the same he couldn't refrain from assuming an air of importance. People noticed a metamorphosis over the past weeks. He appeared to have grown taller and statelier in body, and loftier in mind. Indeed, traits of the former train-jumping hobo were giving way to a new-found gentility.

"He is taking himself for another," people remarked mockingly.

No doubt Briggs emulated notorious characters of the Klondike area; notable Skookum Jim and Dawson Charlie. He expected to be lionised, not treated indifferently like right now. Being greeted with a yawn, as it were, hurt his feelings. They surely must know me, he thought, since every newspaper in the Northwest carried his picture. Concealing his annoyance Briggs presented his free miner's certificate along with Hunt's death attestation. The partnership agreement, being integral to the title, required no proof.

"I want to update the records," he announced.

"Which claim?"

"Wolverine, at Frenchman Lake."

The registrar, raising an eyebrow upon hearing the widely known name, walked slowly towards a cabinet, where he removed a voluminous ledger which he laid on the counter. Briggs was overcome by an odd sensation that made his pulse beat quicker. He resented the official's smirk, as much as he disliked his dilatory tactics. When heads bounced up expectantly of employees sitting at nearby desks, he felt like a manikin on display. While still reading the entries Briggs was asked:

"What would you like to have done?"

"Remove Hunt's name from the registry."

Pursing his lips, poring over the pages once more, shaking his head, the official remarked:

"That's impossible."

"What do you mean?" Briggs barked.

"I can't remove what's not there."

"What are you talking about?"

Briggs soon found out. Speak about somebody stunned. His face, distorted by disbelief, changed into a mask of horror when an awful truth sunk in.

"Have you seen a ghost, Mr Briggs?" the official asked.

Worse than that; he had seen a devastating reality: Les Hunt's name was nowhere on the deed, contrary to Lars Elblang's, whose now as then glowed like St. Anthony's Fire on the main page. Staring at everyone nearby, Briggs moaned:

"I don't understand, it can't be."

Did he hear snickers on his way out? He couldn't say, but the registrar's remarks resounded in his ears:

"Too bad that the wrong man had to die," he called out as Briggs stumbled down the steps onto the street.

Briggs was in a quandary, uncertain of his next moves. As he stood outside, he tried to control his feelings. Chiding himself mercilessly for his gullibility, bemoaning his negligence, he almost cried in despair:

"I should have checked the registry," he reproached himself. Pity, he didn't insist to be present when the transfer was supposed to be made. Then again, why should he have done so? Everything appeared to be above board. He recalled Hunt's reply when asked: "Did you and Lars affect the changes at the title office?" "All done," that barefaced liar answered.

Snow started to fall. A sudden drop in temperature made people muffle up and huddle. Several sturdy fellows armed with axes and bucksaws offered their services as woodcutters. There weren't many takers, for money that is, but ample lunches and barleybree were a welcome substitute.

Shivering from head to toe, Briggs decided to seek accommodation in town. It was high time. The paralysing cold, made unbearable by high wind and blowing snow, conveyed a clear message: Get – and stay inside.

He found a room at the Eldorado where he purchased a bottle of Canadian rye before he went upstairs. Liquor, as we know, not only loosens tongues, but also emboldens minds. Though deemed profane when sober, men bravely wander onto fields made taboo by convention. The gates of intuition start to open; before one's eyes the truth obtains bold outlines. Briggs instinctively knew the score; he had been tricked most famously. He and Elblang were not finished with each other yet.

Outside the storm showed no sign of abatement. The street, normally teeming with folks of every persuasion, race, and opinion, looked forsaken. The storm's fury, never seen before by him, unsettled his nerves.

The dreaded knock came shortly after midnight. Below, the raucous festivities were in full swing, drowning out possible cries for help; he therefore had to deal with his former pal all by himself.

The second rap, more peremptorily, left no doubt who stood at the other side of the door. The hour of reckoning had arrived.

"You almost made it, Lance," were Elblang's first words.

"I don't understand."

"You will in a moment. You see, old buddy, doing away with Les is one thing; but sending Iona to kingdom come is a horse of another colour."

"What are you insinuating? Explain yourself."

"I never tell anyone what they already know. But here is news for you."

"Well, let's hear it," Briggs demanded in a tone meant to sound gruff.

"You checked the registry?"

"Ye – es ."

"That must have been a surprise."

"Sure was. How did you manage that?"

"Never mind. Here is the news: I have sold and deeded my shares to the Hershel brothers."

Briggs appeared not to comprehend immediately, but he seemed visibly rattled. A frown began to darken his countenance, which rapidly changed into a mask of incredulity.

"You have done what?"

"You heard me."

"But – but, they are ruthless gangsters," Briggs exclaimed.

"I know."

"Don't you realise that every man jack of that clan has done time for committing crimes?"

"I do."

"They are killers."

"I know."

"Then how could you..."

Briggs never completed the sentence.

"Guess, Lance, guess," Elblang said on his way out.

Briggs gasped in horror, he understood.

The Walking Stick

The snowfall increased by the minute, as did the wind. Montreal in the winter can be quite blustery; snow unfailingly accumulates wherever one looks. Today the elements seemed united in an effort to wreak havoc on the city that never sleeps. A corn-levelling gale drove sheets of snow across Lac Saint-Louis, piling up drifts that not even an athlete in his prime could have traversed.

The blizzard-like weather drove people indoors. Travellers as much as workers on their way home sought refuge at the nearest bar or lodging in a motel. Every lounge within reach soon filled to standing room capacity. Like the Upper Lachine Motel for instance, a favoured dining and drinking spot, where revellers in the sunken patron's area were gradually reaching a state of inebriation.

Not everyone, mind you, there were some notable exceptions; like the man sitting with two companions at a corner table. Unaffected by the convivial atmosphere, despite his companions' prompting, he touched nothing stronger than ginger ale; in other words he remained sober in the face of overt temptations. Not that former drinking buddies did not try to bring him around as it were, cunningly and no less persuasively.

"The poor man is suffering," they quipped.

"Give him a drink," one said.

"Make it a double," another seconded.

"His tongue must ache for a drain," Greg Varco suggested.

He was one of the men, many in numbers, who for years bent elbows with Kolmar in every bar between the Main and Mercier Bridge. Kolmar accepted the banter good-naturedly, but not a drop of alcohol proffered.

Always self-conscious at such moments, he quickly diverted attention with a jest or two. Since his return from a holiday he had become an enigma to friends, and a curiosity to acquaintances. They expected a relapse any day; none believed that a champion of the whistle would suddenly turn into a confirmed teetotaller. They recalled the party given in his honour, right here six months ago, on the eve of his departure. The newly avowed paragon of temperance drank more than his fill. The truth is he had to be carried to bed; not for the first time to boot.

The memory of that, plus many similar nights, compelled them to consider Kolmar's sobriety with scepticism.

"It will not last," they said.

"Not on your life," some declared who for years tried to cast the same monkey of their backs.

Outside the wind howled unabated. Snowflakes, increasing in size, whirled through the chilly air with frightening abandon. The revellers inside welcomed the rattling fury, for it served as stimulus, and no less as an excuse to kick over the traces.

Not in the case of Baleine and Tobias however, who remained aloof from the bustle. Not on their own volition, but on account of Kolmar's presence. What fun is there in merriment when rubbing elbows with a wet blanket, that makes one feel self-conscious? They drank sparingly; Kolmar's putative sobriety dampened their spirits. As mentioned, they were not convinced that a votary of barley broth almost overnight becomes an inveterate aquarian, who insists that water be substituted for wine at the Lord's Supper. Only yesterday they agreed that backsliding stood in the offing.

Maybe tonight, their suggestive glances implied, for the signs were there.

Indeed, Kolmar appeared to be on edge, unwontedly so. Fidgeting, biting his lips, moving a hand across his face, he gave an impression of irresolution. Like someone trying to stave off an impending evil, his companions thought. They weren't exactly enamoured with him anymore, for several reasons. Though plagued by a spectre arisen from an experience in the islands, he steadfastly refused to unburden his troubled mind. A connection surely exists, they mused, between an unpleasant occurrence and his pledge of temperance. What it was he declined to say. Any allusion to his trip were met with vacant stares, shrugging shoulders, and vague responses like:

"There is nothing to talk about."

Being thus fobbed off, miffed and surprised a good number of people, since they recalled his enthusiastic preparations, accompanied by effusive praise prior to setting out. He practically buttonholed them in order to extol the attractions of this fabulous place in the sun.

"Island of Venus, Elysian fields, that's where I'm going," he sang in their ears till they tingled.

"I might stay there for life," he announced at every opportunity.

Well, he didn't; not even for the duration planned, which was six months. Who could describe their amazement when he returned after one month, suddenly, and furtively it seemed. That in itself created a stir among his coterie, which increased when astounding rumours about his sudden sobriety turned out to be true.

"A miracle," they confessed in disbelief.

"He seems ruffled," more than one noted.

"I wonder why," Greg Varco inquired with Marc Baleine.

"You, his bosom friend should know what bothers him."

Baleine wished it were so, especially after a harrowing experience about two months ago. Barely suppressing an impulse to blazon it abroad, he kept the occurrence to himself; for a while anyway.

One day, however, after an ample meal, fortified by wine, made memorable by snifters of fine brandy, he broached the subject with Tobias.

"By the way, Rudi, did Steve ever show you the walking stick he brought back from the island?"

"I can't say he did. Has he shown it to you?"

"Hm, sort of."

"Quit talking in riddles, Marc."

Contracting both eyes, puckering his brow, Baleine declared:

"I will tell you something that strains credulity and stretches anyone's imagination."

"Well, go on," Baleine was encouraged.

"I will, but remember, keep it to yourself."

"Of course."

"About a week ago I walked in on Steve unannounced."

"At his place?"

Nodding, Baleine went on:

"Since my knock received no response, I turned the knob and went in. It was a mistake, resulting by a hairbreadth in disaster."

"Oh, you startled him?"

"And then some," Baleine emphasised, after which he fell silent.

"There is more?" Tobias asked.

"I say. Standing inside, gaping no doubt at what I saw, I had to fight off an impulse to run headlong outside again."

Trying to ignore his friend's quizzical stare, unsure how to frame his next words, Baleine burst out:

"Laugh, scoff, call me irrational when you hear this. Steve, down on his knees, sobbing his heart out, with both hands gripped what looked like a cane."

"On his knees, sobbing?" Tobias interjected.

"That sounds odd," he added.

"Maybe so, but what followed borders on the grotesque. I tell you with not a word of exaggeration Steve trembled from head to toe, in fear and anguish, it appeared to me. The sight made my head whirl."

"That doesn't make sense," Tobias muttered.

"Hear the rest, then judge," suggested Baleine.

"What happened?"

"Steve went berserk."

"What do you mean?" Tobias cried.

"When he saw me standing there, thunderstruck no doubt, he flinched, then leaped up and lunged at me. You know what?"

"No."

"For an instant I feared for my safety."

"Come now, Steve is a good friend," Tobias objected.

"He wasn't then, far from it. Raising the cane over his head, a sturdy one, I tell you, he aimed it squarely at my skull."

"Did he not recognise you?"

Wide-eyed, tilting his head, Baleine declared:

"Strange to say, I believe he did."

"It sounds bizarre, hard to believe," suggested Tobias.

"Quite so, but anyway, luck was on my side. Anxious to strike, Steve tripped and staggered past me. Mind you, though riveted to the floor for a split second, I regained my wits and stepped aside. Struggling to his feet, uttering a string of imprecations, he tried to hide the cane behind his back."

"Was he embarrassed?"

"Not really, he seemed more concerned with concealing the walking stick from me, than possible disgrace."

"Did he offer an explanation?"

"In a way, yes."

"What did he say?"

"That was close, Marc. I thought you were an intruder, the same fellow that's been lurking about the house lately. I intended to fix his hash for good."

"It's conceivable," acceded Tobias.

Noticing the smirk on his friend's face, he snapped:

"Why are you looking at me like that?"

Indeed, why, Baleine granted, for he realised that his narrative sounded more contrived than realistic. It could easily be taken for a yarn, a tale of the tub. Nevertheless he explained:

"Think what you must, I will tell you anyway. Nearby on the table stood a bottle of brandy beside a glass filled to the brim."

Shrugging his shoulders Tobias conceded:

"It does sound ominous, but hardly strange. After all it used to be his favoured drink, the same as yours."

"And yours," Baleine chuckled.

The words of this conversation were soon forgotten, contrary to conjectures.

As the storm became more intense, patrons drew closer to each other. The place was packed with regulars mostly, yet a few strangers were also present, notable two men who sat at an adjacent table to Kolmar and his friends. They appeared to be unaffected by the hubbub, moreover, showed no visible concern about the inclement weather; in contrast to the others, who became increasingly restive, whose initial jollity subsided as the hour grew late and the storm gained force. At every gust shrieking through the tall pine trees outside, heads turned, brows puckered, and eyes contracted. Apprehension showed on their faces which neither fake cheer nor forced laughter managed to shoo away.

"It's the worst blizzard in thirty years," the bartender announced.

"Did you hear that?" patrons said to each other as their faces dropped.

"We are going to be here all night," some suggested crestfallen.

The realisation rendered them subdued, but also conciliatory. Mutual resentments, nurtured for years, prejudices inherited from their forefathers, were temporarily forgotten. A curious phenomenon prevailed: The raging elements, keeping them confined, imprisoned as it were, accomplished what neither a smiling sun nor mild weather were capable of; it made them more benevolent and tolerant.

Not Steve Kolmar however. His frown, resembling that of elderly disapproving faces, took on aspects of a scowl. Now and then he started a frantic tattoo on the table which raised his friends' eyebrows and made them stir uneasily. He exuded an air of a man fighting temptation. Traces of his usual volubility vanished rapidly; he grew decidedly taciturn.

Shortly after the bartender's announcement about the weather, he jumped up and, prior to disappearing amid the crowd, muttered:

"I will be right back."

Exchanging significant glances, Tobias muttered:

"Steve sure is jumpy tonight."

"I wonder why," Baleine said tongue in cheek.

His friend's mien and tone ruffled Tobias. Glancing at Baleine's smirking face, he chided:

"You are not alluding to that high-flown notion of yours again, about Steve's arcane dependence on a walking stick?"

"I am. My believe has not changed. Some dreadful experience in the islands has altered his life."

"To the better, I say," replied Tobias.

"I am not so sure, he seems to fall away by the week. Mortal fear ages him rapidly."

"Fear from what?"

"Search me. All I know that cane is somehow connected with it. In other words it acts like a friend in need. Anyway, he is coming back."

"What do you know, he has a cane in his hand," remarked Tobias.

"Clutching it for dear life, I wager," suggested Baleine.

Kolmar sat down without uttering a word. His hitherto troubled demeanour had acquired a haggard appearance. He gave the impression of a man shrinking under the talons of a cruel fate.

The cane aroused instant attention, especially from the two strangers sitting nearby. An odd pair that was, drinking sparingly, wrapped in silence, till now that is. Unconcerned they sat for hours amid the raucous crowd, observing the excitement with condescension.

Why this sudden agitation at the sight of a walking stick, not even a clairvoyant could have explained. Yet attentive they became, to Kolmar's dismay, and his friends' astonishment. Their demeanour changed drastically. Before Kolmar sat down, both men, standoffish all evening, became amiable.

"You see what I see?" one of them said louder than his companion appreciated, judging by his frown.

Nevertheless, he too could not contain the spark ignited by Kolmar's walking stick. Obeying an urge, unaccountable to himself, he bent forward to have a closer look.

At that moment a man stepped up, unsteady on his feet, but quite adept with his tongue. As it turned out it was Varco, a regular at the motel, who had been bedevilling Kolmar since his return from the islands. Refusing to give a reason, he nevertheless insinuated that it served a purpose. When he noticed the walking stick which Kolmar tried to safeguard from the strangers' curiosity, he broke out in a hoot that had a mocking ring:

"What do we have here? A walking stick for a lame man?"

Stepping nearer he called out:

"My, a pretty piece of handiwork it is too, here, let me have a look."

With these words Varco tried to gain possession of it. That proved not easy; they soon fought over it tooth and nail. Greg Varco, not exactly pusillanimous when cold sober, in his cups could turn into a regular fire-eater. His strength, never to scoff at, doubled when under the influence. A mighty tug pulled his pal halfway across the table. Bottles tumbled to the floor, glasses spilled, men jumped up.

"Don't be a silly, Steve, I'm not going to swallow your precious stick."

These well-meant words fell on deaf ears. Kolmar, it seemed, felt vulnerable without his cane; like Samson when his hair was trimmed. For although unable to match Varco's strength, who got the better of him, he did not show the white feather. Diving around the table, pushing aside his parrying friends, he bellowed:

"Give me back my cane."

Loath to do so, pricked by mischief, Varco raised the walking stick high over his head.

"Come and get it, come and get it," he taunted.

When Kolmar rushed at him he let out a whoopee and threw the cane behind his back.

Kolmar charged his erstwhile boon companion like an enraged bull. A scuffle ensued, which took several minutes, plus strong hands to subdue. While arms were flailing, voices bellowing, and feet shuffling, a sudden cry arose:

"Where is my walking stick?"

Rummaging furiously around, cursing freely, Kolmar's search proved fruitless; the cane had vanished, no amount of lamenting brought it back. The realisation made him see red. Turning increasingly tumultuous, thus bothersome to others, the publican intervened. Stepping up to Kolmar he admonished:

"That's enough, you settle down, or leave."

"Someone stole my walking stick," Kolmar complained.

"Fiddlesticks! Who would want to steal a walking stick?"

"Well, where is it then?"

Indeed, where? It was neither found on the motel premises nor anywhere else. Despite Kolmar's frantic search, intrusive quizzing and snooping, no trace of it could be detected. His antics, deemed by some of his acquaintances grotesque, perturbed his friends.

"One would think he lost a precious gem," Tobias remarked.

"He lost more than that," suggested Baleine.

"Yes, yes, you told me already," Tobias mocked.

"I will tell you again, that walking stick acts as a fetish for Steve, without it he feels vulnerable."

"Rubbish, plain rot, nothing else," protested Tobias.

A few weeks later a rumour circulated among Kolmar's coterie: "Steve has been arrested. For nonpayment of a traffic ticket probably."

The news was waved aside as a trifle, but then more information leaked out.

"Steve is in custody, he is being accused of a crime."

Then it became hawker's news: "Steve has been charged with murder."

"Steve Kolmar? Our Steve a murderer? Not in a hundred years!" one and all exclaimed.

Alarmed, Tobias and Baleine decided to investigate, albeit hesitantly, because of Kolmar's well understood preoccupation with privacy. What some termed sincere concern, he was apt to call meddling.

Baleine declared:

"He doesn't need our help, should it be the case, surely one of his brothers would have knocked at our door."

Compelled by curiosity as much as convention, Tobias contacted one of Steve's brothers; to his regret. For Wilbur Kolmar curtly let it be known that indeed Steve, being under temporary duress, would soon overcome his difficulties.

"It's a case of mistaken identity," he declared in his condescending way.

"We, the family, appreciate your solicitude, but everything is under control."

It was not, as it turned out.

A few days later the two friends undertook a business trip from which they returned two weeks later. Almost immediately they learned the sad news about Kolmar. He had been arraigned and charged with murder, senseless, brutal, and unprovoked.

"I still don't believe it," Tobias exclaimed.

He and Baleine sat in the sunken lounge of the Upper Lachine Motel, listening to Greg Varco's tidings.

"Neither do I," Baleine seconded.

Varco could barely suppress a gloating grin, which repulsed the friends who never cared much for him. Smacking his lips, Varco said:

"Fair enough, I too shared your sentiments till a few days ago."

Revelling in their quizzical stares, he declared:

"It's that walking stick that sunk him."

"I don't understand," protested Tobias.

Varco had the annoying habit of tilting his head and cocking an eye, while pursing his lips before continuing:

"You remember that blustery night, right in here, when Steve behaved like a fool gone mad?"

They did remember, but also his own offensive antics. Chuckling to himself, Varco remarked:

"That very same cane, evidently so precious to Steve, has been identified as the murder weapon."

"You mean the one you wrenched away from him?" Tobias asked.

"I just wanted to look at it, what's wrong with that? Anyway, it used to belong to an old man who was beaten to death with it."

"You are not saying...." Baleine burst out.

"The authorities seemingly are firm in their belief that Steve did it."

"Where is that cane now?"

"In the hands of the police," Varco replied.

"How did they get a hold of it?" Baleine wanted to know.

Giving them that cockeyed look again, shrugging his shoulders, Varco professed ignorance.

Baleine finally managed to visit Kolmar at the prison where he was held pending bail hearings. It wasn't a happy meeting, chiefly on account of Kolmar's attitude, which for some reason was inimical. Understanding his friend's feelings, where a sufferer blames his intimates for his debacle, Baleine cut the visit short.

"Steve is going through hell," he announced after his return.

"Small wonder, considering the allegations," Tobias commiserated.

"Hm, I don't believe that I should say it, but that is not the underlying cause of his misery."

Smiling indulgently at his friend's stilted language, who after all maintained that brevity is the soul of wit, Tobias inquired:

"Oh, what is?"

"Steve is suffering from withdrawal symptoms."

"Impossible, he hasn't swallowed a drop in more than six months," protested Tobias.

"I am not referring to alcohol."

"To what then?"

"His cane."

"You are not on to that again?"

"Maybe justifiable so after my visit," Baleine hinted, but he shared no desire to go into details.

Although facts concerning Kolmar's situation were difficult to extract, either from his next of kin or the authorities, some information did trickle down the line. It corroborated Varco's assertion about the walking stick, which seemingly served as the authority's fulcrum of their case. In fact, it turned out to be a fatal gift. Kolmar insisted it had been given to him by a total stranger in return for a favour. A clever ruse, the police granted, not readily refuted, yet marred with flaws, which they refused to mention.

As the winter gradually released its grip on the city, Kolmar fell into oblivion, or almost; for Tobias and Baleine were disinclined to stand idly by while their friend languished in jail. Their offer to act as bondsmen, though inconsequent on account of the government's refusal to grant bail, endeared them to Steve's brother Wilbur, who sort of opened up.

"They are groping in the dark," he told Tobias.

"Why then is bail being denied?"

"Difficult to say, since the state's motives are not exactly advertised."

Lifting his head, acquiring that inimitable haughty look, Wilbur Kolmar added:

"But to give the devil his due, the authorities do have grounds to be hesitant. For even I, his brother, can not help being racked by doubts."

Nothing further could be elicited from that martinet, strictly honourable, but no less foolish, in Tobia's opinion.

"What a stiff. He is more concerned with disgrace, his own that is, than Steve's plight," he told Baleine.

Meanwhile spring was on its way. Layers of snow covering the still frozen ground melted rapidly under a climbing sun. Ponds and small lakes formed on the flats, large and deep enough to take a spin in a boat.

Just as Baleine prepared to visit Montserrat, a small, quiet island in the Caribbean Sea, the news broke. Kolmar's trial was going to be held in Montreal at the end of March. Extradition to Montserrat, the locality of the homicide, could not take place without the accused's consent. Baleine, expecting to be subpoenaed, cancelled his scheduled trip.

Soon the newspapers started to show interest in Kolmar's upcoming trial. True to form, they delved into the story headfirst. As usual their reports were a mixture of imaginary fiction, with a sprinkling of facts added, which they stirred lustily till that notorious concoction called huggermugger emerged. Servicing the public, they called it overtly; tickling the palate of Lord Belch among themselves, it was referred to.

Anyway the puzzle started to be pieced together. An old Negro, known as Rufus, had been bludgeoned to death near his home on the outskirts of Plymouth, pretty well the sole town in the island of Montserrat. He was a solitary man, a recluse really, yet distinctly remembered especially by the expatriates. His small hut, place of his birth, he seldom left, except when guiding tourists to the Great Alps Waterfall. Seemingly there existed a controversy concerning this service in view of a well-maintained path, clearly depicted for all to see. Of course Rufus expected a tip for services rendered. To tell the truth, old Rufus was running a racket, one newspaper suggested.

A reporter, writing for the Montreal Gazette being due for a holiday, decided to spend his vacation in Montserrat. Combining pleasure with business always stood high on his agenda. Prior to departure he talked to Keith Bramont, Kolmar's lawyer, whom he knew from numerous courtroom meetings.

Maitre Bramont enjoined him with an errand tailored to his mettle. Not without good reason was he nicknamed 'Warren the sleuth'.

Warren Kent, the reporter, returned with his quiver overflowing with hearsay; a notebook filled with innuendoes, and tales describing the human angle. Not much could be gleamed from these ramblings, but of course he didn't tell all; notable the part of maitre Bramont's interest. On his return he went to the lawyer's office, who greeted him with the words:

"I have read your articles."

"Now you want to hear what hasn't been written," teased Kent.

"I sure do."

"First, your client is remembered as a toper; second, no one I spoke to could, or would state with assurance the time or day when Kolmar left the island. I tell you, Keith, my consensus is this: Old Rufus was not a favourite in the island, certainly not among the expatriates. Some openly call him an old rascal, others an extortioner."

"Fair enough. But what about the owners or occupants of the guest house where Kolmar stayed?"

"McLeods you mean?"

Acknowledging Bramont's nod, Kent declared:

"Kolmar was the sole guest during that time."

"But the owners surely must know."

"She is a Miss Allen, with whom your client seemingly did part of his carousing."

Reflecting a moment, the lawyer mused:

"Of course there is still the matter of the registry to be considered, plus Miss Allen's deposition."

"I am glad you mentioned it. She has made a statement to the police, plus voluntarily handed over the registry for copying."

Bramont, unable to hide his disappointment, declared with a frown:

"Well, so be it. Thanks, Warren, for your help."

"What's the smirk for?" he then asked.

"Don't you want to know what Miss Allen said?"

"Tell me."

"She confirmed the date and time entered in the book; here is a copy."

One glance at it told a mighty story. Kolmar, as he steadfastly maintained, left Montserrat two days prior to the murder.

"Now to the walking stick," maitre Bramont said to his assistant.

At the outset of the trial the defence introduced a motion for dismissal, in view of the latest discovery. The prosecution objected, saying that witnesses were at hand who will disprove the defence's assertions. The judge decided on continuation, albeit reluctantly. But the suspicious circumstances surrounding the walking stick left him no choice, he explained.

Indeed, how did the slain man's property end up with the accused? Rufus, the crown attorney insisted, who shaped and carved the cane, clung to it like an abalone to a rock in a raging sea. Never would he have parted with it voluntarily, nor sold or traded it for all the gold of the Chibchas. Indeed, substantial, verifiable offers were turned down. A surprising fact, considering the old man's poverty. Rufus, who never left the island, shaped and carved his cane into an incomparable object. Once seen, always remembered.

On the second day of the trial the defence lawyers relaxed; came day three they smiled. The prosecution had overreached itself by declaring exhibit one, the walking stick, as the murder weapon. When challenged by the defence, the crown attorney hurled expressions like balance of probability and probabilism at the jury, pronouncing them a science. It even made the judge wince. The notion weakened the crown's case for the simple reason that no sane person could be expected to wander around with an incriminating object of no benefit to him.

"It doesn't make sense," maitre Bramont pointed out.

It didn't to the jury anyway, whose verdict, not guilty, resonated through the courtroom.

A few days later Baleine went on a trip. Quoting urgent business he set out in the morning. Two weeks later, when he returned, he was greeted by appalling news: Steve Kolmar had shot himself. Contacting Tobias without delay they agreed to meet for breakfast at the Seaway Hotel.

"I can not believe it. Why should Steve do such a thing?" Tobias explained without preamble.

"It does seem strange on the surface," Baleine admitted.

Lifting his head, Tobias remarked:

"What's that supposed to mean? After his acquittal one should think he was in good pasture."

"Evidently not," Baleine suggested as he set his eyes towards the Great Lakes Waterway where a ship turned around the bend.

It gives one an eerie feeling, sitting on the mole watching the giants of the sea plying the mighty St. Lawrence River. So close to land that one instinctively shrinks back.

Baleine, squinting, puckering his brow, visibly wavering, finally said what seemingly lay on his tongue.

"Rudi, there is something I have never told you: Steve is guilty as charged."

"How do you know?"

"He told me."

"He what? When?"

"The night he almost struck me with that walking stick. I only related part of the incident, besides, I falsified it."

"What did you leave out or change?"

"Steve was drunk when I arrived, blind to the world. After his attempted attack he broke down and wept like a forsaken child. Haunted by remorse on account of his relapse, maudlin like only a besotted man can be, he made a confession."

"Incriminating himself? Hm, that doesn't sound like Steve."

"Not really, but he said: 'Marc, I have to tell someone, so it might as well be you. Should push come to shove I can always deny everything.' "

"That's more like it," Tobias chuckled.

"Anyway, it's quite a story, grotesque and somewhat macabre. Seeing Steve in a state of diminished responsibility, I promised to be back in the morning, then left. Not, however, prior to exhorting him to rest his tired body and weary mind. Besides, keeping mum, not to breathe a word to a soul till my return."

"Good advise," praised Tobias.

"Next morning at the crack of dawn I knocked at his door. He was waiting for me by the looks of it. His eyes lit up as his hand, a bit shaky, reached out to grab mine. 'I'm glad you came,' he stammered.

"Hoping Steve had forgotten last night's avowal, I had decided to leave well enough alone."

"But he didn't, I presume," Tobias suggested.

"No, he repeated everything verbatim which now can be related, since Steve is out of harms way. Of course what I say must remain between us."

"That is understood," Tobias assured.

"When Steve elected me father confessor I was not exactly enthused. Even less after he told me what should have remained unsaid, and frankly sounded like hysteria to me, triggered by repressed guilt."

"Let's hear it anyway," prodded Tobias.

"As we heard at the courthouse, Steve lodged at Mc Leod's Guesthouse, owned by Edna Allen, a latter day Messalina."

"You met her?"

"I did. But back to Steve's lamentable narrative which bears the stamp of a Greek tragedy; this is what he said:

" 'When I arrived in Montserrat I felt elevated to the seventh heaven, which sentiment soon yielded to abject discord.' 'What happened?' I asked. 'I met Edna Allen.'

"At that time of course I had no idea who Miss Allen was. Steve went on: 'She became my fatal attraction. From the moment I saw her I was infatuated to the point of slavish dependence.' "

"An odd thing to say for a prosaic man," Tobias interrupted.

"Hear the rest, but hold on to your chair. Miss Allen, neither young nor comely, as I can bear witness to, induced Steve to stay at her place, where she wined and dined him. She gained ascendance over his body and soul."

"I don't want to be indelicate, did they become lovers?"

"Strangely enough, no. When I hinted at it he had this to say: 'Though enticing me with seductive smiles, inviting gestures and amorous eyes, I didn't get to first base with her, if you know what I mean.' "

Squinting, Tobias interposed:

"Hm, that sounds odd in view of your remark that this Miss Allen wasn't exactly niggardly with her favours. Besides, Steve is easy to look at."

"I asked him that. You know what his answer was?"

"I couldn't even guess."

"He said: 'First I had to do a job.' 'What kind of a job?' I exclaimed. 'Kill a man called Rufus,' he replied with a rueful smile.

"You could have bowled me over with a bobbin. 'You are not serious,' I protested. 'I wish you were right, but that is what she wanted from me,' he averred.

"I asked Steve: 'Did she tell you that?' 'Not in so many words.' 'Then how did you know, Steve, how?' I cried.

"Then he dropped a bombshell: 'By the medium of subliminal messages.' "

"Subliminal messages? What on earth does that mean?" Tobias interjected.

"That's what I wanted to know. Surprisingly Steve appeared to be well informed about this theory expounded by Carl Jung. Back to Steve's narration.

" 'Her finely honed woman's instinct must have told her instantly that I was the answer to her prayers. My not so slumbering ardour she fanned like only a scheming woman will. How? Through suggestive glances, inviting gestures, and languishing sighs, meant to be tokens of suppressed passion. Believe me, Marc, I felt like Tannhäuser on the way to Venusberg.' 'But gained no admission,' I couldn't help remarking.

"Steve just grinned prior to continuing:

" 'Haunted by unholy desires, weakened by excessive liquor consumption, I gradually became irrational. In fact, without realising it, I had turned into a libertine in bondage who could no longer separate reality from fancy. Miss Allen did her part; she stoked the flame that consumed me. Whether deliberately, or unwittingly, I can not say.'

"I asked him with a measure of incredulity how she managed that, for I concluded that he imagined things which never happened."

"You mean he felt compelled to do what he was incapable of, hence he took flight to the world of subconsciousness, where contradictory perceptions have a rightful place?" Tobias asked.

"Something like that. He insisted to tell me more.

" 'One day Edna was particularly distraught. Dim with suppressed tears, she walked around as though smitten with grief. Seeing my solicitous demeanour, hearing my repeated worried inquiries, she unburdened her heart. 'Rufus is out to ruin me, he is spreading rumours, imputing shameful deeds to me that no woman can endure.'

" 'Although too upset to mention details, her silent plea rang in my ears like a scream for delivery. Feeling enjoined with a knight's errand, I decided to act. Rufus shall be silenced today, before the sun dips into the Caribbean Sea, I promised myself. Fortifying my pounding heart with potent drinks, not just a few, I might add, I set out. Edna was nowhere to be found, a fact that suited me well. It was late afternoon when I stepped onto the path leading to the much extolled waterfall. Staggering more than walking, I saw the world through an alcoholic fog.

" 'Rufus came limping out of his hut. The moment I laid eyes on him my bewilderment grew to the nth degree. 'Are you Rufus?' I called out. 'Yes, sir,' he answered.

" 'Despite my befuddled state it flashed through my mind that something was amiss here. Shaking myself like a wet poodle, trying to penetrate a haze getting denser by the second, I stammered: But – but, you are old. It was a reproach which he accepted as good-natured banter. 'True, sir, but I am still up and going. I will guide you to the waterfall, have no worry about that. But not now, it will be dark in minutes, come back tomorrow, sir.'

" 'As we talked I sidled into the woods. Why, I could not explain even today. Was it to lure the old man off the path, or did I attempt to flee from a dreaded responsibility? Rufus followed on my heels which infuriated me. Overwhelmed by a surge of hate for this chattering creature I fell upon him. What exactly happened I do not remember. I must have lost consciousness, awareness in any case. When I regained a semblance of composure, darkness was rapidly setting in. Hunted by fear, sobering up quickly, I fled without troubling about Rufus.' "

"It sounds weird to say the least," remarked Tobias.

"Wait, it gets weirder," declared Baleine.

"When I implied that his narrative sounded like a fantasy, he glanced at me with doleful eyes. Pointing at the cane he murmured: 'Where it not for that I would concur with you.' 'What has this walking stick got to do with it?' 'Everything, Marc, everything,' he sighed."

The two friends looked at each other, both recalling maitre Bramont's court performance concerning the walking stick, identified as the murder weapon. His incisive words, born by sarcasm, still rang in their ears: 'Who in the world would believe that a sane person with an iota of wits walks around with a murder weapon for all to see? Certainly not the murderer,' he proclaimed.

As mentioned the jury entertained similar notions.

"The cane is a mystery alright, it certainly caused Steve a lot of grief," Tobias mused.

"It did," agreed Baleine as he turned fully towards the Seaway where a passing freighter attracted people's attention. Small wonder, considering the hubbub. Two sailors played the accordion while others sang lusty songs of faraway lands. Guests at a nearby table rose and walked closer towards the shore. They waved, and evidently familiar with the melody, they joined in. Sitting down again their eyes were no longer dry, their voices became subdued. Signs of nostalgia appeared on countenances attempting to hide emotions awakened by childhood memories.

"You implied there is more to come," remarked Tobias.

"Yes. To begin with Steve had it all wrong. Miss Allen was undoubtedly infuriated when her lover jilted her."

"What?" cried Tobias in a voice that made heads turn.

Raising a hand Baleine cautioned:

"Take it easy, Rudi."

"Hearing a shocker like that how can I remain calm. Imagine, an old, decrepit man, a Negro to boot, being the fancy-man of a woman in full bloom," Tobias protested.

"As I said, like you, Steve laboured under an erroneous concept. You almost repeated verbatim what he mentioned to me: 'The sight of that senile remnant of a man, who harboured filthy desires towards my coveted lady, drove me into a frenzy.' "

Cocking an eye, knitting his brow, Tobias obviously at sea, observed dryly:

"Shouldn't that anger have been directed at the woman?"

Grinning broadly, Baleine declared:

"Perhaps so, but as I just explained, Steve had it all wrong. Miss Allen's estranged lover's name is Len Rufous, known throughout the island as Red. In fact, as I found out, very few, if anybody, know his last name."

Shaking himself like a wet poodle, totally bewildered, Tobias stammered:

"You lost me, Marc."

"Let me expound. Miss Allen no doubt heaped fiery scorn onto the head of the man who left her in the lurch; openly and virulently, according to Steve. For some perverse reason, contrary to her wont, she didn't refer to him by his moniker Red, but by his family name Rufous."

Falling silent, Baleine looked at his friend as if to say:

"Do you see it now?"

"I am still in the dark," Tobias admitted.

"Steve's smouldering animosity, culminating in calamity, was aimed at a man who most likely never laid eyes on Miss Allen. Hearing the name Rufus, Steve wrongly thought she meant the hapless guide living near the waterfall. Of course he expected to see a much younger man, plus certainly someone not coal black. The rest you know."

"Good gracious, what a mess," Tobias moaned.

Charlie

"I have a room reserved for you at the Frobisher Inn," Corbett advised as they shook hands.

After Wayne Sloan had moved in, his friend suggested: "How about supper tonight?"

"Sounds fine. Where at?"

Steve Corbett chuckled.

"Where all the Bigbrows eat, down below in the dining room. Will eight o'clock be suitable?"

"I shall be ready."

Both men were Montrealers, old acquaintances, who kept in touch. Corbett, employed with Lavalin, resided permanently in Frobisher Bay, a windswept town on Baffin Island. He considered himself a dyed-in-the-wool Northerner, contrary to Wayne Sloan, who stepped onto the barrens the first time in his life. He intended to vie for a government contract whose leads were provided by Corbett. Steve, so it appeared, cast a long shadow among influential people in the area.

The half-empty dining room, though lacking opulence, radiated comfort and good taste. The friends had much to talk about, especially concerning conditions in the Arctic, and no less its prevalent mores.

Considering Sloan's need for information, one should have thought that he be attentive. Not so. A diminutive figure slouching between tables seemed to captivate him. Never had he seen such abject resignation in so small a boy.

"What a pitiful sight," he murmured.

Corbett looked at his friend inquiringly.

"I mean that boy over there," explained Sloan.

"Charlie? Don't mind him," Corbett remarked curtly, indicating displeasure over the interruption.

Feeling a twinge of remorse, he added:

"Really, Wayne, he is clearing tables, what's so pathetic about that?"

"But he picks up crumbs and eats scraps from the plates," Sloan noted.

Corbett shrugged his shoulders, implying indifference. Sensing a silent rebuke in his friend's manner, Sloan tried to avoid glancing at the wretched figure evoking compassion. Yet a force stronger than mere intent directed his eyes, furtively, mind you, towards the boy shrouded in misery.

"He is just a child," he muttered involuntarily.

"A child? Far from it," responded Corbett against his will.

"But he is so small and frail. Do his parents know he is cadging?"

"They do, but couldn't care less; in fact, they kicked him out."

"But – but, how can they?"

"They can, and they did. After all he has reached majority. Besides, he is an unmitigated parasite, indolent, and a sneak."

Noticing his friend's shocked demeanour, Corbett emphasised:

"Let me tell you, Wayne, this fellow is unworthy to be spoken about, he is a wastrel."

"Do you expect him to work in his condition?"

"Yes."

Eyeing his friend censoriously, Sloan suggested:

"Aren't you a bit callous, Steve?"

Corbett didn't think so. With the smell of the north in both wings of his nose, he abhorred namby-pambies who attempt to shape reality to suit their bleeding hearts.

Prematurely aged, wrangling with fate, Corbett was prone to be querulous. Waving a hand deprecatingly, he said:

"Don't be sentimental, Wayne. If you intend to work and live in the Arctic, leave daintiness at home. The tundra deplores pity; the natives fear and hate it."

This was sound advice, deserving to be taken to heart.

"By the way, I'm going on a business trip for two weeks, starting Thursday. You can stay at my place till I return, if you wish."

"Sounds good."

Next day Corbett introduced Sloan to various business and government leaders who without exception welcomed his presence. What an ennui-ridden crowd that is, Sloan couldn't help thinking. And so they were after months of long nights, short days, assailed by terrible cold and howling winds. At that time few white people resided permanently in the Arctic.

Sloan soon found out a surprising fact: The old-timers were a shiftless lot, who almost upon arrival graduated from has-beens down south to worthies up north. A spurious coterie that was, Sloan decided, united by benign contempt for the natives. With the exception of the priest, none spoke Inuktitut, therefore rendering them deaf and mute amid the vast majority.

Sloan vowed to shun these Adullamites, as he called them. To begin with he would learn the native language, beginning tomorrow that is. How to go about it? Well now, that should prove easy enough. Having kept his eyes peeled, and ears pricked, he noticed that Charlie, the outcast Inuit boy, spoke good English. Thus an opportunity existed to kill two birds with one stone; learning the native language while simultaneously salving his conscience. For the stunted flotsam seen at the Frobisher Inn refused to yield from his thoughts.

January had arrived, accompanied by the usual bluster and bone-numbing cold.

Sloan, who made himself comfortable in Corbett's house, lost not an hour of daylight to make his rounds. On the second evening, fortified with altruistic sentiments, he visited the Frobisher Inn. Charlie was there. His face lit up when he caught sight of Sloan. As they made eye contact, the misshapen youngster quickly lowered his head. A sign of deference, Sloan surmised with satisfaction, for he liked to be esteemed.

Silently savouring the presumed respect accorded him, Sloan took scant notice of Charlie's furtive grin, who divined the older man's intentions. The management, though willing to show mercy towards the ill-fated waif, was disinclined to allow mingling with guests. Instructions were strict and succinct:

"Answer when spoken to, but do not linger, nor ever accept an invitation to sit down."

Although weak-limbed and frail in body, attributes utterly despised by the gypsies of the north, Charlie possessed inherent Inuit qualities. He was endowed with an eagle's sight and instinct of the wild. Sloan's come-hither demeanour spoke louder than words; it sent a message readily understood. But remembering restrictions imposed, Charlie hesitated to obey Sloan's broad hint, who had chosen a corner table somewhat segregated. Prudence was advisable, for only yesterday a patron complained about Charlie's presence.

"His proximity spoils my appetite," he told the waitress.

A man bent on doing good deeds rebuffs restraint; he resembles a hungry wolf on the prowl who will not, rather can not, rest till a prey is found. Watching the woeful figure shuffling about raised Sloan's hackle, a column of righteous anger against his parents rose within him. Waves of resentment were directed towards a society living on the fat of the land, yet failed to take under its wings a fellow being sorely tested by fate. His indignation turned to bitterness upon learning a disgraceful fact: Charlie had no home of any kind.

"But where does he sleep?" Sloan asked.

"Anywhere," he was told.

Annoyed by the seemingly frivolous information, Sloan glowered at his informant.

"You are putting me on, how could anyone survive in weather like this?" he remonstrated.

"Charlie seems to manage somehow," he was reminded.

Sloan sneered at the notion of Charlie's presumed homelessness, till others confirmed what he strenuously repudiated. Words of rebuttal remained stuck in his throat when the truth unfolded. Charlie was indeed homeless, a pariah scorned by the Inuit, and shunned by the inhabitants from outside. He had been disowned by his relatives about a year ago, and shamelessly ignored by the rest of the community ever since. Even the priests, declaring Charlie incorrigible, turned their backs on him.

What kept the stray among the living were two facts: The hotel staff's graciousness, plus a lucky circumstance. Below the hotel a small shopping mall existed, whose access corridor remained unlocked in the cold season. This had become the outcast's lair, which protected him from bitter chills and horrendous storms, plus provided a place to sleep.

Thinking about the hapless outcast's predicament, as he presently did, made Sloan blush in anger. He decided to lighten the unfortunate youngster's privation, and possibly eliminate it.

From thereon events took a course best described as singular. Sloan, like the princes of Serendip in quest of worldly possessions, found something more precious; that is, a sense of fulfilment. Inner contentment, which eluded his anxious grasp till now, fell into his lap. Philanthropy conferred upon him harmony and a feeling of worth not perceived till now. In decades of frantic pursuit of values, deemed essential to a happy life, bitter disappointment was always his lot. Material success, ardently sought, once acquired failed to mitigate a gnawing emptiness. Love, persistently chased, turned out to be a source of discontent. But now the search for a mission had ended. Easing Charlie's dire existence, whom he considered a blunder of nature, bestowed Sloan the sorely coveted purpose of life.

Several days later a letter of intent arrived from the territorial government in Yellowknife.

"A formal contract is being drawn up," the administrator advised.

Sloan lost no time to seek suitable quarters, preferable a detached house with sufficient space for an office. Finding such premises proved not easy, certainly not on short notice.

A lucky circumstance alleviated his anxiety. Corbett sent word that he will not return prior to the middle of February. Company demands dictated a prolonged stay in Montreal.

Heaving a sigh of relief, Sloan relaxed, then took Charlie in tow. He provided him with clothes, small amounts of money, plus other amenities. To his surprise the little tramp displayed scant enthusiasm to avail himself of the proffered shakedown at the house.

"Thank you, sir," Charlie said, yet spent nights now as before at his usual haunt.

Thinking he had been misunderstood, Sloan repeated the offer.

"Thank you, sir," Charlie murmured, but stayed away.

At first Sloan chuckled over his charge's presumed bashfulness, it somehow caught his fancy. But his spiritual welfare, serendipity as it were, demanded pliancy. Charlie, Sloan resolved, must be persuaded, subliminally or otherwise, to spend nights in comfortable surrounding. With that in mind his search for accommodation included a bedroom intended for his adopted ward.

"Tonight I shall apprise Charlie of that fact," he announced to the bare walls, in a voice crackling with remorse.

For guilt, the beast that never smiles, began stretching its mangling claws, reminding him of a disquieting fact: Charlie, till recently obliging to a fault, grew increasingly sulky and unhappy, which circumstance Sloan attributed to his own failing. He frowned like a man bedevilled by emotions, wavering between self-reproach and annoyance.

Three weeks had passed since he took the frail pariah under his wing. It changed his life, the quest for a mission had ended miraculously. But the initial bliss accorded him, and Charlie for that matter, gradually waned for inexplicable reasons. His magnanimity, once welcomed with grateful smiles and words of gratitude, now barely received acknowledgement.

What was happening? Another factor disconcerted Sloan: His charge's changing demeanour. Whereas previously Charlie's face perked up at the sight of him, he now acquired that former doleful expression in his presence.

"I must be doing something wrong," Sloan admitted. Charlie's desires were evidently not fulfilled.

"Tonight I shall sound him out," he resolved.

"Charlie, have I neglected you lately?"

"Oh no," came a hasty reply.

"You need money?"

"No, sir."

"Here, take a few dollars anyway," Sloan insisted, as he stuffed several bills into the boy's pockets.

"How about clothing?"

"I have enough," Charlie countered, visibly on edge.

"Don't be bashful, you need a warmer coat. February, I understand, is a brutal month."

This encounter, similar to others before, took place on a late evening in the mall's corridor. Charlie seemed strangely restive; he gave the impression that he wanted to get away.

"Why? From whom? Surely not himself, his benefactor," Sloan surmised.

Noticing his furtive glances directed at some boys at the far end, he asked:

"Are these boys bothering you, Charlie?"

The respondent's chuckle surprised Sloan. Had he not felt assured of his adopted ward's meek character, he might have been tempted to deem it derisive.

"Oh no," Charlie answered with conviction.

Sloan felt content as never before, his quest for a mission in life had ended. So he thought, till Charlie started to act up. Shying away from seeking shelter in Corbett's house was understandable, in view of his friend's undisguised dislike for the little outcast. But not his increasing odd behaviour towards him. He could no longer stave off the impression that Charlie avoided him. It made no sense. A starveling taking to his heels at the sight of his benefactor, who asked nothing in return for his charitable deeds? Who ever heard of such a paradoxical conduct which nevertheless pricked Sloan's spiritual welfare.

Of course he wasn't honest with himself, his professed unselfishness did not exist; quite the contrary. Demands were made, conveyed silently, or through subtle hints, which Charlie failed to fulfil. Though cap in hand, deferential to a fault, he lacked enthusiasm to express his gratitude in words; repeatedly to boot. Possessing a native's reticence, he abhorred hackneyed utterances; besides, his instinct told him that giving is more satisfying than receiving. Sloan's craving for appreciation, quintessence of his being, suffered on account of this cultural divergence. Nothing loath he remained steadfast in his endeavour to keep his adopted waif in clover, even if it discomfited Charlie.

"The little fellow is just shy, and awed by my generosity," Sloan explained to himself the youngster's odd deportment.

His own feelings he forbore to admit; the gratification accorded him by these benevolent acts. The satisfaction derived from them he would not have traded for all the gold of the Chibchas.

How Charlie perceived Sloan's relentless charity never came to light. He vaguely did grouch about it to some of his vagabond chums, but being Inuit, their lips remained sealed.

A silent contest ensued between Sloan, the bleeding heart, and his beneficiary, which the great blizzard brought to an end.

What a storm that was! Memories are still aglow with its destructive force. Like an infuriated monster, intent to ravage everything in its path, it came roaring down Cumberland Sound, laying the entire peninsula under siege. Old men still talk about that raging hell; old women cover their faces at the slightest mention of it.

"No one dared to leave the house for weeks," Okalik, the elder declared. His assertion, while falling short of the truth, wasn't that far off. No sensible being, man, or beast, ventured outside after darkness.

It started innocent enough. Strange to say the temperature became suspiciously mild; an eerie silence engulfed the land. Snow started to fall after darkness, soon big flakes whirled through the air and in no time covered the ground with a carpet of soft, white powder.

"What a wondrous sight," recent arrivals proclaimed, while old-timers got busy boarding up windows.

Shortly before midnight an ominous stir woke up old Tegeluk. He knew the signs; the shrieking monster was about to be unleashed. By mid-morning of the following day the wind had reached gale strength, and was gaining force by the hour. The accumulated snow, raised by a howling wind, scoured over the ground, creating a condition known as whiteout. Visibility, barely a few feet at times, seldom attained more than twenty yards. Within hours temperatures tumbled to record lows. Fifty degrees Fahrenheit below zero was registered, which, adding the wind-chill factor, defies description how cold that is.

After a solitary nightlong drinking bout, Sloan fell into a leaden sleep, racked by horrendous dreams. Incubus after incubus, one more ponderous than the next, pommeled his chest and shrieked in his ears. Walls of ice seemed to hem him in, gradually freezing the blood in his veins.

Alarmed, fearing for his life, he tried to hurl these demons from his chest. Rising, still in a torpor-like state, an awful realisation hit him: The heat was off!

"That's impossible," he murmured aghast, with incredulity written all over his face. The huge fuel tank, he knew, had been filled three days ago, at which time the heating system underwent a thorough overhaul.

"Yes, yes, Steve, the heating system works like a charm," he mocked his friend's reassuring words.

Though dazed and chilled to the marrow, he realised that prompt action was essential to avoid a looming disaster. Calling for help would be futile, Sloan decided, as much as seeking shelter at a neighbour's house. For though unable to get a glimpse through the frozen windows, the roar of the wind, and rattle of driving snow told him everything. Besides, when he tried to open the front door it budged not an inch.

Muffling up with failing strength and waning spirit, Sloan started to investigate.

"Why is there no heat?" he mumbled repeatedly.

Both stoves were cold, neither a gleam of light nor a speck of oil could be seen.

"The oil supply is blocked, must be the main valve," Sloan decided.

It was closed as it turned out. That much could be seen at a glance by the stem's position.

Stunned, Sloan nevertheless reached out involuntarily to open it. A hoarse cry escaped his throat as he withdrew his hands. Ice, his instinct said; impossible, reason countered. Yet a closer look revealed a startling fact: The valve was frozen solidly, no force on earth could open it, except heat of course.

Gaping aghast at the source of his distress, Sloan realised what must be done.

"Pile every traceable blanket onto the bed and crawl underneath them," he told himself. He would soon be missed. No doubt Charlie could be relied on to alarm the authorities.

Trembling with cold, shaking in every limb, Sloan went at it, or rather tried to. Enfeebled in body, disheartened in spirit, chilled to the marrow, he stumbled and fell.

There he was found, stiff and lifeless, on the concrete steps leading from the tank's shelter to the house.

Constable Carey conducted an investigation.

"Someone tempered with the oil supply line," he reported to the sergeant.

"In what way?"

"The main valve, closed tightly, flooded with water which filled the gate's chamber, had turned to solid ice."

"Meaning?"

"Not even an earthquake could have opened it."

"Except heat," the sergeant offered.

"Except heat," the constable agreed.

The police inquiries came to very little. Sloan had neither enemies nor detractors; in fact, he was universally liked by white people. The Inuit voiced no opinion. They answered constable Carey's probing questions with a curt yes, no, but mostly with, I don't know. To them he was just another double talking Bigbrow, whose insinuated authority was met with smirks.

When after several months not a single clue turned up, constable Carey closed the file. His conclusion: A tragic accident.

June drew near. The sun was up twenty-two hours a day, bestowing warmth as much as brightness peculiar to the Arctic. People were glad to be alive, when almost overnight the tundra acquired a carpet of fiery colours.

The huskies, short-tempered in the winter, lazed about peacefully, blinking in awe at the sudden splendour. A promise lay in the air, touching all but the dead.

Charlie trudged on as before, with a difference however. The shuffle of the past had given way to sprightly steps. His mien, hitherto crestfallen, now sported a smile. At one time he felt tempted to confess, after listening to Naujuk's wondrous tale, who had served a jail term in Edmonton.

Indeed, the old rascal set the town agog upon his return. When he was hauled off he resembled a corpse warmed over. At his return he was the picture of health.

"What happened? What happened?" young and old people asked.

"I spent a wonderful time in a place the Bigbrows call prison. Ample meals are delivered to you three times a day; dry and warm beds are provided, all at no cost. Did you have to work, you ask? Not a stitch, not a stitch."

Yes, Naujuk's wondrous sojourn down south nearly encouraged Charlie to admit his guilt. But the temptation faded at the sight of the returning snow buntings, who filled the air with their sweet, rippling whistles.

Maria

The wind showed no sign of abatement; if anything its fury increased. Maria Abel anxiously scoured the eastern sky for traces of dawn, hidden somewhere amid shrouds of dust. She fervently hoped that Mr Pulko would stop on his way to the outer fields, as he unfailingly did in foul weather.

"Just want to make sure that you are hale and safe," were his usual pat remarks.

He seldom lingered, for small talk he didn't relish, certainly not on the way to work. Yet he never failed to give her the once-over while nodding mutely. Sometimes Maria suspected the long-standing widower of entertaining amorous intentions.

Maria cast a sidewise glance at the prostrate man at her feet, strangely convulsed, his body grotesquely wrenched out of shape. Judging by his rigid limbs and motionless frame, she reckoned he was dead. He would never cause her another moment's distress. The realisation eased her soul and smoothened her countenance. Tears of relief welled up in her eyes; fate had finally removed a lingering scourge, evaded for a while, but never forgotten.

The homestead, place of her birth, situated between Regina and Moose Jaw, though not far from either city, might as well have been located in the sticks, considering its seclusion. Mr Pulko's farm, about three kilometres distant, was the only one visible from her own.

Maria stepped outside to survey the sky once more. She had to shield her eyes from the wind-lashed dust that became entangled in her hair.

There now, to her relief, the heavens commenced to acquire the hue of dawn; the clouds of dust could no longer hide the presence of the sun. Though unable to penetrate the layers of floating powdered earth, her quick ear perceived the peculiar chug-chug of her neighbour's tractor.

"How is Maria?"

"I am fine, Mr Pulko."

"Well, in that case I will be on my way," the farmer offered; not of course prior to giving the solitary woman the usual esteemed glance, whereby he sensed her discomfiture.

"Anything wrong, Maria?" he asked in German.

"In a way, yes," she answered in the same language.

"Tell me," the older man requested.

"Come in, I will show you."

At the sight of the prone man lying there motionless and grotesquely contorted, the farmer drew a deep breath.

"What gives, who is it?"

"My husband."

"I didn't know you where married."

"I forgot to mention it," she countered his hidden rebuke.

"What's the matter with him?"

"He suddenly collapsed."

"Is he, is he..."

"Dead as a doornail," Maria advised.

Mr Pulko's bland, honest eyes wandered from the unperturbed woman to the stiff-limbed man on the floor. He lacked the words to say anything. Being a man of rustic simplicity he scratched his head, inwardly that is, for he prided himself to be a man of sensibility. Yet in his book, a woman whose husband died under her nose, should show a different deportment.

Maria neither displayed grief nor surprise; in fact, she gave the impression of a smug-faced individual confronted by everyday occurrences. True, Maria's demeanour had always been a source of bafflement to Mr Pulko, who knew her parents, and Maria from birth. She left with her folks when quite young, never to return till recently. He had lost track of the family, who presumably moved east.

When Maria returned he barely recognised her. The youngster had become a full-bodied woman, graced with a charm of her own. Her personality, however, underwent few changes; in fact, some traits were etched deeper onto her character than before. The tendency towards taciturnity for one, endured the passage of time. Eliciting information from her deemed Mr Pulko more strenuous than cultivating a section of land. He did find out, however, that her parents had died, and that she intended to run the farm with no help, if possible.

Mr Pulko had leased the Abel's quarter section in the past, which included looking after the place.

"Have you notified the authorities yet?" he inquired.

Instead of an answer Maria viewed him with that quizzical smile of hers, which he liked, yet also resented – you know I have no means too communicate with the outside – her reproachful stare seemed to say.

"Oh, I forgot, shall I notify them?"

"Yes."

After Mr Pulko's departure, Maria cast a mocking glance at the prone figure. She felt tempted to bend down and whisper in his ears: "There now, Wilf Procter, you have reckoned without your host once too often." But she decided it might be undignified, not befitting the grisly situation. Would there be an inquest? Whatever, she had no grounds for concern. Her testimony, no doubt playing a decisive role, would prove to be inconsequential. In short, her husband came to visit her in a state of mental anguish and physical discomfort.

In the early morning hours she tore herself out of a nightmare, which turned out to be more than that. Wilf had risen from the sofa, his bedstead for the night, and lamented as if beset by Dante's twelve devils. Suddenly he gripped his throat and pressed a hand against his chest. Then, groaning piteously, he gyrated as if mortally wounded and slammed to the floor. A minute later he lay there, as the police can attest, a heap of twisted limbs exuding the smell of death. Mr Pulko can tell you the rest, she intended to depose.

There was no inquest, nor undertakings of stringent examinations, after two doctors diagnosed heart attack. True, the police left no stone unturned to find evidence of skulduggery on her part. Soon, however, they declared her innocent of any wrongdoing. Ha, what a bunch of amateurs, who merely see what hits their eyes, and hear what's said aloud. Ha, ha, and ha again, Maria uttered to herself.

The Abel family had moved eastwards, hoping to escape backbreaking toil, bone-numbing cold in the winter, and parching heat in the summer; not to mention the discomfort of those odious dust storms.

Mr Abel found work at the Mannesmann Tube Mill in Sault Ste. Marie, given his knowledge of German. Maria, a young woman now, met Wilf Procter who sort of wooed her in the fashion of a clodhopper. One glance at him made Mr Abel cringe, the young man's deportment evoked spectres of bleached hearts and stifled souls. He resented the type with unbridled vehemence.

"Anna, that fellow gives me the shivers," he told his wife who, though equally repulsed by Maria's friend, managed to hide her misgivings.

"Don't worry, Kurt, their liaison will soon end," she consoled.

"Did she say so?"

"Yes," she lied.

When Maria announced her betrothal to Procter, her parents were thunderstruck. Mr Abel, who referred to the daughter's prospective husband as fidgets for obvious reasons, felt particularly offended, so much so that he remained tongue-tied. Reaching for his hat he stormed out. Blinded by anger, saddened by the daughter's putative treachery, he stumbled along Queen Street where he stopped in front of an establishment he labelled unfit for cattle, after taking a glimpse inside some years ago. Yet he entered, and despite the stale smell and drab windowless interior, he sat down at a rickety table hardly larger than a good-sized plate.

While still staring at the walls, unadorned and stained, two bottles were set in front of him. Glasses? "Drink from the bottle," he was told. Indeed, swigging was the manly thing to do, not sipping from a glass, like a sissy. Despite his grief Mr Abel couldn't find it in his heart to touch one of the bottles, much less drink from it; in fact, he rose and fled.

The wedding took place six months later. The Procter marriage unfolded as expected by the parents. Within a year it turned sour, then bitter, and finally brutal.

Maria, a dutiful daughter and submissive wife, found herself at the mercy of frightful emotions; she staggered from the arms of love into the clutches of hate. At first she accepted her husband's ill-treatment as the norm, accorded an unsatisfactory wife. But after years of similar, steadily worsening abuse, Maria grew despondent; in fact, she practically took leave of life. Overwhelmed by shame she hid her sorrow from the world.

When Wilf received an offer of employment at the Sudbury Nickel Mines, Maria urged him to accept. She thought that leaving the place of misery behind might improve their harsh relationship. Besides, living some distance from her parents, once unthinkable, she now welcomed. At least they would be less exposed to her growing degradation, nor have to see signs, carefully concealed mind you, of her husband's maltreatment. Moreover, she didn't want them to witness her steady transformation from a spirited young woman to an automaton.

Nothing changed in the new surrounding, if anything Wilf's antagonism towards her became more vitriolic. Nevertheless, Maria did not lose hope entirely. "Things will improve, they will, they will," she encouraged herself.

Then destiny intervened. Her parents met with a fatal accident. Although cut to the quick Maria heaved a sigh of relief. They would no longer have to bear the shame, for which she still took most of the responsibility. Being alone, living with a man who pretended to love her, yet acted as if he loathed the ground she walked on, oddly enough honed her mettle. She no longer feared nor pitied her husband, whom she recognised as a wind egg not containing the principle of life.

With her parents gone she was alone as never before. Yet, strange to say, she felt no longer hapless, and even less helpless. She knew what needed to be done, and she resolved to do it. Her parents had bequeathed all their possession to her, including a tidy sum of money.

One morning, after Wilf's departure for work, she packed up and left. She cast a last glance around the rooms pervaded by odours of malevolence, then lifting her head to the soot draped sky, she said:

"Farewell, misery, may I never meet you again."

Sitting in the westbound train her courage sagged; uncertainty reared its head. In what condition will she find the farm? Is it still workable, could she manage it alone? What about Wilf? Will he try to get her back, avail himself of the law perhaps or, heavens forbid, follow her? Pangs of anxiety plagued her, as much as dread of the unknown. The grey sky over Lake Superior seemed like a harbinger of evil tidings. Wherever she looked, traces of an impending misfortune glared at her. Contrary feelings of guilt and defiance prevailed till the train crossed the border and steamed towards Winnipeg.

Maria's demeanour underwent a change. The scowl disappeared as did the sorrow in her eyes. Upon sighting the sentinels of the prairie the veils of melancholy lifted; sentiments, unknown since heaven knows when, tugged shyly at her heartstrings. When they passed through fields of wheat swaying in the wind, Maria's heart leaped for joy. The sight of prairie lilies nodding in the morning sun brought tears of delight to her eyes. "Home at last," she whispered. Her face lit up, as did many of her fellow travellers'. Talk grew louder, more animated, banter arose, light-heartedness filled the air. The train's movement felt different, less bumpy, as if gliding rather than rolling. Its whistle, cautious before, indicating fear to be heard, now let go with abandon.

Life on the Saskatchewan prairie is not meant for the weak and squeamish, certainly not during the long winter. Maria felt daunted by isolation, the furious wind seemingly bent to blow the house down, and the onslaught of an early winter. But all was overshadowed by nagging anxieties concerning her husband. Though hardly a sophisticated woman, her intuition spoke louder than books of psychology. As sure as God made little apples, Wilf would show up at the farm one day, laying claim to his elusive possession. Yes, Wilf's character held no secrets for her; he was a product, in her father's words, of a counterfeit society with twisted morals. Love, to Wilf, must be countered with debasement, hers in this case, only thus can a man maintain his pride.

After a harsh winter, spring suddenly arrived. By mid-March not a flake of snow lay on the ground. Sun and wind combined forces to turn the soil to powder. Maria no longer cowered at the thought of Wilf's appearance; quite the contrary, she chuckled in expectation.

What had happened? Just this: The magic of the plain started to enter her bloodstream. In short, she lay in the grip of prairie fever, which is said to strengthen one's strength, and weakens one's weaknesses. Unforgettable sunrises and sunsets invigorated her spirit; the eerie singsong of coyotes endowed her with courage; in fact, she felt intoxicated with new life. She no longer feared her husband.

Wilf showed up one afternoon in April. Glancing at the sky, Maria chuckled. Observing her husband closer nearly made her break out in peals of laughter. He decidedly looked wizened and forlorn, evidently intimidated by the vast treeless land. As he approached Maria, standing in the doorway like a fatal sister guarding Valhalla, his steps became hesitant, for a moment that is. For he remembered that after all she was only his wife whom he had debased at will for years.

Producing a piece of paper which he crumpled, then threw angrily at her feet, he barked:

"The note says you are leaving me."

"You are wrong. It says I have left you."

"It will never happen. Get ready, we are going back," her husband growled.

"Not on your life." That retort lay on her tongue, but she swallowed the words.

Looking heavenwards again, then at the wretched man shivering in the strength gathering wind, an idea struck her.

She said smilingly:

"Come inside, Wilf."

What made her affable all of a sudden? Memories of her childhood, plus the darkening sky. She knew from experience a black blizzard was on its way.

"Make yourself comfortable, Wilf, I need a while to pack and put things in order," she remarked timidly.

Drawing a long breath, Wilf nodded assent. There now, he thought, my hold over her is still intact.

A tug of war ensued, not unlike between Phaedrus' donkey and driver, where the wish of one is the other's bane. The husband desired the wife to make haste, but the wife aimed at tardiness. Although bustling without rest, she made scant progress.

"Be patient," she countered his promptings.

"If you stopped gazing about every few minutes we would be in Regina by now," he growled.

Stepping up to a window, letting his eyes rove, Wilf scolded:

"What's there to see anyway?"

To see? Plenty, Maria could have told him, but she held her tongue, for a great spectacle unfolded over the vast plain, which evidently left the citified man unconcerned, contrary to herself. She observed with every fibre of her being what happened outside, as much as inside, where Wilf had reached a state of extreme agitation; a condition well known to her, hitherto dreaded, now eliciting but a passing sneer, for she sensed his growing disorientation and irresoluteness; in fact, he shuffled around like someone wishing to be elsewhere.

Nevertheless, he made several attempts to assert himself as in the past. But Maria nipped such endeavours in the bud. Drawing herself up, arms akimbo, looking daggers, sufficed to set him right.

It happened so suddenly that even Maria was caught unawares. A gust of wind, she knew, was the precursor of the yearned for spectacle. It came with a vengeance, all hell broke loose within minutes. Clouds, massive and portentous, blotted out the sun. Dark columns of dust rose, which, uniting in midair, rolled in billows towards them.

Noticing Maria lingering and glancing at the sky, Wilf inveighed:

"What are you gazing at now? Move it, I want to reach the border by nightfall."

"Not today, nor tomorrow either," she advised.

The comment brought him to his feet. Sawing the air with both hands, he barked:

"Don't be daft, woman, we are leaving right now, I say."

Maria, unperturbed, beckoned mutely with her head.

"Take a look," she remarked dryly.

One glance made Wilf's blood freeze, all vestiges of bravado drained from his features. Small wonder; the vast prairie had disappeared amid whirling clouds of dark brown dust. Objects, visible a moment ago, were totally obliterated.

Thunderstruck by the weird spectacle unfolding before his dilated eyes, he lost all desire to set out for home. He just stood there, gaping from Maria to the inferno outside. When a sudden squall shook the house to its foundations, he expelled a cry and jumped back.

Maria observed her husband with mocking disbelief as he collapsed within himself. Indeed, he acted like a man pursued by spectres rising from the bowels of the earth, screaming for victims. No doubt, she intended to scare him away, once and for all wean him from notions to ever again make her his chattel. Then, she hoped, he will consent to a divorce. For surely a wife meant to be daunted, under the protecting wings of a snarling and shrieking nature, must lose allurement.

Fate had smiled at her, Wilf showed up at a most opportune time. Hardly did he step into view when the prairie came to life. Forces gathered quickly, as if in anticipation of his visit, ready to unleash a fury that can not be tamed. Although Maria knew that a prairie storm can play the deuce with anybody's nerves, she took no chances. Plans, contrived long ago, rehearsed many times, were put into motion.

Under the pretext of acquiescing to his demands, she pretended to pack with deft hands and twinkling feet. Rushing about, occasionally scurrying outside, she set the stage where

Wilf would meet his Waterloo. Her father's invention should be able to chase his daughter's tormentor away for good. The voice of the Wendigo, he called these uncanny sounds; doomsday wailings, her mother named them, devilries that had no place in a Christian home.

"Ah, Anna, don't knock it, it's ideal to keep unwelcome visitors from our necks," he always countered.

True enough, these contrivances, consisting of tubes and funnels mounted at a certain angle, produced sounds causing white-knuckle terror in the stoutest heart. Maria recalled too late that Wilf neither possessed physical courage nor mental strength. Her intended cure turned out to be too drastic for him.

The wind's increasing fury brought to life the macabre sounds expected, with a devastating vengeance to boot.

Wilf, recoiling, cried out:

"What's this? What's this?"

"The voices of the Wendigos," Maria said, feigning abject fear.

"Listen, listen, do you hear it?" she uttered.

"Yes, yes," Wilf moaned, visibly cowed.

For indeed, stomping feet and pawing hoofs could seemingly be heard prowling around the house.

Wilf, muttering to himself, casting haunted glances around the room, clapped both hands over his ears, hoping to muffle the hellish racket outside; to little avail however. The eerie sounds of denizens from another world were audible just the same.

Stumbling from wall to wall, approaching the wife like a supplicant at the end of his tether, he gazed at her imploringly. Maria took pity on this heap of misery; for an instant she felt tempted to reveal all. But memories of mental and physical sufferings made her decide otherwise. So there and then, amid an atmosphere of growing frenzy, she related the story, heard from her father, of a mythical Algonquian tribe, known as Wendigo.

"They are cannibals, roaming the Saskatchewan prairie in a storm, searching for victims," she told her terrified husband; then added:

“I recognise them by their gnashing teeth, and hungry growls.”

Hardly had Maria said that, when an inhuman shriek interrupted her narrative. Aghast she gasped:

“They have found us, Wilf, they have found us.”

To be sure, hers was a fantastic tale, convincingly told, guided by ulterior motives, which her husband never divined.

Being utterly distraught, he took her narration as gospel truth. Thus, that horrid sound, known and anticipated by Maria, sealed his fate.

Reeling back, clutching his throat with one hand, pressing the other to his chest, he groaningly collapsed. Bedevilled by rampant hysteria, suffering from an incurable heart disease, Wilf Procter ended his life on that floor.

Maria told the truth. Though plagued by the question of omitting certain facts for a while, she stifled her scruples quickly; in fact, prior to Mr Pulko’s arrival.

The Report

Rita Dither had reasons to celebrate. Her unremitting endeavours, spanning more than a decade, finally bore fruit. The distinguished magazine 'Strange World' not only accepted one of her submissions, but agreed to sign her up for future consideration. An enormous weight lifted from her ample chest; tears of joy flowed from her kohl ringed eyes, washing out, for a moment that is, accumulated insincerity. Her future as an author seemed assured. The realisation rendered her step bouncier, and buoyed up her spirit. To be sure, a shadow did mar the light of glory in the form of the editor's criticism. Adam Kohn found fault with her flowery style. In his opinion repeated taffata phrases weaken a narrative's penetrating power. Besides, they distract the reader's sense of realism, paramount to the magazine.

He wrote: Idealism, cleverly wrapped in pretentious verbiage, often referred to as literature, is anathema to the Strange World. Our goal is to entertain readers with well written reports, not stories, about occurrences which captivate the mind and stir the intellect. We understand the difficulty in ferreting out such events, for which reason we pay triple the going rate. Never forget, submissions to be considered must be matter-of-fact renderings as stated in our guidelines. Take a look at the agreement signed by you. All must be provable if requested.

Rita Dither, though resentful of the editor's didactic lines, nevertheless took his admonition to heart. She had no choice for now, but she felt disinclined to forget or forgive the slight.

Mrs Dither's stamping grounds were the Lesser Antilles, in particular the island of Barbados, where she presently investigated the sugar cane debacle.

What took place there was this: Cane reapers, being on piece work, deeming their progress impeded by dense underbrush, consistently set the fields ablaze prior to harvesting. The owners resented it for several reasons. Chiefly on account of revenue losses, but strange to say also because burning increased the presence of instar borers in subsequent growth.

They hired a detective from England, enjoining him to hunt down the culprits who, upon conviction, could expect a jail term. When the agent, locally known as 'Lord Sniff', was rescued one night from the licking flames, a narrow escape it was, Mrs Dither entered the breach with might and main. Articles were compiled and submitted in record time which soon landed on Adam Kohn's desk. They were steeped in spurious presumptions, and peppered with wild insinuations, which grossly contravened the magazine's rules.

Having no inkling of the misrepresentations, the editor of the Strange World included the submissions with pride. 'Our woman in the Antilles' Kohn had christened Mrs Dither, whom he praised loudly, in contrast to his assistant who cursed her silently. Hubert Margolis neither liked nor trusted the contributions by Rita Dither. He found her narrative power wanting, the never-ending similes vexing, and her vapid metaphors nerve-rattling. "Pure obfuscation, literary gymnastics intended to avert suspicion," he mused.

Mr Margolis wasn't far off the mark. Rita Dither walked a fine line between imagery and reality, rather her pen did. Adhering to the guidelines of the Strange World proved not as easy as it sounded, since unusual occurrences in that peaceful island were rare. Not particularly fazed by this, she grew into the habit of embellishing insignificant episodes till they attained sinister aspects which met the Strange World's standard.

Take the sugar cane affair for instance, called a disaster by Mrs Dither. Her narrative, blithely received and promptly printed, asserted that the English detective was waylaid by ruffians, overpowered, and dumped in the middle of a cane field. Satisfying themselves that he was unconscious, they set the cane ablaze. His subsequent rescue, termed a miracle by Dither, she attributed to her unswerving vigilance; in other words, observing the event, she alerted passers-by who aided her efforts to carry the unfortunate detective to safety. It was a good story, related in a dramatic style, but not coinciding with facts.

Detective Clark, whose cover was blown before his shadow fell on the first cane field, had much to endure. The locals, tractable on the surface, proved to be a mischievous lot; the sugar cane reapers in any case. Set on burning, they devised plots that would have done honour to Guy Fawkes. One of them was this:

After nightfall two or three youngsters lit crudely made torches, which they paraded along roads skirting the cane fields. As intended the darting tongues of light caught the agent's attention, who in no time pursued the presumed firebugs. No match for their nimbleness, he nevertheless chased them through the rustling, swaying stalks. Leeward it went, right to the field's extremity. Ignoring his repeated commands to stop, they ran out onto the road and disappeared in the Egyptian darkness. Not, however, before expelling eerie cries that resounded through the night, which were signals to waiting men at the opposite end, who promptly started the fire. It was a clear ruse, obviating the possibility of getting caught red-handed.

It so happened, while chasing the two scampers through a field, Mr Clark stumbled and rammed his head against a post. The impact rendered him unconscious, thereby exposing him to the mercy of encroaching flames. Luck was on his side. The youngsters, divining a mishap, raced back towards the crackling wall of fire, from which they rescued him in the nick of time.

Rita Dither's misreport about the incident, plus her vituperations directed against Barbados, almost remained undetected, since editions of the Strange World were not sold in the Caribbean. But somehow that particular copy, containing her misrepresentation of the incident, spiced by denigration directed against Barbados, landed on Gil Hanson's desk. He took immediate umbrage. Not a man given to procrastination, he sent a note to his friend Bertram Gaunt – Let's meet for lunch at the Pelican – the communication read.

The Pelican is a tiny village of gift stores and a restaurant. Its setting amid a profusion of blooming shrubs and trees, and cobblestone pathways, appealed to Hanson's turn of mind. Indeed, the unhurried pace, particularly in the summer months, has a bewitching effect. One can sit there for hours listening to the distant drone of the sea and the rustle in shrubs and trees. Added to it the lilt of native voices and the fragrance of sweet scented frangipani, it may happen that one gradually drifts into a world of imagery.

Right now Gil Hanson felt no inclination to succumb to such reveries. Sitting there, scowling at the magazine before him, he played the devil's tattoo on its cover.

"Ah, there you are," his friend called out.

"In body only, my mind is elsewhere," Hanson growled, as he pushed the opened magazine towards Gaunt.

"Here, read, and try to remain calm."

After a minute's perusal, Gaunt exclaimed:

"That's outrageous, a blatant distortion of the facts. I happen to know detective Clark fairly well, he explained the circumstances of the incident to me, which entirely differ from this drivel. Who wrote this tripe?"

"A certain Rita Dither, but read on."

As Gaunt skimmed over the article, he repeatedly burst out in imprecations, which Hanson waved off.

"Keep reading," he bid.

When Gaunt reached the end, he broke out into a torrent of maledictions. Discussing the situation, deemed untenable, amid curses and threads, though soothing their tempers, led nowhere.

"She should be deported," expelled Hanson.

"It will never happen," replied Gaunt, then suggested:

"I should go and talk to her, after all I am the director of the tourist board. Besides, a conciliatory approach is usually more effective than harsh rebuke."

Rita Dither was on the prowl again. Her promised contribution for the coming month's issue trembled in the balance. In fact, seven days prior to the submission deadline, she hadn't written a word of it. To tell the truth, she couldn't even think of what to write. The sugar cane affair had been milked to the last drop, squeezing out another believable story seemed impossible; besides, the harvest rapidly neared its end.

Mrs Dither had the wind up, no question about it. Inventing a zesty story outright deemed her too risky, and no less beyond her ability.

As before, when strapped for time and ideas, she went to the Fiesta Club, where she chose a table somewhat distant from the others. While sitting there, silently inveighing against the peacefulness of the island, a stranger walked up. Bowing gallantly, he said:

"Forgive me, madam, aren't you the famous author Rita Dither?"

Looking up surprised, and no less pleased, she saw a man well turned out, considering her favourably. Mrs Dither did something that would have confounded her husband for days, had he witnessed it; she smiled.

"My name is Bertram Gaunt. I am the director of the Barbados Tourist Board."

Mrs Dither, while casting anxious glances at Gaunt, wondered whether having gotten wind of her unflattering portrayals occasioned this visit. Anticipating criticism, if not stern rebukes, she took on a defiant stance. Nothing of the sort happened. After asking and being granted permission to sit down, he explained:

"My errand, a delicate one, is simply to ask a favour."

"From me?"

"Yes."

Relieved, because she wasn't going to be raked over the coals, she gestured willingness to oblige.

"If I can, of course."

A nod and smile expressed Gaunt's appreciation.

"Are you familiar with the Sighing Cliffs?" he inquired.

"Never heard of them," she admitted.

"Small wonder. Their existence, a stain on our lovely island, is not exactly trumpeted abroad."

Intrigued, Mrs Dither remarked:

"You are making me curious, please do go on."

Acquiring a mournful demeanour, moaning audible, Gaunt elucidated:

"At the extreme northern point where nature is in the raw, loom rocks which over the years have gained a controversial reputation; baneful to most, a blessing to few, who seem fatally attracted by these mist shrouded cliffs."

"Who are they?"

"Adventurers to some, deviates to others, like myself."

Sensing a subject for her clueless contribution, Mrs Dither encouraged him to say more.

"Over the years accidents happened there, fatal ones that is, and no less freakish."

"Oh, tell me about it."

"I will in a moment. But first let's speak about the favour we are asking of you."

Though not particularly enthused by the change in subject, she nodded assent.

"The Sighing Cliffs, christened thus by unscrupulous operators, are on private property, which we want the government to expropriate and permanently close."

Sensing the drift of Gaunt's request, she asked:

"For what reason?"

"They have become sort of an altar for people inclined towards morbidity."

Seeing her raised eyebrows, Gaunt hastened to forestall questions.

"You are familiar with Stevenson's suicide club story, I take it?"

"Yes, a sinister tale that one is," she granted.

"Well, our situation is more than a tale, it's an ignominious reality. The Sighing Cliffs serve a similar purpose as Stevenson's club. In other words, men, bored with life, come from far away to challenge fate, while others, ghouls in my opinion, watch, hoping they will plunge to their death."

"Sounds gruesome," Dither conceded with scant conviction.

She felt a surge of excitement racing through her veins, for what she heard raised her hopes. Hungry for more details, desirous to suppress a rising agitation, she inquired:

"What is the favour you want from me?"

"Write letters to the government, plus to our board, and don't forget the local newspaper. Berate the authority's criminal indifference, make them aware of this brand of infamy's detrimental influence. Don't mince the matter, help us to keep the dregs of society from our gates."

Cocking her head significantly, Dither inquired:

"Do I detect an ulterior motive here?"

"In a way, yes. I do have a personal bias."

Noticing his inviting glances, she ventured to ask:

"May I ask what it is?"

"You may. I lost a dear friend under gruesome circumstances at those cursed cliffs. Exactly a week ago Carl Benson, whom I knew since childhood, fell to his death right under my eyes."

"How did it happen?"

"On one of our inspection tours he stumbled, and before I was able to extend a hand he staggered downwards. My heart leaped up when he gained a hold on a ledge, but it cut me to the quick the next moment, for I realised that clinging to precipitous rocks, while dangling in midair, can not last long. Losing strength by the second, moaning piteously, he implored me to rescue him. But how could a man like I, stricken with muscular dystrophy, clamber over rocks no mountain goat dares to approach?

"For several minutes Carl held on bravely, never ceasing his lamentations and desperate cries for help though. In a panic by now, I was rendered paralytic. I was unable to move, let alone lend a hand to the man dear to my heart, who was obviously doomed. Then followed an eerie shriek, which signalled the end."

"Was there an inquest?"

"Yes. The coroner recommended that the area be permanently closed."

"Will it be, you think?"

"With your assistance it might be."

Dither, visibly shaken, raised her head and leaned back.

"Where exactly are these Sighing Cliffs?" she wanted to know.

With quick fingers Gaunt produced a sheet of paper from a folder.

"Here is a sketch, but no need to fret, every taxi driver knows the place."

Then touching his brow, he exclaimed:

"Dear me, I almost forgot."

Reaching inside the folder again, he removed an envelope which he pushed across the table.

"This arrived in the mail, sent no doubt by someone gloating. Take a look at the pictures inside, I can't find it in my heart to touch them."

Dither pulled out two photographs which at first sight made her wince. High above a raging sea a man could be seen holding on for dear life at the brink of a cliff. Never before had she seen such agony in a man's face.

"What a horrendous sight," she uttered.

"Thank heaven one can not hear his bloodcurdling screams and piteous pleas for help," Gaunt rasped in a heart-stricken tone.

As Mrs Dither perused the photographs, she became peculiarly excited. Why her brow creased, her eyes contracted, only she knew, as much as the reason of her reluctance to return the pictures.

"Would you like to keep them?" Gaunt offered.

Pleasantly surprised, her head came up.

"Hm, not a bad idea, they might come in handy," she commented.

With the words: "Well, Mrs Dither, we rely on your assistance," he rose and walked away.

Dither's submission reached the editor's desk hours before the deadline. Annoyed, yet equally grateful, he barked at no one in particular:

"I feel inclined to throw the thing into the wastebasket."

Taking another look, however, convinced him otherwise.

'I watched a man die,' the title read.

"A stirring caption," Mr Kohn granted, "which alone will enhance the edition's sale."

"Read it, Hubert, let me know what you think," he bid his assistant.

Though vexed on account of the submission's late arrival, Margolis read and edited it with his customary thoroughness. Progress was slow. Despite an acknowledged urgency, he made little headway. After reading the manuscript three times, the assistant was none the wiser. Something didn't add up. No matter which way he looked at it, he was unable to rid himself of an uneasiness that defied mention.

There was something peculiar about 'I watched a man die'. It roused the assistant's suspicion which no amount of wincing, head scratching, or desk drumming could dispel. Take the pictures for instance, they looked bogus from every angle. The expression on the man's face perplexed him; it resembled the sneer of an imp rather than the mien of a panic-stricken being. Her descriptions, never exactly palatable to him, seemed contrived. But also, strange to say, they appeared to be overflowing with trepidation.

Being aware however of their dilemma, since space had been reserved for Dither's promised report, he felt obliged to vote for its inclusion, yet without the pictures.

"There is something amiss with these photographs," he commented.

"In what way?"

"I can't rightly say, but…"

"Don't be such a wet blanket, Hubert, these pictures are the icing on the cake, they are essential to the story."

The month's copy created a sensation, chiefly attributable to Dither's 'I watched a man die'. The magazine's staff and management reeled from euphoria to ecstasy. Not so much on account of impressive sales, but also because of praising letters to the editor, preponderantly aimed at 'I watched a man die'.

Rita Dither had found the path leading to fame and riches. Her self-conceit, never insignificant, acquired Gargantuan proportions, especially when other publishers showed interest in her.

Three weeks later a man announced himself at the offices of the Strange World. He caused a flurry of excitement with the staff, and deep consternation with the assistant editor, who was hastily summoned. Hubert Margolis visibly started at the sight of him, then flinched when the irate stranger slammed the offending copy of the Strange World onto the receptionist's desk, while bellowing at the top of his voice:

"What's the meaning of this?"

Mr Margolis, trying to remain composed, wanted to know:

"Who are you?"

"Who I am, who I am? Don't you have eyes in your head? I am the man this – this penny-dreadful says plunged to his death, while being watched to boot. A true story? My eye, it's bogus from line to line. Those pictures were not taken by your correspondent, as you claim, far from it."

Attracted by the commotion, employees came rushing to the reception room. Some had difficulties to comprehend, others understood instantly. All cast glances from the picture on the magazine cover to the irate man glowering at Margolis.

Benson, supposedly dashed to pieces on the rocky shore, pounded by the Atlantic Ocean, got into full swing. Grabbing the magazine with both hands, he read:

"Hearing bloodcurdling screams, followed by a bone crushing thud, I realised it was the end. The man whom I had watched helplessly, was dead."

Snickers, suppressed, yet still audible, elicited a frown from Mr Margolis. Words, uttered mockingly, made him wince.

"For a dead man he seems pretty sprightly."

"Smashed to smithereens he was? Hm, I wonder who glued him together again."

So it went, one gibe barely ended when another one followed. Anxious to diffuse a tickling situation, the assistant manoeuvred Benson to the editor's private rooms.

Adam Kohn needed no clairvoyant to guess the truth: Their woman in the Lesser Antilles had hoodwinked them. Glancing from the picture on the magazine's cover to the man glowering alternately at him and Margolis, he groaned:

"What a mess."

Turning to his assistant, he observed mournfully:

"I should have taken your advice."

Being a pragmatic individual, however, the editor sought assurances. After all the fellow confronting him might pursue an ulterior motive. Could he not be an identical twin of the man in the picture? That notion, however, received short shrift.

"Nice try, but no applause," Benson snorted.

While scrutinising the editor and his assistant more intensely, his demeanour changed. At the sight of their dumbfounded faces, doubts about their culpability seized him.

"You are either two consummate dolts, or unmitigated knaves. Tell me, did she con you?" Benson chuckled.

Instead of a reply Adam Kohn asked, while tapping the magazine on his desk:

"Aren't these the Sighing Cliffs?"

"Nonsense, the place is known as North Point Surf Resort. We shoot films there at times, as we did recently. In fact, that picture of me, seemingly hanging on for dear life, stems from it, I was the lead actor."

The editor, visibly shaken, gazed at his assistant as if to say: "What now?"

"You will hear from our lawyers," were Benson's parting words.

Rita Dither's career came to a sudden end. Even worse, the Strange World's management threatened with legal proceedings. She realised of course that the hoaxer had been hoaxed. Furthermore, that finding work with other publishers might no longer be in the cards. Just the same she made inquiries, which to her surprise showed promise. Quite a few magazines imposed less stringent standards than the Strange

World. To be sure, they too demanded submissions glowing with excellence, but in reality preferred contributions teeming with inferiority, especially if steeped in prurience. True, the honorarium offered fell considerably short of her wonted recompense. But can beggars be choosers?

Three submissions in a row had been accepted by the Tatler, a periodical aimed at the disciples of inanity, who were easy to entertain. It was a comedown, no denying it, yet in her inimitable capacity for self-deceit she managed to term it an enormous step ahead.

She told her husband a cock-and-bull story, which she repeated within her close circle, about quarrels over dilatory payments, and the editor's insupportable high-handedness. Heads were nodding, signifying understanding, and no less approval, although not even her husband believed her; for the grapevine, always whirring among friends, told a different tale.

To say that Rita Dither harboured no qualms concerning her recent flop, would have stretched the truth. In fact, for quite a while uneasiness never budged from her side. But gradually she relaxed when the Strange World neither bothered nor pursued her. But then, as the last wrinkles on her brow smoothened, dark clouds gathered over her head once more, getting ready to burst.

The winter months in Barbados are delightful. Admitted, the throng of bulky, boisterous tourists around hotels and beaches are a nuisance which, however, can be circumvented. Besides, one can enjoy benefits like the absence of sweltering heat, and pesky mosquitoes, whom the strong and steady wind from the North Atlantic Ocean forces to seek shelter rather than bare skins to prick.

Nights are cooler then, days sunnier; the inevitable rain showers of months past become nonexistent. The waves on the north and east shores are a sight to behold. Tossed up by high winds, far out in unruly water, they break thunderously on rugged cliffs.

April was nearing, heralding summer's approach, that would bring sultry days and sweltering nights. The local colour, soothing to one's mind, overshadowed by dwindling crowds of raucous, importunate voluptuaries for a while, exerted its dominance again.

Rita Dither had neither forgotten, nor forgiven Gaunt's nasty trick at her expense. Though seeking means to pay him back in his own coin, she let well enough alone for now. Such sentiments, however, were not reciprocated by Bertram Gaunt, who agitated against her with undiminished fervour, as soon became evident.

"They want you off the island," Bruce, her husband, announced one evening.

Never quick on the uptake, grown more obtuse by constant brooding, it took a moment to sink in.

"Who wants us off the island?" she snapped.

"Not us, you, Rita."

More aghast at her husband's temerity to repeat such notions, than being upset over the suggestion, she glowered at him wordlessly. They sat outside on a small porch watching the sun disappear beyond the horizon. Night descends quickly in these latitudes where myriad voices strike up a shrill concert at the first sign of darkness. Tension had of late crept between them, rendering a relationship, never whole-souled to begin with, a burden born with acrimony.

Mulling over the words she had just heard, Rita Dither harboured no doubts about their meaning, and even less about her husband's thoughts, for which she intended to make him suffer; more so after hearing his comments:

"As I see it, Rita, you might have to comply," he advised.

Suppressing an impulse to flare up and overwhelm him with a string of invectives, she decided on a more severe punishment: Prolonged silence steeped in malevolence, accompanied by an unyielding aloofness, characteristic of a catatonic.

Bruce Dither knew the routine; its rigour had left many scars on his psyche. Although he did not clearly see her face, he could well imagine what she was up to. Weaving once again, in the spirit, a crown of thorns intended for him to wear.

Not this time, he nearly said aloud, nor ever after. The thought made him chuckle, which confounded his wife of twenty years to such an extent that she hesitated to rush from his side, as usually happened when vexed.

Although egged on by indignant voices from within to decamp in a huff, she remained glued to her chair. Something was up she sensed. Her compliant, easily led husband harboured notions she could not brook. No denying it, since their sojourn in Barbados her tractable consort gradually transformed into a rebellious independent. It appeared that the unrestrained ambience in a salubrious environment, awakened mutinous instincts so far kept safely under lock and key by mothers and wives.

"Let him have his fun," she said to herself. "Let him believe that he is kicking over the traces. I will soon wean him from such inclinations; right after I have settled with Gaunt." Who, she understood, agitated against her with undiminished fervour.

Indeed, he did; for reasons not readily fathomed. As his friends pointed out she had been exposed as a fraud, thus decried in publishing circles, plus deprived of a plenteous honorarium.

"What more do you want?" they asked.

Treating his evasive answers with a grain of salt, smiling at his shrugs and grimaces, he was told to lay off.

Well, that was easier advised than obeyed, for reasons he dared not reveal. This mindless zeal, bordering on persecution, seemed to be out of character for a staid businessman no longer young. Granted, settling her hash was deemed necessary under the circumstances; but once achieved, why pursue her any longer, people argued, why, indeed?

The reasons Gaunt kept prudently to himself, for he thought them dishonourable, undeserving of a reputable man. It was nothing less than a personal dislike, a revulsion really, which he could not suppress. Those kohl-adjusted eyes, a sight that in his opinion drove cattle afield, and made pigs lean, haunted him. Her kookaburra laugh and jettatura squint, triggered sentiments which he preferred to hush up.

Nevertheless, she must leave the island, he resolved. His attempts to harness the immigration department's authority led nowhere. Mr Backman, the minister, overwhelmed him with hollow words and velvety phrases, but did not act beyond having a word with Bruce Dither, the husband.

Rita Dither neither forgot nor forgave Gaunt's trickery. How could she in view of the aftermath? Adversely affecting her career and prestige was one thing; but knocking down the pedestal on which her husband had placed her, she considered to be a horse of a different colour. No doubt Bruce knew what happened, judging by his ill-concealed sneers and snickers when she related her quarrel with the Strange World; untruthfully that is. Yes, the husband, hitherto awed by her literary achievements, now openly denigrated them.

"Run-of-the-mill," he said aloud.

"Penny-dreadfuls," he labelled the magazines with which she now dealt.

Mrs Dither batted more than an eyelash, but still said little, although her belligerent instincts were in full array.

Undecided what to do, or where to go, she drifted one morning to the North Point cliffs. As she stood there, gazing from the wave-washed rocks to the billowing sea, many thoughts coursed through her head. Questions arose which to date begged to be answered. Gaunt's stratagem, though rankling, paled in comparison to her concerns about her husband, whose contrary attitude towards her she found vexing, and no less worrying.

With the thunderous roar of pounding waves in both ears, her hair tousled by high winds, she commenced walking to and fro. Mind you, at a respectable distance from the precipice; for Mrs Dither was plagued by a few weaknesses; fear of heights was one of them.

The exercise, spurred by the sounds of breaking waves, kindled her power of deduction. Gaunt's machinations, amid raw nature plus the passage of time, defied understanding. Did he stage that cliffhanger episode merely to discredit or harm her? She no longer thought so, but rather believed Benson, the actor's explanation.

Something else baffled her; namely, how the Strange World ended up in Gaunt's hands. After all, its distribution never went beyond North America's borders.

That was it! Bruce, her husband, had engineered the whole thing. Yes, he had a motive, plus the opportunity to get her out of his way. Didn't he say: 'You might have to comply with the minister's request to return to Canada'?

"It will never happen," she announced to the foaming sea below.

Ignoring the burning sun above, oblivious to the raging ocean beneath, Mrs Dither's strides became brisker, while talking to herself.

"How mean, how perfidious," she moaned, as the whole scheme unfolded before her infuriated eyes.

Reading her articles, as Bruce invariable did, an idea reared its ugly head. She always wondered why instead of criticising these spurious reports, he rather egged her on.

"What a Judas," she growled, while hastening her steps.

His motives were clear and no less shameful. The local belles, or rather his fascination with them, was the mainspring of these machinations. His roving eyes spoke volumes; he found them more attractive than his wife. Although feeling abased by this ogling, she treated it lightly. True, their marriage lacked passion, but loyalty and chivalry she deemed commendable substitutes.

By now Rita Dither had worked herself into a regular snit.

"Leave the island, Bruce, to let you philander? Not on your life," she screamed into the wind.

"Just wait" she pledged, "I will pay you back, with a wronged woman's sting."

Just then a mighty roller broke thunderously down below, making her bound. She tripped, then stumbled forward. But alas! in the wrong direction.

Rita Dither had left the island.

Priming Tobacco

With a bit more knowledge in English, this would probably have turned out less serious. But what am I saying? A few connected sentences, accompanied by sign language would have helped. Oh well, it was not meant to be. In those days even the German language caused me nothing but grief. True, I was German, but from a region outside Germany and Austria. On the flats of the Woiwodina German was spoken and written like six hundred years ago. To tell the truth, peasants like myself grew up to speak a tongue-breaking dialect, and wrote as they spoke. But all that lay far behind me. Germany affected me like a fleeting kiss that went no further. Now I stood in that immense country called Canada; to be more exact, at the corner of Bloor and Bathurst, two of the busiest streets in Toronto.

What a bustle that was! With dilated eyes I stared at this new world, strange, from an oppressive heat to the hubbub on the streets. People moved differently here, much quicker and tenser, jumpy, as if on the way to great events, which might end before they got there. About tarrying these people had heard little, if anything at all. I must say this bustle affected me in no small way. Should I happen to look closer at one of these scurrying men, I was promptly greeted, mostly followed by a few words that I could not understand.

One thing manifested itself clearly: My attire had to change, because with corduroy pants and fancy jacket I stuck out from afar as a recent arrival. It did not escape my notice for long that I was eyed briefly at times, then smiled at condescendingly, most likely by immigrants of six months or so. But six months in those days counted for something, certainly enough to be entitled to make patronising remarks about an evident greenhorn.

Despite my efforts to give the impression of an arch-Canadian, I was at times spoken to in German. Well, as I said, my attire had to go. But before I was able to dress in accordance with local customs, several months would have to pass, since my pockets were empty to the seams. But what of it? That's why I undertook the trip across the great pond, to fill them to the brim.

There I stood, like a hundred times after, waiting for shadowy events that would lift me to Eldorado in one heave. Exciting those notions were, but regrettable they proved from year to year more like flights of fancies. Reality forced itself again and again between me and my dreams. But why drag tomorrow's shadows over today's sun. I was young then, barely twenty years old, propelled by intoxicating thoughts, imbued with an irresistible thirst for action. I could have snared every blinking star in the sky; indeed, I had the world by the hinges, the way I felt.

The unknown renders one either faint-hearted or more daring. Myself it drove to the summit of venturousness. I felt elated to be surrounded by people who were not forever searching with punitive eyes, if perchance uncertified people pushed to the foreground, or walk around without proper identification in their pockets. Fear of failure seemed not to exist here. Like the spider picks up its thread again after every tumble, so proceeded the people in the new world. Only temporisers were despised, never one who tried and foundered, as long as he made another attempt. Canada's inhabitants and I were evidently cut from the same cloth. Unfortunately this assumption changed after I got to know them better.

But first to my monetary trouble, which could have been called impecuniosity without exaggerating. Even in the land of milk and honey, where a large carton of milk sold for fifteen cents, five dollars would not set the world on fire. My intention to make that big catch in the mines of Sudbury or Elliot Lake, had to be put on the back burner for now. My immediate needs were an income without further expenditures; that is, without delay, as soon as today, or tomorrow. Whoever believes this sounds high-flown or foolish, simply has no knowledge of Canada in the fifties. Was I in the land of unlimited opportunities or not? Lingering about while waiting for Menetekel's handwriting on the wall did not suit me, especially since fame and fortune beckoned from every corner.

Undaunted I lifted my feet and marched in step of the new world. With the stirring beat of drums in my ears, I sauntered up and down the busy streets. Suddenly my eyes caught a sign in one of the windows. – German spoken here – it said. One glance told me it was a dinette offering a complete meal for less than a dollar.

Being hungry, but also desirous of talking in my own language to someone, I stepped inside. In a jiffy I sat down on one of the bar stools on which I swirled to and fro in the manner of a real Canadian, I hoped. I took my time while eating, more so since two men beside me started talking in German. Now there was news to my ears, which were pricked in anticipation.

I soon became privy to the fact that work was to be had for the asking. Priming tobacco they called it, Delhi they named as the industry's centre. My ears tingled upon hearing that a diligent primer could earn twenty dollars a day, in addition to free room and board. Calculating quickly, which to this day I consider to be my forte, an astounding sum of five hundred dollars clear hovered before my eyes. Of course I knew nothing about priming tobacco, nor did I have an inkling were Delhi was. Did that deter me? Not in the least.

By two o'clock in the afternoon I sat in a bus, which rolled steadily towards those promising fields.Upon arrival, however, my heart sank low and lower. I have no idea how many people live there today, but at that time a youngster like myself could have thrown a stone from one end of the street to the other, without taking much of a run.

What a sight awaited me. Both sides of the main street were lined with men and women. Almost shoulder to shoulder they stood or sat, laughing and chatting excitedly. I quickly got the drift; like myself they were seeking work. But here I erred; some were there for the fun, others to panhandle. How shocked and embarrassed I was to see them plying such a trade I can not, rather dare not, declare. They were professional beggars I learned later, who tapped already impecunious men for their last two bits. I watched them open-mouthed I am sure, cringing and lamenting while holding out their hands. Never had I seen something similar before.

Immediately I joined the rows of job seekers. There we stood, lined up like prostitutes along Jarvis Street in Toronto, hoping to catch the eye of a passing employer. The farmers drove up and down the street at a slow pace. Some silently, others with cheerful banter on their lips. My chances to be favoured stood near zero, I thought, considering my European appearance and nonexistent knowledge of English. I got a surprise.

Within the hour I was selected; unfortunately only after I had been relieved of my last dollar by a seedy looking man on the prowl. But what did I care? because for now I was rescued. Thinking about a conversation between the farmer and myself was wishful. Just one thing I deduced from his talk; we were heading towards Tillsonburg. That was fine with me, had he said Timbuktu it would have been equally fine.

Next morning shortly after sunrise we went to work. Someone who never primed tobacco has no clue what work means. Hopping along forever in a half-kneeling position from plant to plant, is no fun. Add to it the burning sun beating down on our bent backs, and one might understand the meaning of upper Gehenna. To straighten up once in a while is not advisable, for fear of falling prey to a desire to remain standing. Kneeling down for a breather? Don't even think of it, it might be the end of one's priming career, since an overpowering yen to stretch out flat could win out. I have seen several primers collapse at the end of the second row.

Fourteen dollars per day I received, a considerable sum in those days, if room and board is added. We worked six days a week, from sunrise to sunset, right into October. Towards the end, fields and meadows were covered with hoarfrost in the morning, that melted quickly however under the inevitable sun, which made our lives miserable. Since I never spent a cent, I was handed a little over five hundred dollars at departure time. A substantial sum, that put more than one tempting idea into my head.

On the way back I intended to look around Hamilton, a city of smoke, mainly to buy new clothes for my onward journey to Sudbury's mines. My old attire, besides being tinted green as grass from tobacco leaves, began to peel off my body.

In Tillsonburg a youngster stepped onto the bus whom I recognised as a compatriot. One glance at each other sufficed, everything else took its course from thereon.

His name was Fritz König, a roguish fellow, who hailed from far above the Danube. He too was en route to nowhere in particular, except of course to places one had never seen before. Regrettably he understood no more English than myself. Time spent on the farm contributed very little to my proficiency in the language, because the crew I worked with, albeit consisting of three Dutch brothers, plus one Mexican, surprisingly spoke German fluently.

That, however, could not dampen our spirits. It did not affect two youngsters with the fire of adventure under their soles, and the lure of success before their eyes. Fritz König possessed a waggish bent; moreover, he at times kicked over the traces which nonplussed my shy nature.

While searching for a clothing store we were exposed to many a sideways glances. A sight for sore eyes we surely were not; alone our splattered pants, coloured would be a more appropriate description, warranted more than disapproval. Added to it the foreign language, moreover our un-Canadian deportment, indeed, how could one fault the worthy citizens' slanted glances.

This overt attention appealed to Fritz, until he became aware how censorious it was. Some people turned around, making remarks which we could not understand, but their deprecating tone affected our sensibility.

I urged Fritz to distance ourselves from this embarrassing situation with all available tact. More so when I noticed two policemen observing us intently from across the street. They were putting their heads together while pointing repeatedly in our direction. Before I looked around they had crossed the street and now followed on our heels. Nudging my companion I made him aware of this, hoping to persuade him to make ourselves scarce.

The contrary happened. For a moment I thought my comrade was going to thumb his nose at the constables. But I was mistaken, he did something far more dreadful. I should mention that Fritz possessed the skill to walk on his hands almost nimbler than many people do it on their feet. Before I could say: "Oh no!" he already stood upside down and started to hand-walk in circles around the policemen. They were baffled, undecided what to do at first. Some pedestrians stopped, voices and laughter arose from all sides.

The lawmen's consternation changed to anger, which was fanned by the onlookers' behaviour who had meanwhile started to hoot noisily. If I am not mistaken they cheered my companion on, while making fun of the two policemen. That of course the gentlemen in uniform could not accept, although they remained undecided how to act. Accosting a hand-walker, much less apprehending him, lay outside their bailiwick. In the meantime I harboured but one wish, namely, that the earth should open and swallow me.

Suddenly I heard utterances sounding like an order, after which the policemen moved into action. They approached Fritz with set miens.

Then it happened: Fritz, the wag on hands, discharged a string of yelps, then making an about-turn, started to cross the busy street on his hands.

Now the police felt forced to act, their cups had run over. A number of brisk steps brought them within reach of the wandering Fritz. One grabbed him under his arms, the other by the legs, and so he was whisked off like a drunken man. In the meantime two additional constables had joined their colleagues, who, after exchanging a few words with them, grabbed me ungently and, upsy-daisy, I landed in the Black Maria, where Fritz already occupied another seat.

We remained behind bars overnight. Next morning we were taken to the courthouse before a magistrate. Through an interpreter, a Pole barely sufficient in German, we were advised of the following offences: Disturbance of the peace; endangering public safety; and resisting arrest. Sentence: One month in jail or two hundred and fifty dollars each. Soon I could see my dreams fluttering out of the window, because it came to light that Fritz had no money. He had only worked a few days in the fields which, besides yielding little, he had squandered that small amount before it warmed his pockets. Therefore I felt obliged to pay his part also.

One thing I learned from that episode. From now on I would heed my forebears' warning, never to trust a person from above the Danube.

Madame Xiang

One morning Picard received an invitation from Rolland Mercier, the deputy minister. Things were done in style in those days, particularly among French Canadians. A messenger, dressed up to the nines, handed a nicely framed card to Picard, on a silver salver of course.

"The deputy minister and his wife request the presence of Mr Maurice Picard at our birthday party, held at the Polar Bear Club next Friday at 8pm."

Thankful for the distraction, Picard accepted with alacrity.

It turned out to be a grand affair, so much so, that he entirely forgot the gnawing concerns which lately beset him.

At the end of the meal each guest was presented with a Chinese silk cookie, which one after the other opened affectedly amid laughter and teasing. When Picard's turn came he put on a good act. Screwing up his face in the manner of a mime, making roguish movements, he opened his cookie with deliberation. It was a commendable performance, worthy of a Thespian in his prime, eliciting applause from the women, and nodding approval from the men.

It all stopped abruptly when Picard, turning deathly pale, moaning piteously, slumped down in his chair, lamenting repeatedly:

"No, no, oh no."

Stunned, uncertain whether to construe his behaviour as further histrionics, or an expression of genuine grief, the company fell silent. Someone nearby took up the small roll of paper, unfurled it, and read:

"I have found you at last. Signed: Madame Xiang."

Hands were stretched out by others who wished to see with their own eyes what just had been heard.

Meanwhile Picard, forcibly trying to regain his composure, announced with a pained grin:

"Forgive me, I had a sudden attack of faintness."

"Any cause to worry?" the deputy minister's wife inquired solicitously.

Shaking his head Picard replied:

"None at all. Just the same it's best for me to leave. A good night's rest will restore my strength."

Chuckling he added:

"Don't forget, I'm not a spring chicken anymore."

On Monday Picard showed up at his office a changed man. His eyes, always bright, possessing that inquiring look of alert men, were dull and downcast. The hitherto bold, purposeful stride, a distinctive trait, had become hesitant. He left behind an impression of a man with fear on his neck and lead at his feet.

"Did a black dog walk over you, my dear colleague?" he was asked.

Grimacing annoyed, silently appealing for compassion, he protested:

"What a notion! I am just a bit under the weather, that's all."

"On account of that Chinese cookie?" his colleague was about to say, but bit his lips.

Of course the tattletale drums were busy, they resounded throughout the ministry and beyond. Tongues wagged, ears were strained in an endeavour not to miss a single beat. The whispers grew more insistent in view of Picard's relentless probings about people, women in particular. Subordinates as much as colleagues were confounded by this increasing interest in females, deemed prurient by some, unseemly by others for a department head getting on in years.

Thus ribald jests started to circulate, evoked more by sentiments of discomfort than conviction. No one rightly understood what the chief was after, yet many were annoyed by the persistent questioning.

A week later Picard failed to show up at the office. For three days running he missed appointments, a fact that struck others as unusual, since he seldom, if ever, remained absent; certainly not without leaving behind detailed information where he could be reached, plus what he wished done while being away. Questions were asked, eyebrows were raised, but none felt inclined to investigate further.

"The minister must surely be aware of the situation," was the consensus. Besides, not even his colleagues knew where Picard lived, or which places he frequented. His small home, sitting secluded on the banks of the Ottawa River, suited the single, unattached chief to a tee.

A woman, Mrs Prat, had been engaged to maintain the place. Having been away a few days, therefore feeling guilty, she approached the house with a measure of anxiety. To her surprise she found the front door not only unlocked but left ajar. Upon entering she called out:

"Are you home, Mr Picard?"

Not a whisper could be heard, nothing was stirring in the house.

"Mr Picard, I am back," she announced a bit louder.

A disquieting silence reigned, inexplicable so since signs of Picard's presence caught her eyes. His jacket hung on a peg; his hat lay on the rack above; shoes were carelessly placed.

"Strange, very strange," Mrs Prat said to herself, for Picard, doubtlessly nearby, could hardly be called a quietist; far from it. His Falstaffian rumblings were well known to her. Tiptoeing about with abated breath, strained ears, and wide-open eyes, she suddenly flinched upon hearing moans coming from above.

"Is that you, Mr Picard?"

"Yes, yes," came a muffled reply.

Reluctant, yet also relieved, she climbed the stairs. What she saw made her gasp. Blinking several times, wiping putative gossamer from both eyes, she stood there gasping in astonishment. Seeing her employer in bed on a sunny morning deemed her a trick of the senses. Noticing his ravaged condition made her wince. How could a man, brimming with good health a week ago, an epitome of vitality, now resemble death's head on a mopstick?

"What happened, did you have an accident?" she asked baffled to the core.

Picard shook his head:

"No."

"Have you seen a doctor?"

The question, innocent enough, made Picard bolt upright.

"I don't want a doctor," he expelled, then added: "See if you can contact Mr Basil. Ask him to come."

Bruno Basil, his friend, arrived later that afternoon.

"What's up, Maurice?" he inquired in his breezy way.

"She was here."

Taken aback, Basil remarked:

"Who was here?"

"Madame Xiang."

Recalling the episode at the Polar Bear Club, Basil cast an oblique glance at his friend, who lamented:

"All is lost, I am done for."

"Nonsense, you are out of sorts, that's all."

Knitting his brow, squinting at his friend, Basil exclaimed:

"Who is this Madame Xiang anyway? Does she exist, or is it an apparition evoked for self-punishment?"

"She is my nemesis."

"Fiddlesticks! Quit snivelling and tell me about it."

"Not here, let's meet at the Country Club later tonight."

"If you are up to it, I'm willing."

They met as arranged. Picard, assuredly not his bouncy self, did show vestiges of his former vigour, albeit not for long.

"Alright, old horse, tell me all about it," Basil encouraged.

His words instantly brought a pained expression to Picard's countenance, who exclaimed:

"I will follow you to the Pillars of Hercules."

"I don't understand."

"You know the expression, don't you?"

"Yes, but I fail to see the connection."

"Those were her last words, spat at me with the virulence of a rinkhals cobra ejecting her venom."

Basil, smacking the table with the flat of his hand, declared under his breath:

"Enough with this biblical talk, what are you driving at?"

Bowing his head, heaving a sigh, Picard announced:

"I am poisoned."

Stung, his friend snapped:

"Come off it, Maurice! How can you be poisoned and still walk around?"

He felt a temptation to add: "You do look like a walking corpse," but checked himself.

"Say what you want, the silent death is stalking me. I know the symptoms, and worst of all I am aware of her intentions."

"Her? You are not referring to that dratted woman again, which most likely is nothing but a spectre invoked by your feverish condition?"

The gaze Picard hurled at his friend would have angered a more squeamish man. Basil kept his composure, he just smiled and declared:

"Start at the beginning."

Picard took a deep breath. Closing his eyes he called into being those eventful days, rather months, spent on the windswept, snow-blown tundra. He was younger then, resilient in body, afire in spirit.

It was in June when he stepped into a wondrous world that took his breath away. Though treeless as far as the eye could see, the land teemed with life. He expected snow on the ground and heavy vapour in the air, yet was met by a lush carpet of flaming colours spread across the vast land, aglow under bright sunshine.

A promise he never felt before lay in the air; the hills resounded from myriad voices vying with each other to herald the arrival of summer. How short that summer was he could never forget.

"Do you know Lake Harbour?" Picard asked.

"Never heard of it," his friend replied.

"I fervently wish I could say the same. Anyway, here is what happened:

"About twenty years ago my employer, Roonex International, sent me up to Lake Harbour, a small settlement south of Frobisher Bay. Four men were there already, in a small camp set apart from the hamlet, inhabited mainly by nomadic Inuit."

"What were you doing there?"

"Enlarging a tank farm. Everything went like clock-work, till Henry Montour, a half-breed, started to act up."

"Act up?" Basil interrupted.

"Yes. One morning he planted himself before the window and refused to budge. There he stood, gazing towards the rising sun, mumbling to himself gibberish no one understood. 'Is it Cree?' I asked the foreman, who shook his head and replied: 'No, it's Esperanza.'

"Seeing our questioning glances, he explained: 'He is praying for hope.'

"A peculiar remark we thought, especially if made by a staid man of substance. When he added: 'Let him be,' our glances turned to stares of disbelief.

"A boss, who advocated bounden duty, allowed a subordinate to loaf during working hours? It seemed incredulous, but true. When we returned at noon, Montour stood there as before, like a statue nailed to the floor. 'He is bushed,' Hartwig announced."

"Bushed?" Basil echoed.

"That was exactly my response, to which I received no reply. At quitting time when we entered the camp a remarkable sight awaited us."

"Oh, what was that?" Basil asked with rising interest.

"Montour sat on his cot. Glowering, pointing at two broadaxes driven to their cheeks into the floor, he threatened: 'Don't cross the line, stay on your side.'

"Believe me, we were undecided whether to guffaw or take to our heels. Younger then, prone to fits of temper, I was about to challenge these interdictions, when the foreman held me back. It was a mistake; we should have tackled him there and then, it would have saved a lot of grief."

When Picard paused, his friend's brow started to crease, as if perplexed for reasons he could not fathom. Picard continued:

"We were at a loss what to say, or even what to think. Trying to make small talk proved futile, for our eyes continually wandered towards Montour. When he produced a formidable knife and started to grind away at it with a fiendish grin, they bulged."

"He sharpened his knife?"

"It wasn't a knife, but a mixture of cleaver and sabre with a curved handle and a broad blade, sturdy enough to hew down an oak tree. Hartwig, signalling for us to be quiet, rose and approached Montour with measured steps. 'Henry, what's up? Just take it easy,' he said in a soothing tone. Ha, it would have been simpler trying to pacify an enraged Tasmanian devil."

"What happened?" inquired Basil, all ears by now.

"The hitherto peaceful half-breed turned into a ball of fury. Snarling like a cornered wolverine, he hurled himself at the foreman and pinned him down with arms, as Hartwig afterwards declared, forged of steel."

"How did it end?"

"Not so agreeable, far from it. As I suggested we should have confronted him in the morning. Anyway, seeing Hartwig's life endangered, for Montour had somehow managed to get a hand on his Dussack knife which he wielded over the struggling foreman, galvanised us into action. I moved first, the others followed suit. Montour, a raving maniac by now, was finally subdued and fettered to his cot."

The frown on Basil's brow deepened, he failed to perceive a thread between his friend's narrative and the dreaded Madame Xiang. He grew restive; yet noticing that recounting these events lightened Picard's mind, he resolved to remain patient. He let his friend continue.

"Meanwhile darkness had set in. With neither a star nor the moon visible we had the impression of a huge pitch-black canopy descending on us. Consternation prevailed, more so after making a disquieting discovery."

Seeing his friend's raised eyebrows, Picard hastened to explain:

"Our radio had been tampered with, thus rendering it impossible to obtain outside help."

Considering Basil closer he remarked irresolutely:

"Before I say more be prepared for a shock; also understand that it may not be communicated to another living soul."

"Of course not," Basil promised.

Expelling a heartfelt sigh Picard continued his narrative.

"That night, twenty years ago, an incubus was born whose gnashing teeth and crushing weight I thought to have escaped, besets me again. Thinking of that fateful night makes me shudder even today. Sleep was out of the question, although we tried. Montour's moans and wails, interrupted by weird incantations kept us tossing from side to side.

Then suddenly silence reigned, which allowed us to catch a few winks till a desperate voice put an end to that. 'Henry is dead,' Hartwig called out.

"Jumping from our cots, half-dazed, heavy with sorely needed sleep, we rushed towards Montour. Exclamations like: 'Impossible, he is probably sleeping, feel his pulse,' resounded through the camp. From that moment good sense flew out of the window, reason left the camp."

Picard fell silent; he seemed reluctant to continue.

"What are you referring to?" Basil inquired, quite intrigued, and anxious to hear more.

Picard's mien darkened. Visibly shaking, he declared:

"We completely lost our composure when the licking flame of the lamp revealed distinct weals on Montour's neck."

Basil, drawing himself up, instinctively expelled:

"Weals?"

"Yes, unmistakable signs of strangulation."

"But – but," Basil protested.

"Exactly our sentiments, expressed more through stares than words. You can imagine our consternation. An innocent, albeit disturbing situation, took on a more sinister aspect. One of us had choked the tied-up half-breed to death. But who?"

"And why, I should have asked," interposed Basil.

"That question entered my mind later on, but not instantly."

"Could not someone else have entered the camp, for unknown reasons strangle the hapless half-breed, and disappear silently into the night?"

"Possibly, but in the end it didn't matter, for, as I mentioned, we lost our nerves, totally and irreversibly. Listen to what follows, and you will agree.

"Signs of daylight had not yet appeared, it was still pitch-dark outside. Inside the flickering flame of the kerosene lamp created shapes pregnant with doomsday messages. What happened next can neither be explained, nor vindicated in a normal surrounding, where tenets of studied refinements prevail. Yet in the land of permafrost, amid a world of haunting ghosts from medieval times, it seemed quite natural.

"Hartwig spoke first: 'We are in a pickle,' he announced. I, the youngest, protested loudly: 'We? Only one I venture to say.'

"It earned me a withering look from the foreman, plus snickers from the others. John Miller, the welder, evidently quicker on the uptake than I, explained what Hartwig had insinuated. 'You see, fellows, the situation is this: The authorities will accuse us of manhandling Henry with excessive force, thus causing his death.'

"Baxter, the electrician concurred: 'Seeing the welts around his neck might even induce them to conclude that we choked him intentionally.' 'Well, somebody did,' I meant to say, but swallowed my words. Guy Benoit lamented: 'What now?'

"Hartwig put things in perspective: 'Henry is dead, that's a fact. Another one is we all laid more than one hand on him, besides tying him down tight and good. Manslaughter will be a likely charge, upheld no doubt by the courts.' "

"I question that," Basil interjected.

"So do I, now that is; but then, as mentioned, our judgement was impaired."

Basil, on tenterhooks to learn the mysterious Madame Xiang's involvement, urged his friend to continue.

"Did I say impaired? It's an understatement. Our discernment was hiding in the folds of doltishness. In short, we caused Montour to disappear."

"How was that done?" wondered Basil.

Picard looked up. His face acquired an impish expression which his friend had hitherto not observed in that broad, honest countenance; even less the cunning smile whisking around his lips, which he pursed prior to replying:

"Well, he disappeared during the night, never to return. That is what we reported to the police, the company, and anyone else.

"Three days later a woman appeared at the camp, who seemed to be a mixture of Inuit, Native Indian, plus Canadienne. 'I am Madame Xiang,' she announced, then added: 'I will cook for you, plus manage the camp.'

"Now, that seemed like good news, a godsend really, no mistake about it, for none of us considered himself a chef worth a pinch of salt. Besides, kitchen and housekeeping work consumed time, better employed to accelerate the work, which had fallen behind.

"You should have seen our efforts of silent persuasion directed at Hartwig, to engage her for the duration of our stay. For since Montour sort of left us, who was the only crew member capable of doing more than warming up a tin of beans, we felt undernourished."

"Didn't Montour's disappearance cause a stir?" Basil asked.

"Hardly a ripple. It happened, still happens, that occasionally men disappear without a trace in the Artic. Since the Inuit never make a fuss concerning such incidents, nor report or talk about them, investigations quickly fizzle out. As I said we silently wished that the foreman come to terms with this Madame Xiang.

"Noticing Hartwig's puckering face deemed us a sign of interest. We heaved a sigh of relief, which ended in suppressed groans upon hearing his next words: 'This is no place for a woman, we haven't any lodging for you,' he advised. 'I don't need one, I live in the village,' she told him with an alluring smile.

"I tell you, Bruno, that woman possessed the gene of a Jezebel, seemingly ready to deliver what she silently advertised. But strange to say, despite her seductive demeanour, she insisted on formality. 'You address me as Madame Xiang,' she announced with an air of finality.

"For inexplicable reasons, to me anyway, the men resented her airs, as they termed these demands, thus they missed no opportunity to deride her. 'What's your real name?' she was twitted. 'Madame Xiang; you call me Madame Xiang,' she sternly advised. 'And if I don't?'

"My word, Bruno, that was a foolish challenge, made flippantly by Miller, the welder. Her response could only be described as drastic and frightening. Turning slowly, taking two steps towards him, she stretched herself beyond her height, it seemed. I swear by all the saints there were red-hot darts shooting from her eyes. Neither before nor after have I witnessed such fierce, suppressed anger. In a voice trenchant and menacing, she repeated: 'You will call me Madame Xiang!'

"Did Miller flinch? I thought so. His attempt at bravado deceived nobody. The tough hombre, as he liked to refer to himself, withered visibly under her burning gaze. Small wonder, considering the amazing transformation from a pliant womanly shape to a figure of wrath, which in a twinkle took on the former feminine grace again. Nevertheless, I became aware that she was no daughter of Canada."

"Didn't you say she was part Inuit, Native Indian, and Canadienne?"

"Quite so; but her spat with Miller taught me otherwise. Our soil does not produce such women, I realised, who could muster a savage gaze, nor that hellkite's determination. Soon enough I found out where her cradle stood."

"Tell me." Basil requested.

"She hailed from the wild mountains of Yucatan, Guatemala; in other words, she was a Chorti Indian.

"Miller, the welder collapsed first."

"Collapsed? Why?"

"We didn't know, it happened after supper. As we carried him to his cot, Hartwig slumped to the floor, groaning as if Dante's twelve devils were wrangling over his soul. Baxter and Benoit were not spared either. I helped them lie down on their beds where they writhed and groaned as if vying with each other.

"I was in a dither. My head whirled, my mind could not formulate a single thought. Madame Xiang had left some hours ago. I was alone with four whimpering men. Baxter, who appeared not to suffer as much as the others, managed to stammer: 'The radio, call for help.' That was easier said than done, because for some mysterious reasons our wireless hardly functioned after nightfall. I finally reached the police station in Frobisher Bay. Constable Ritchie promised to set out in the morning. Being versed in first aid, he told me what to do in the meantime. 'It sounds like food poisoning,' he suggested."

"Where you not affected?" Basil interrupted.

"To some extend, yes, but not as severely as my co-workers."

"That's strange," Basil conjectured.

"Perhaps not. You see I ate sparingly that evening, especially from the meat. In any case I spent a harrowing night among four suffering men, delirious, and judging by their wails in the throes of death.

"Next morning at daybreak, as was her wont, Madame Xiang arrived to prepare our breakfast. At the sight of me she uttered a muffled cry. Her face, wreathed in surprise initially, quickly turned into a mask of hate. I still see her in my dreams, bent forward, evincing sounds of a laughing hyena, hissing words that sounded like 'next time, next time.' Prior to turning and walking away, she spat out a final threat: 'I will follow you to the Pillars of Hercules.' "

"Meaning to the end of the world," Basil offered.

"Exactly. But back to me on that lonely windswept barrens, with four men hanging onto life's thread. Thoroughly baffled, shaking my head incredulously, I made an attempt to call her back and tell me what this was all about. 'Stop! Talk to me!' I meant to shout, but not a word rolled over my tongue. Why? Because an awful thought struck me, so hideous I dared not whisper it to myself. Aghast, feeling the clammy breath of a hundred fiends creeping up my spine, I went inside again, realising she had poisoned us, every man jack."

"Not you, obviously," Basil interjected.

The remark elicited a wry smile from Picard, who murmured:

"Not yet, not yet. But let me continue. The police arrived late afternoon. Digesting the situation quickly, they acted without reservation. When I tried to voice my suspicions, constable Ritchie waved them aside: 'No time, no time,' he declared, then added: 'Tell me about it on the way.' 'I must come with you?' The policeman cast a glance at me as if he had heard wrong. 'Didn't you say you felt nauseated, sick as a dog? You certainly look it. Besides, we need your statement,' he said brusquely. 'What about Madame Xiang?' I ventured to ask. 'Who is she?' he snapped. 'The cook; she might be the cause of our plight' I started to explain, but was cut off by constable Ritchie. 'Later, later. Get on the boat, it's a long ride to Frobisher,' he reminded.

"Indeed, it was. The police had brought a doctor along who, after a cursory examination declared: 'Botulism, hardly life threatening.' He administered medicine which improved everyone's condition."

"Did they recover?"

"Yes, and no."

"How is that to be taken?"

"They didn't die, but just wasted away. The last I heard of them, about a year after the incident, they had become inanimate beings."

"There was an investigation, I presume?" Basil inquired.

"A perfunctory one, in my reckoning."

"What was the conclusion?"

"Extreme botulism, ascribed to the consumption of contaminated meat. Nothing serious, the doctors decided, curable in time."

"What about the cook?"

"Madame Xiang? She was absolved of any malfeasance, though chided for preparing tainted meat. My statement, incriminating enough to have her indicted, I thought, received scant attention. A nod, plus a pat was all I got, in view of the medical findings."

As his friend talked, Basil listened less. His thoughts became inundated by a sea of scepticism. The jigsaw puzzle painted and stamped by Picard did not fit; the pieces were too rough on the edges. His narrative made little sense; the reason for relating it even less. Was it done to allay fear, perhaps to confound, or to ease a belaboured conscience? Why would this mysterious Madame Xiang wish to harm him, or for that matter the four men up in the Arctic, whose culpability consisted of nothing more than a breach of etiquette?

Basil was not an obtuse man, he knew the truth as a fickle dame, weaving webs with lisles of confusion, and knots of deceit. Quite frankly, he didn't belief his friend's story, for such he deemed it, a tale like from the Arabian Nights, meant to distract. Something was amiss here. No doubt his friend tried to lead him up the garden path. Why? What for?

An odd sensation gripped Basil. His friend wanted to confess something too dreadful to be mentioned. He decided to draw him out.

"Maurice, a while ago you said: 'We made Montour disappear.' What did you mean by it?"

Picard flinched. His eyes, unsteady before, acquired a hunted expression. He sighed as if tormented to the marrow. In a voice choked with emotion, he said:

"First let me tell you something about Bruce Hartwig."

"The foreman?"

Nodding, Picard continued:

"He was older than any of us, though still sinewy like a practising athlete. A more overbearing man you can not imagine; but granted, he possessed a fair and alert mind which he demonstrated on that fateful morning. Not prone to shilly-shally in a crisis, he came to the point in a deliberate fashion, brooking neither censure nor opposition. 'Fellows, we are in this together, we either all swim or drown, no ifs or buts. There is only one thing left to do.' 'What's that?' Miller wanted to know. 'Montour must disappear.' 'Why?' I interposed.

"I can neither describe nor imitate Hartwig's withering glance, or my fellow workers' nervous chuckles."

Looking his friend full in the face, Picard commented:

"Here is the part that haunts me."

"Tell me about it," Basil encouraged.

"As if in a trance we not only acquiesced in Hartwig's action, but lent a hand. As mentioned we had reached a state best described as delusory; we obeyed the foreman's orders. None of us protested when he announced: 'We will send him to the bottom of the inlet.'

"Not a word was uttered while we helped to remove Montour's fetters; not a syllable of objection escaped our throats as we carried him to the boat, in which we laid the corpse. Rowing stealthily to a narrow fjord, indicated by Hartwig, we stopped and heaved Montour overboard."

Visibly disturbed, Picard made several attempts to utter something evidently painful. Deciding otherwise, he added:

"Not of course before tying the weights to his legs."

"Is that the end?" Basil asked.

Looking at his friend suggestively, then lowering his head, Picard replied:

"Pretty well. I might add, however, that afterwards Hartwig enjoined us to say that Montour disappeared during the night, whereto, we have no idea."

Two weeks later an urgent message reached Basil – Come at once, I am at the General Hospital, room 112.

When Basil stepped through the doorway, he almost sank to his knees. He could have sworn to hear death bells ringing in his ears. His dear friend had become a wizened man; he resembled a corpse prior to internment.

"Maurice, what in the world has happened?" he cried.

"I told you, she has found me," Picard panted.

"What's the diagnosis?"

Chortling resignedly, with a sneer on his lips, Picard replied:

"Botulism."

"Just like the others," Basil burst out.

"Yes, just like the others, poisoned with a substance, undetectable, immune to any antidote which turns a living being into a rotting vegetable."

Staring into space, Picard, who meanwhile had propped himself up in bed, moaned under his breath:

"But we deserve it, everyone of us got his just deserts."

"You are talking in riddles," Basil protested.

"Maybe. Sit down and I shall unveil them."

Basil did as requested. He took a seat beside the bed and waited patiently for his friend's explanation. He felt intrigued by this spectral Madame Xiang and her loathsome habits, but even more so by Picard's ghastliness and alarming behaviour.

Sitting up in bed, Picard managed a wan smile while saying:

"Remember, Bruno, what I said at the Country Club?"

"Most of it, but I still don't understand why this Madame Xiang should want to poison you."

"You will in a moment. When I stated that we dumped Henry's corpse in the water, I lied."

Shrugging his shoulders as if to say, what of it? Basil commented:

"That's neither here nor there now."

"So you say, old chap, so you say," Picard murmured.

His demeanour acquired the wild-eyed expression of a man trying to fend off spectres of the past. Suddenly he burst out:

"I will never forget those screams."

Startled, Basil asked:

"Whose screams?"

"Henry's, when we threw him overboard."

"But he was dead," Basil protested.

"I lied, we did not chuck a corpse over the gunwale, Bruno, but a living, struggling man."

"What do you mean?" Basil exclaimed.

"This: When we lifted the presumed corpse up, Montour opened his eyes and called out: 'What's going on here?' They were his last words, followed by shrieks which the lapping water soon drowned."

Dismayed, staring at his friend as if struck dumb, Basil commented:

"By all saints, Maurice, how could that happen?"

"I told you, we were in a state of dementia, circumstances beyond comprehension had turned us into mechanical men scared out of our wits."

Still in shock Basil inquired:

"Where does Madame Xiang fit in?"

"Yes, the Chorti Indian, our bane and nemesis. She is Montour's wife, I found out after."

Noticing his friend's uncomprehending look, Picard explained:

"The company hired only single men for their remote projects. Henry must have lied, pretending to be unmarried. But that hellcat harboured different notions by the looks of it. As I understood she took a job with the Hudson Bay Company under her maiden name."

"To be near her husband, I presume."

"Yes."

Basil's brow creased and his eyes narrowed, indicating bewilderment. I still don't understand why she poisoned you, or did she?"

"No doubt about it. Having presumably witnessed everything, she must have decided on the spot to be the plaintive, judge, and executioner."

Shaking his head vigorously, Bruno Basil remarked:

"How weird, why should she not go to the police like other people?"

Picard, appearing somewhat relaxed after disburdening his mind, smiled broadly.

"The answer most likely lies in the wilds of Yucatan, amid the ruins of the Maya."

Printed in the United States
68202LVS00002B/30

9 780973 470321